Posthumanism

About the future of mankind

MIEKE MOSMULLER

POSTHUMANISM

About the future of mankind

OCCIDENT • PUBLISHERS

Translated from Dutch by

Kathryn Harington
and
Christopher Guilfoil

Band MM 57

Occident Publishers
Geerstraat 1
5111 PS Baarle Nassau
The Netherlands
Phone: +31 (0)13 - 5079948
E-mail: info@occidentpublishers.com
Website: www.occidentpublishers.com

Cover image: Ruth Franssen
Graphic design: Carina van den Bergh

ISBN/EAN: 978-90-75240-62-7

In my book 'Singularity', I made an attempt to contradict the current vision of the future of the human being from the vision of Artificial Intelligence with the vision of the human being as we see it from anthroposophy, which does not bear that name without reason: wisdom of the human being, or a wise image of the human being. At the end of the book, the friends who have discussed this theme separate and agree to meet again a few months later to develop a concrete vision of human development, based on the sovereignty of the mind.

This current book, 'Posthumanism', is the account of that meeting of thirteen friends in the high mountains. It has become a condensed description of human development on earth, described from the time of early Lemuria to the end of the Post-Atlantean era. It will not be easy to read, I count on the activity of the engaged reader both in a thinking and in an imaginative capacity. Without this activity, it can be nothing but a curious accumulation of facts of the past and the future. If, on the other hand, the reader is prepared to engage actively in both thinking and imagining, an infinitely rich future will appear before the inner eye. The post-humanism of singularity will pale into an inanimate insignificance. If there is a sense of truth inherent in the human being, in which I have the full most confidence, then the joyful recognition of this vision of the future should enlighten us.

The only thing that can undermine it is unwillingness, in all its forms, from a lack of will to outright repugnance.

They sat together in the meeting room, Johannes and Philippe. It was a sunny day in June, at the beginning of a busy summer season. Johannes looked at Philippe and said:

"In a fortnight time, our Amsterdam friends, our new ones, will visit us here and we have agreed to present a different view of trans and posthumanism. Now, our friend Raymond is a specialist in the future vision of singularity and transhumanism. This offers us, as it were, a miraculously complete foundation on which to build our spiritual vision of the future of 'the human being after the human being'."

Philippe nodded and said:

"That's going to be quite a task, Johannes. I have devoted a great deal of meditative power to it over the past few months, but it will not be easy to express what one recognises in the unspeakable. After all, we have always confined ourselves to teaching spiritual thinking here in this institution in the mountains, and we have revealed only a very small part of the way to initiation. Now we have decided to put a prophetic area of human development into words, and we will, of course, hardly be able to do so with words. We will have to use those words to paint images so that we can get an impression of what will happen to mankind in the future, when evolution has reached the point where the need for life and death in a physical body will be over. At the moment this is still unimaginable. And if Raymond had not come our way, we would have left it to the unimaginable. Of course, he has come because it is time for this which is unimaginable to become imagined. I do wonder if I will be able to depict what lies in an unrevealed future in colourful images... and I am also full of expectation to experience how you will do that!"

Johannes said:

"I have similar feelings, Philippe. We'll have to prepare this thoroughly; we can't just sit down with Els and Raymond and hope it will all reveal itself. The same thoroughness with which Raymond underpinned his vision of the future of singularity and post and trans-humanism will also have to be the foundation for us. In the work of the Master of the Occident, I believe there are only two places where this future of mankind is clearly pointed out. In one place it is said that around the year 5700 mankind will have developed in such a way that women will have become infertile and that humans will then move on to an earthly existence in which the physical body will have been conquered, as it were – where one should not imagine that the whole miraculous construction of the physical body decays, of course, but where one should imagine that this miraculous construction takes on an immaterial form… In the other place the Master of the Occident does not speak about the year 5700 but about the eighth millennium and says something similar there. To me, the fact that these two years do not correspond just means that they are probably two different aspects that are described. How one has to imagine the survival of man without a material body is indeed inconceivable! And there is no clear literature about it, except in the field of science fiction – and that is not what we are talking about…"

Philippe let Johannes's words sink in and said:

"The vision of singularity and transhumanism is based on the idea that there will be a new phase in the development of mankind, in which biological intelligence will be supported or even replaced by artificial technical intelligence, which will then have assumed a speed, a range and a form that will be impossible to follow from a biological point of view. It is envisaged that it will then be possible to draw together the essence of a human being living on earth in an algorithm, to upload this algorithm into a computer – and when it is then combined with artificial intelligence, technically intelligent beings will emerge which will by far surpass man in his so-called biological intelligence and which will introduce a new era on earth, in which first there will be a kind of mixture of biological human beings and technical human beings for some time to make way for post-human beings. It is hard to imagine who will be in charge there…"

"Partly," said Johannes, "I can't help but see this as a science fiction world, which will remain fiction. But the arrival of Raymond in spring has made it clear to me that one has to take this kind of science fiction-like prediction more seriously. Even if this cannot be realised fully – as is believed and hoped – if only a fraction of it were to become possible, it would already be a great disaster for the spiritual human being… That is why we have also decided to take a different, a spiritual view of the future, one based on certain truth. If only to show that we can expect a being living on earth who follows the human being as we know him in evolution, also in a perfect spiritual form. Of course, it is not impossible that both one and the other will be realised. But if we succeed in making a spiritual form conceivable opposed to the post-human beings in a technical sense, then this will bring about an indescribable effect in the human world of thought."

Philippe nodded and said:

"That's why we're going to do this..."

"We have to realise that the motivation to believe in these technical solutions is that man is a mortal being and one loses one's loved ones. In fact, this dying is experienced as a form of amputation. That is why humans look for ways to escape death that is inexorable for everyone at the end of the road."

Johannes took Kurzweil's book about the singularity from the table and read a piece:

> "Substrate is morally irrelevant, assuming it doesn't affect functionality or consciousness. It doesn't matter, from a moral point of view, whether somebody runs on silicon or biological neurons (just as it doesn't matter whether you have dark or pale skin). On the same grounds, that we reject racism and speciesism, we should also reject carbon-chauvinism, or bioism."[1]

"It is the fear of loss of self, of the loss of the loved one that ultimately leads the human being to conceive these kinds of ungodly ideas – because religion, too, has become completely powerless. People no longer have any use for the belief in God as we used to because the mind, as it shades reality in the rational realm, leaves no room for the existence of a transcendental being like God... And so these people, who are in fact extremely lonely, are looking for solutions to sustain themselves above the mortality of the body and to do the same with their loved ones."

Philippe said, after a brief reflection:

"Still, it's strange that such a lack of perception of reality occurs among these thinkers. I can also read you a quote, from the same book:

---

1 Nick Bostrom, "Ethics for Intelligent Machines: A Proposal, 2001" in Ray Kurzweil, "The Singularity Is Near: When Humans Transcend Biology".

"Death is a tragedy. It is not demeaning to regard a person as a profound pattern (a form of knowledge), which is lost when he or she dies. That, at least, is the case today, since we do not yet have the means to access and back up this knowledge. When people speak of losing part of themselves when a loved one dies, they are speaking quite literally, since we lose the ability to effectively use the neural patterns in our brain that had self-organized to interact with that person."[2]

"It is clear that a sensible person can believe that it doesn't matter whether you express yourself as an algorithmic being in a silicon carrier, in a nanobot or in a biological body. It is curious that the aspect of self-awareness is simply overlooked. It is believed that if you could recognise such an algorithm, such a pattern, and you were able to implant this into a device in such a way that the device would function according to that algorithm, that the device would have a consciousness of itself after all. In evolution, we see the development up to the homo sapiens, to the development of the 'homo sapiens sapiens', don't we? In other words: the human being who not only can know, but who can also have that wonderful motto: Know yourself! By knowing himself, that human being knows everything he has acquired through the process of knowledge. He sees this with a new perspective... We, as occult researchers, are also convinced that this could lead to another stage of development. But it is incomprehensible to imagine that the powerless step would have to be taken in order to achieve that which nature has brought to us as the supreme artistic refinement – namely self-consciousness – really could be surpassed by transforming it into a formula and introducing it into a device. The fact that these scientists can assume that self-consciousness – the second sapiens – will then be preserved is truly incomprehensible to me. Such a blind spot can only occur when you have no idea of what the second sapiens actually is, when you see it all as products of the activity of the brain. Then, of course, the second sapiens can be transferred back into a device just like that. But if you take even a fraction of a step towards becoming aware of what you are actually doing, when you are engaged in the process of knowledge, and what you are doing, when you are engaged in the

2 Ray Kurzweil, in his book "Singularity".

process of self-knowledge, then it should be so that in experiencing this activity you would immediately know: all technical possibilities stop here! Technology can only relapse into powerlessness! When people ask themselves what the next step of development should be, it is an increase of the second sapiens, namely of self-knowledge that cannot be grasped in a device. Do you understand, Johannes, I cannot understand at all how a thinker can be so narrow-minded that he can overlook this great abyss of being conscious. They have left religion behind… If that is not the case – even though you may have left the church behind - sooner or later, you will come across a passage in the Bible in which John the Baptist appears. Through what he says and preaches and through what Christ says about him, you know: This man is the representative of the transition from only being occupied with the highest part of the soul to being fully conscious of the spirit, albeit still with, say, the lowest form. There you have visualised, personified the experience of that transcendence of self-consciousness into a new form of consciousness. But if you use this as an argument, then of course he who is sitting opposite you and who thinks very differently is immediately led to say: Oh yes, well, you have read that and it fits in with your vision! In this way, you can never come to a fruitful dialogue, for it is the great difficulty that we are familiar with concrete inner experiences, which we then have to transfer in usual forms. Our conversation partners who are not occult researchers then say: But we have known that for a long time anyway!

I can sometimes become desperate about that. How do you find a way out of this confusion of speech?"

Johannes said:

"It is true that Raymond is no longer a fully convinced representative of singularity and trans- and post-humanism, but he has 'hung on' to it for decades and his whole way of arguing has been shaped by it. So, you can expect that to recur regularly when we try to make our occult positions clear. Perhaps this exercise that we are about to embark upon will help us understand more clearly how we should argue against it…"

So, we realise that these people, like us, ask questions about the development of mankind. What will happen when the biological body will have lost its function and the human being will be able to find another form of life, a form of life in which there is no longer any need to die? The transhumanists cannot wait, as it were, for the development of mankind to reach the point at which that biological body can truly be missed, and the human being will be able to intervene as an individual in the earth's existence without the skin in which you feel your "I" – not only knowing! These transhumanists are not prepared to delve into the meaning and significance of the physical body itself. They simply want to get rid of it, having distilled from it what is most important to them: an algorithm based on computer science, which also contains certain creativity, as we know it in gaming. You have to be content with that creativity, further developed, of course. You then have to be happy with the unprecedented computing capacity as a basis for intelligence. Those future machine people, who will be something completely different from robots, will then take the place of biological humans.

There is also, of course, a very large number of scientists who do not believe in this hard artificial intelligence and who see the artificial intelligence more in the sense of supporting the human intellect. That is how I myself have seen it for years, and in that area you cannot see it as something negative. From the beginning there has also been a tendency to extend the respect you can have for an artificial intelligence and its possibilities to an evolutionary step in which it is really hoped that the artificial intelligence will take an enormous flight and also become the cosmic intelligence."

Philippe said:

"When you meditatively absorb these insights, you find the opposite image and you more or less spontaneously arrive at the step in the development of humanity which is the 'other half' of this and which still lies in a distant future."

"But now, for Raymond, we will also want to become concrete with regard to what the human being will be like then. He will no longer be incarnated in the flesh, he will no longer have to leave the body. The woman no longer has to bear children. The distinction in gender will cease to exist. And yet, that existence must have a different quality than life after death... The states of consciousness on earth and after death will then correspond far more to each other than they do now, but one difference will still be that with your individuality you surrender yourself to earthly existence and all the beings that belong to it – or that you withdraw from it and turn your gaze to the heavenly realms and the beings that take care of the progress of mankind there."

"I think it would be best that our explanations begin with a description of our occult knowing in relation to the very beginning of human development on earth, when the human being, as a high spiritual being who already had a history, connected himself with earthly existence. The bodies living on earth were not adapted to that high spiritual human quality at all. Then we describe the occult knowing in relation to what in the Old Testament is called the *Fall of Man*, namely the separation of the sexes, the premature access to knowledge, the loss of that which as in an image is called the *Tree of Life* – and the first occurrence of that extraordinarily painful phenomenon of death and birth. When we can bring that which we know from the past through contemplative consciousness into a reflection of the future, so that we can give a perspective of what happened so long ago and what has yet to come into a metamorphosis when time has passed, it seems to me that it will be most understandable not only for our friends, but also for ourselves. For it is, of course, something quite different when you describe the events that have taken place - even if they are spiritual - in the past, or when you look for an expression for what is yet to come. In the Bible that is called the *Apocalypse*, that is which is to come, which has not yet been fulfilled. This requires a completely different kind of clairvoyance than that required to be able to look into the past. When you go into the time flowing back, that leads back to the pre-birth, to previous incarnations, previous eras, to previous great earthly states, to previous planetary states, then you move into the realm of thinking that has become the world thoughts. But if you want to look into the future, then you have to find a way to perceive, as it were, preformed expressions in that still completely unformed area of will. You can only do this if you have learned in the present, not only to fathom homo sapiens with self-consciousness, but also to participate fully and consciously in that 'second sapiens'. This willpower also carries a thinking in it, and with it you can unfold and contemplate that which is, as it were, completely rolled up in the future. But of course, it is clear that this is very ethereal…"

"With the help of the same knowledge we have acquired in the occult sense in the present, we shall have to look ahead, as it were, to how this ability will develop in the future, and see that it will become possible for mankind to reach a state comparable to the descent of the high spiritual human being in the past, in a transformation and reflection. Only the whole human development from then till then lies in between… But through the possibilities which then light up, the whole will be filled with self-consciousness – and not only with self-consciousness in knowing, but also in the principle of independent moral intuition, through which the human being becomes able to take full control of himself and creation, more and more."

Philippe said:

"Such words you indeed hear in the circle of post-and transhumanism too, and I am so surprised by them every time, but it is really incomprehensible that these highly educated people – because they usually are – believe that when mankind has developed a mechanical intelligence, that would mean that you take complete control of yourself and creation. Surely, it should be clear at a glance that you are then handing over control to the machine… But if you think about it longer, then of course you understand. For these people only have access to their sharp intellect, which can only think in shadow images. Shadows only have the shape of the original object, but otherwise all shadows are equal. And then it really doesn't matter if you think of occult knowledge of the spiritual human or think of great mathematical knowledge of technology. Shadowed, the two are very difficult to distinguish.

But of course they bring us a feeling of desperation and hopelessness. Because after all these years of work here, we can hardly say that there is an increase in people who have risen from the shadow to the sun. A small group of people with whom we work intensively here will, of course, achieve this, but one would have expected that after all those spring, summer, autumn and even winter courses, a community of people would emerge who had really come to an awareness of their own *homo sapiens sapiens*. The question remains: what can we do to make it even clearer, to make it even more intense, to transmit the enthusiasm even more strongly?"

Johannes said:

"I am really very curious to know in what condition we will find our friends Raymond and Els. They have only been out of our sight for two months and we have, of course, had occasional written contact – but the question will be whether the intensive conversations we have had here in a fortnight have triumphed over there in Amsterdam in the midst of their busy daily lives...."

*

Els and Raymond sat together at the table in their flat in Amsterdam.
Raymond said:
"I am really looking forward to our trip to Switzerland, to the mountains! I have good memories of our time there in the spring and I am also looking forward to talking to Philippe and Johannes again."
Els replied:
"Yes, I am really looking forward to it too. But I'm also a little reluctant. Those two men have remained in my memory as giant human spirits, and I do wonder what we actually have to offer."
"Above all, that they share their occult knowledge of the future ... What we have to offer is a listening and observant ear. I think that is already very special. I have, of course, my experience with the knowledge of singularity and of trans- and post-humanism, an area in which I am very much at home and for which I have lived and worked for many years, and which I have now been looking at with some detachment for a few months. I am very curious to see what 'other post-humanism' will be like, now that I have also come to know a 'different way of thinking' since we have been there. Can you really make those two men appear before your inner eye? All I really have is a memory of the spiritual greatness of each of them, no matter how many differences there are..."
Els said:
"Yes, of course I do! I always look very precisely and that's why I also remember a lot of external details."
"Then describe Johannes again,' he asked. "Maybe I'll envisage him in front of me again?"
"Johannes is a rather tall man, who certainly looks much livelier and younger than he is. He has a head like that of a harmonious Greek statue and he has a luxuriant head of hair, which is slightly greying. His eyes are as blue as the southern summer sky, but they can sometimes take on a somewhat greyish hue, a more 'North Sea' aspect. I would imagine that if you have more to do with him, it could be a sign that you need to be a little careful. He is very kind, extremely charming, would certainly be very successful with women - if he wanted to. I don't see

auras, but I do feel something around this man that stretches far and wide, that must be his spirituality. He is always well-dressed, usually wears a jacket, no tie, has a wedding ring on his left finger, wears a simple wristwatch. His shoes are not really very new, but they are well polished, and he always wears matching socks."

"God Almighty!" exclaimed Raymond, "how is it possible that you see all these details and remember them too! Indeed, his outward appearance now reappears in my memory, and I think: I don't remember him either, because I'm a little scared of him. He's an amazing figure, so you ask yourself: How can I stand in that overwhelming solar power?"

"Yes, I haven't" said Els. "I like the sun's power to be warm and light and it's kind to me."

"But he knows overwhelmingly more!" objected Raymond.

"Yes, that's what is so nice about him, that you know: I'm talking to someone who's at home in all areas of science, art and religion. He laughs very kindly, taps you on the shoulder more often than not as if to encourage you. I remember him as a very good speaker, his speech was clear and comprehensive."

"Yes, I had a bit more difficulty with that, you know." Raymond said, thinking back to that first lecture he had heard, where he had felt that his sympathy for artificial intelligence had been trampled on - even though the man didn't even know he was there - or perhaps he did?

"Apparently," said Els, "you are more in competition with him. I'm not in competition with him at all, I think it's pretty pointless being a dwarf if you want to take on a giant. You might think you're a giant yourself, and then things would be different."

"That sounds really nice! I think I am a giant! I do have some respect for myself, yes that's right. But that's because, as you know, my environment has always made me feel so special. At a certain point, you believe that yourself. And when you are suddenly confronted with someone like Johannes, you are speechless and you lose your mind. I can't compete with someone like that either. And Philippe? Can you describe him for me as well?"

"Philippe seems smaller, but is certainly as big as Johannes, in every respect. He doesn't look like a Greek god, though in his heart he probably is... He is quiet, taciturn, extraordinarily friendly, expectant. You have the feeling that you could pour out your heart to him and that you would be cured of all your imperfections, that he would accept them from you. Something like that … Philippe is really an extraordinarily kind person. He has an interesting face, you could say inconspicuous… But in that modest way it is very meaningful. His eyes have all the colours that eyes could have. He has nice regular teeth, his hair is greyish, a bit less thick, but certainly not balding like yours," she said, pointing at his head. "His clothes are also modest, I think he wears what his wife buys him, just like you do. He also has a wedding ring on the left and he wears a wristwatch which is probably made of silver. He's a bit fatter than Johannes but not really fat - and if I had to sum up how I experience him, I would say: A very great restraint, but with clear boundaries. He is not a man you could walk over. When he finally starts to speak, only pieces of gold come out of his mouth. Everything he says seems to me to be meaningful, a final expression of something that is in fact far bigger and greater in him. It's as if he eventually manages to combine all the gold that is ethereally distributed throughout the cosmos into those gold pieces that are his words. And although when you listen to him, you know that all this is accompanied by a great clear consciousness, you feel totally at ease with him. I'm sure you are too."

"Well, no," said Raymond, smiling. "Now that you mention it, I feel too what you experience about this man and I understand why he makes me a little nervous. It must be the ethereal gold from which his words are forged."

"And furthermore, I believe that with him, even more so than with Johannes, there is a danger that you could become the object of a divine wrath, which is also part of this golden resignation."

"Yes, but, as you say, with clear boundaries. I can also imagine him as an authoritative priest or a monk, who knows the whole divine revelation by heart, and could confront you in the Middle Ages. It seems to me that this comprehensive knowledge is part of the gold dust that he uses to form his words. A priest-philosopher or something…"

"Interesting," Els said. "You can see that you're very observant too!"

"Yes, but these are more inner experiences and not the colour of his shirt. Which doesn't mean that you shouldn't see that too…"

"Yes, when we talk about it like that," Els said, "I do get a bit nervous and my feeling of 'what am I supposed to do in return' is only reinforced. All right, they must know what they're doing. That they invited the two of us specifically to share their spiritual knowledge with. Maybe I only get that honour because I'm with you?"

"I don't think so, Els. They're modern people and if that were appropriate, they would have invited just me for that."

"Luckily we can live in the same house of my colleague again, and I'm sure we'll have plenty of time to take some of those lovely walks, which have brought us such great physical vitality…"

A week later, Johannes and Philippe were sitting together again in the meeting room, but this time they were expecting their closest co-workers, one might say their friends or perhaps even their brothers and sisters…

First to enter was the old Indian master. He had been the leader of this institute in the Swiss high mountains in the past and after the encounter with Johannes, who at that time was still a professor of internal medicine in Amsterdam, he had decided to make his entire spiritual school available for the path in which Johannes could point to the goal of earthly development. If you wanted to give a name to that goal, you could say: love. But for the human being of the Occident that love has to be achieved by the way of wisdom. That was the nature of Johannes and ever since then he was in charge of this wonderful school of spiritual thought in the Swiss high mountains. The Master was called 'master' by everyone and so he was. He had been initiated into Buddhism and he was a very disciplined person with a great all-embracing love of nature and the cosmos. He was small, had a head like a lion and a great grey bush of hair surrounding his beautiful features. Usually, he wore a grey suit, sometimes black, which gave him a priestly appearance. And from an outer appearance, he was definitely the most striking figure in the whole environment. His personality was characterised, on the one hand, by the deeply active reverential surrender to everything worthy of admiration, and on the other hand, by being straightforward, not holding back his judgement, which was formed in surrender, and sometimes frightened people.

He lived in a chalet on the grounds with his partner Marie, whom he had met in the Netherlands. In the conversations about singularity and transhumanism that they had recently had with Raymond and Els in the spring, the Master had been most direct in his horror about this and had not concealed it from Raymond. Yes, he had even reproached him directly. He had blamed him for the fact that a man as gifted as he was, could be so stupid as to fall for this nonsense. Another characteristic of the Master was that he never regretted such a sudden attack… When you saw him, he seemed gentleness personified, but he could be seized by a frightening wrath.

Johannes had had frequent disagreements with the Master in the early years, but afterwards their relationship was imbued with harmony, and they felt united in the best and most beloved friendship that can only be among people. Philippe had joined this company in the mountains many years later and the Master had received him with great admiration and caution. Between the Master and Philippe there had probably never been a word of discourtesy. The Master looked straight through the people and always encountered shadows and resistances. With Philippe he had not…

They greeted each other warmly and the Master sat down.

"Tell me," he said, "what exactly are your plans? How do you think you are going to make them take shape? In the holy nights, between Christmas and Epiphany, we had already decided to listen to both of you this summer, to what you have to say about humanity's development towards the future, so that we would experience it together in a closed group. Then in the spring these two young people from Amsterdam accidentally ended up here" – the master laughed, because he knew of course that there are no coincidences, "and I can completely understand that they belong here. I think it is extremely important and also interesting that this young man, who has so much talent, should get to know the spiritual side of what I consider to be an idiotic development, but of which, I am of course well aware, there is a dangerous and also a real side. If we were to succeed in ensuring that this young, gifted man, would be able to think about and adopt a different vision of the future, it would certainly be of world importance.

Els, who will be his wife, is gifted in another way. She has a certain mastery in directly recording the facts, whether they are sensory impressions, or people's thoughts… She absorbs them as they are, and in her comes the truth as it should sometimes be seen as an addition, but in most cases as a counter-image. That is a remarkable gift, and it is a miracle that a woman who is so gifted lives beside a man who plays havoc with his gift. It is horrific for that woman to live in a constant inner contradiction with the man she really loves."

Philippe said:

"But by doing so, she saves him too!"

"Certainly…" admitted the Master. "Imagine, however, that you have to listen to this nonsense day in, and day out, or have to live in it unsaid, and that your inner self is such that it blossoms truth repeatedly

– and that you have no choice but to retort incessantly!"

"He does have a great respect for her," said Johannes.

"Of course," said the Master. "Otherwise, this relationship could only fail. I can see that this is a very special couple, not only her but also him. And that we should be thankful that it started to rain when they were here on holiday last time, so they looked for some distraction..."

Johannes laughed and said:

"That distraction must have got way out of hand!"

The door opened, and a sunny young Italian man entered the meeting room. He walked towards them with his arms outstretched, exclaiming:

"Buongiorno singori!"

Because Johannes was a doctor, some of his meetings with important people had taken place in medical circles. For example, this sunny Italian, born in South Tyrol, was a surgeon working at the hospital in Milan. He worked three days a week to spend the rest of the time with his friends at the institute in the mountains. His wife Chiara was there sometimes and at other times not. Beato took a seat. He had met Johannes at a congress in Leiden where they were both participants. From the very first meeting, there had been a warm recognition of each other's being. An important period in Beato's life had been the meeting with a remarkable Dutchman, Gerrit, whom he had ultimately surrounded with medical and spiritual care, until his death here at the institute in the mountains. Beato was remarkable for his outward beauty, his truly masculine vigour, his openness, and his balance. He had an extraordinarily rich inner life and much was achieved in the Institute by the questions he always knew how to ask his colleagues so that he, in particular, had persuaded the silent and withdrawn Philippe to come more to the fore. This initiative, too, to reveal some of the occult knowledge, had come about because of Beato's request for it. The time would certainly come when he himself would come forward with spiritual experiences, but he did not think that time had yet come.

The Master said:

"I asked, when I came in, to tell me what these two gentlemen have been discussing, but we haven't got around to that yet - and of course we have to wait until the others are here too."

The door opened and a new colleague entered. He was also a little older too, maybe about 60. He stood out because of his healthy vitality.

You could immediately tell that he had a choleric temperament. He had black eyes, pitch-black eyebrows, light greying hair… But it was in his posture above all and his way of moving, that you could see and suspect, a concentrated will power that could occasionally erupt. He worked as a doctor at the outpatients' clinic, they had opened here on the premises – years ago – and which was especially popular with the tourists in the area. He was an experienced doctor with a thorough clinical view, he never made a mistake in his diagnosis due to his great intuitive ability to know immediately what was wrong and whether it was something serious or not. He maintained good contacts with the hospitals in the neighbourhood and a fruitful collaboration had developed. He had an enthusiastic interest in the spirituality of Johannes in particular, but he himself was too restless to make any real progress in his meditation, which he practised. In the years, however, he had changed from a rather aggressive, hot-tempered man to a more contemplative type, and it was as if his anger power had transformed into an unshakeable reliability and loyalty. Eva, Johannes's wife, the only woman in the company for the time being, entered behind him. She worked as a doctor in the small clinical ward they had, where mainly chronic patients, who were looking for alternative treatment, could be admitted. She had a rich spiritual experience. She had lived with Johannes for decades, had given him children and shared his meditative journey, it was as if he took her on his inner journeys, and she drew her own inner spirit and self-confidence from them. It was difficult to estimate her age. She was around fifty, but she could also have been ten years younger. She had something girlish of a heavenly beauty about her… The most characteristic feature of Eva was that she was never artificial, that she was a woman who spoke and acted with complete truth – in an apparently effortless way. She was simply like that.

After she had greeted the others, she said:

"Sophie can't be here today, she has another concert, but she'll be here tomorrow. Someone has to fetch her at the airport."

"I'll do that," said Beato. "It will be nice to see her again…"

Johannes spoke and said:

"Good, then we'll give a brief overview of how we'll proceed. We're going to start next Sunday, and we'll meet here in this room for at least an hour every day to discuss the theme together – and that will mean in the first instance that Philippe will speak and that I will join in. At Christmastime, we decided to do this now in summer. You have all made yourselves available, so that we can actually do this – and, as you know, our new friends Raymond and Els are coming from Amsterdam. They give our undertaking an extra dimension. At Christmas we envisaged that it was important here on earth, in this world where spirituality, the very essence, is hardly to be found, to pronounce the development of mankind, from the moment that the human being has essentially become that which is born and has to die again, to the moment and beyond that period of birth and death. That will be the focal point of our consideration, the answer - in as far as it is possible – to the question: How will the human being be conscious, perceive, think, know, experience, communicate, learn, when he no longer has the resistance of the physical body? In what kind of metamorphosis will life and death then be, what are the differences between life on earth and life in the spiritual world, when the boundaries between earthly life and spiritual life no longer have that sharpness which they now have because of the phenomenon of death? And how can we contrast this vision of the future of human development with the vision of transhumanism and posthumanism, whose representatives believe that this phase will begin as early as this century, although we recognise that it is necessary for the development in the biological body, with the phenomenon of birth and death, to continue for millennia? This is the dimension that has been added by the arrival of Raymond and Els, and which gives this undertaking great topicality.

That is what we want to discuss with you every day in this circle, here in this room. We cannot say exactly how much time we will need for this. You have all taken three weeks off. There is no need to write anything down because we will record the whole thing – in the awareness that this is not an ideal form of recording and that in fact this content should not be recorded at all. But because of the undeniably special and unrepeatable aspect of this, we have decided to use this method of recording anyway.

Later in the summer our other friends, who are working at a greater distance from us, will come here to us and perhaps we will have the opportunity to discuss this content again on the same or a different level. Just think of Agnes and Maria, of, for example, Tom from Amsterdam,

Paul from Frankfurt, with his wife Helena…, Anna and Jakob…"

Peter said:

"May I ask something?"

"Always!"

"Isn't it possible that Angelique - she is, after all, Philippe's life companion - and Elisabeth, mine, who after all live so close to us, also participate in these discussions? Maybe also Marie from the Master? Chiara?"

Johannes nodded and said:

"Of course, we've already talked about that! They are welcome … in as far as they wish to."

*

Meanwhile, Els and Raymond were on their way to their rented house in the mountains. He had driven for the first hour, now Els was at the wheel.

"What are you doing on your phone all the time?"

He put it away and said:

"I'm doing some more reading about the spiritualisation of thought."

"You're so good at concentrating!"

"Yes, but it does make me nauseous, so I'll stop anyway…"

"What have you read?"

"I've read that not only the nature of thinking itself has to change - it has to be transformed into pure sense-free thinking - but also the relationship to sense-perception and imagination has to change. You look into the senses with your shadow mind and thereby bring everything into that shadow area. I know that only too well. Because one lives in it so strongly, one can also accept that it would be possible to replace or enrich the still potentiated shadow thinking of the computer with it. Of course, I can see in the meantime what an impoverishment that is…"

"So what has to change?"

"You have to get so far, through the power developed by pure thinking, that you can let that thinking be completely silent so that it is not active in that shadow mind without being noticed, that it is completely silent and that you then use that power of pure thinking to weave along artistically with sensory perception."

"That sounds quite impossible!"

"I don't know…" objected Raymond. "I think you already have a preliminary stage of that, Els. When I read this, I think of you. The way you describe your observations leads me to suspect that you don't submerge everything in these shadow thoughts, but that you imbue everything you observe with a kind of astonishment and therefore see and hear things in it that, for example, totally escape me. It must be a kind of surrender to the world of the senses, without interpretation, but purely in what you see, hear, smell and so on."

"I can't do it now," Els laughed, "because I really need that shadow understanding now to stay in the right lane! But it is recognisable, yes. Only I can't say that I can use the power of pure thinking to replace shadow reasoning, because I'm not aware of having developed pure thinking…"

"Perhaps not yet as a force, but as a quality, namely that you can stop interpreting and explaining and combining and analysing. That you simply live with your sense perception. I don't mean that you let things speak, but that you hear what they have to say while speaking with them."

Els laughed and said:

"It may be that I have something of that quality, but the clarity with which you can explain it really exceeds it! They should be careful in that institute in the mountains that you don't turn out to be a spiritual teacher!"

"Well, they know that my thinking is still far too abstract for that. But the door is ajar, I can feel it. In this lecture, which I have just read, there is constant reference to Goethe, and I have already read a piece from Goethe's writings on natural sciences in recent months. Then you will understand what is meant here. Because he was a master of that contemplative judgment. So, that was not a judgement that is formed by having sensory perceptions which you subsequently arrange and then think about. While you are absorbing something, at the same time, by the very nature of absorbing, you have to know what it is. That is called contemplative consciousness, a viewing consciousness, but also imaginative consciousness. That would be the first spiritual consciousness, which goes beyond pure thinking. Of course, I can do some of that… I am fortunate that I have learned to play the piano and that I have been able to develop that to a certain degree, so that now, when I master a piece, I can indeed move with my whole experience with what I am doing when I play, but which then results in something being performed where you can be happy with your whole experience, as it were, in the hearing. That is a form of artistic bliss that I have always known in all my abstractness. But now, the last few months since the encounter with Johannes and his friends, that artistic bliss also begins to awaken while I am forming thoughts. So, what I do when I form imaginations goes on, as it were, in shaping the thoughts. I am then extremely surprised myself that I apparently have an inner sense for this, while I have neglected it so much."

"Dear Raymond, I feel jubilation when I hear you talk like this! For what you say shows that your highly giftedness is not only a physical disposition based on your DNA, but that it actually flows from a higher area within you. Because otherwise you wouldn't appear to have an aptitude for this higher area."

"Be that as it may," said Raymond, "I would enjoy another of your descriptions of one of the other giants up in the mountains..."

"I'll see if I can do it at the wheel. Who shall I describe? Eva?"

"Fine!"

"Then I must go back to the first real meeting with her. That was when we met her and Johannes more or less by chance at the hotel, where they were having dinner and where we wanted to have dinner too. You would have preferred to leave, but he had already seen us and there was no escape. We then sat down at their table. But you started a conversation with Johannes. I was afraid that it would turn into a discussion, and I would have preferred to run away. I wasn't sitting directly opposite Eva either, so I couldn't withdraw into a conversation with her. But that gave me an inkling of what she is like. When I go back to what I felt then, a very deep sense of nostalgia comes to me. I think she is the archetypal image of a girl, even though she is probably fifty by now, and at the same time the archetypal image of a mother, as a mother is ideally experienced. Someone who understands everything, who can comfort, who is completely open through interest, who does not judge - although I think she too looks straight through you - and who can mediate between father and child, something like that. Johannes is a charming man, but you sense that behind him there is a great severity. She knows how to deal with it and you have the feeling that if you have her on your side, nothing can happen to you. A very strong personality, but someone who has so much self-insight that she keeps that strength in a golden balance. One wonders how someone can be like that… I am sure she will do a very good job as a doctor."

Raymond put his hand on her leg and said:

"If you go on any longer, I won't dare face her!"

"You ask me to describe her, and I will. It is the inner side of her that I have especially noticed, whereas on the outer side is a very special beauty. She is slim, but not too slim, she is graciously feminine, she has dark hair, it could be that it is actually greying, I am not sure. She also has blue eyes, just like Johannes, but of a totally different quality. Her eyes never turn grey, and they radiate what I have just described. She wears beautiful dresses, sometimes jeans and a T-shirt. I haven't seen much jewellery, but she doesn't need it, because she is a diamond herself… With these people, it is quite easy to look at their being in such a way, because that really becomes visible, especially in the conversations we have with them. But actually, one should be able to do that with every human being. One can imagine that critical people who come to that institute in the mountains make very different judgements about these people. For example, I could say of you that you are a bourgeois nerd…"

"Thank you!" he interrupted.

"Well, you know that, that I think that sometimes…. But I can also very well see and describe you as a spiritually gifted young man, who will show a lot in life if only he finds the spirituality. And in self-knowledge, of course, it is already quite clear! When I look at myself with the eyes of an outsider, of course he does not see the quality that I have in sensory perception and the process of knowing. He only sees my outward appearance, my gestures, hears my words, sees my profession and so on… Then it will depend on the circumstances of the moment, how the verdict will turn out. That is what I wanted to add, to put my praise of Eve into perspective."

"Yes," Raymond said, "it is a wonderful combination of areas of life that we have ended up in. I have been very busy in the last few months preparing my work for the university, writing an inaugural address, familiarising myself with different contents – that on the one hand, and on the other hand, I have been engrossed in what we have called 'that other thinking,' which has something in it that looks directly at the truth. I have become really enthusiastic about that and I also feel that in a way I want to dedicate my life to that, although that may sound exaggerated. But at the same time one feels that in doing so one is also saying goodbye to the life we have had up to now, which seems to be a unity, which consisted of that which is accepted in the world as science and art, far from all religion, and that by doing so one is in a way making oneself a laughing stock for that world. For some reason I do not care, it is probably because of those giants there on that mountain, who also made such a choice. With them, it is clear that they are not exactly suckers, engaging in this content and these metamorphoses of soul and spirit. But you do in fact stand with one foot on land and the other in the flowing water and just try to keep your balance!"

"We will learn that," said Els confidently. "You too can feel joy surging in your heart when you think of the coming weeks, can't you?"

"Yes," said Raymond. "I feel it too."

On Sunday morning, at precisely eleven o'clock, the first meeting on the subject of *human development in the future* took place.

Johannes and Philippe had gone to the meeting room early to discuss exactly how they wanted to start.

Philippe was never nervous when he had to speak in public and certainly not when in front of a group of friends. But this time he felt some tension that accompanied the feeling of great responsibility. Were they capable of expressing this responsibly? He had shared his concerns with Johannes and he had replied:

"No Philippe! Of course we are not capable of it! And yet it must be done, a counterweight must be created in the public arena against the anti-Christian tendency that is present in the development of artificial intelligence. If you take John's Gospel seriously, then the Word: 'Everything has become through the Logos and without Him nothing has become of what has become' means that the artificial intelligence has also become through Him. After all, you can see it that way. But if we, as part of that humanity, endowed with occult knowledge, do not raise our voices in relation to the true task of intelligence, then we have not properly understood the principle of human freedom. So, although we cannot do it, we will do it anyway. What then becomes revelation in all its imperfection will certainly be sufficient to provide the right counterbalance, even if this revelation were to remain exclusively within the four walls of this room. After all, we are not alone in our thinking, feeling and willing. The higher hierarchies are at work there as well. Now if only we can manage to direct our spirit strength in such a way that the occult knowing appears in ourselves in the right way, then we will also find the right thoughts and the right words, in which this knowing can be expressed."

"I know!" Philippe sighed. "I know it only too well! But one cannot help continuously thinking of such a great Christian teacher as Dionysius the Areopagite, who in his mystical theology so clearly emphasises the unspeakable and unthinkable of the divine. I know only too well that we really have a task to do in order to clarify this unthinkable and inexpressible in ourselves so consciously that it becomes communicable after all, but I do feel something of a sigh of heaviness in the process. The responsibility is great, Johannes!"

At about a quarter to eleven the friends came in one by one, thirteen in number... Raymond and Els felt strange in this group of people who had known each other very well for years. But they were warmly received and at the same time felt a kind of happiness that they could be here.

Exactly at eleven o'clock Johannes started speaking.

"Dear friends, today we are beginning a work that we hope to carry on for twenty-one days, every day at eleven o'clock in this room. If we use the work of the Master of the Occident, of Rudolf Steiner as a foundation, we have a rich content concerning the development of the world and the human being up to our time, and in the lectures on the Apocalypse we also have a perspective rich in imagery on the development towards the future. But in Rudolf Steiner's work there are at least two places where he points out that in the course of a few thousand years – in one place he speaks of the eighth millennium, in another place of the year 5700 – and describes that the development of humankind will take place in such a way that the physical body will become less and less vital, which will ultimately lead to women losing their fertility and to humans continuing their lives on earth without the incisive events of birth and death. In our time, we seem to see the opposite happening. It seems as though women can still have children up to an increasingly advanced age, which indicates that the physical body is gaining vitality, so that people are reaching an older age. However, in both cases, this is the result of technical intervention; it is not a natural development. We have to distinguish between the two, and it is very important that we keep sharpening our discernment of what technology adds to our evolution and what development actually is. From Christmas onwards, both Philippe and I have been intensely meditating on this process of human development on earth. Philippe will speak, I will add if necessary.

The first question, the question we are asking ourselves today, is: Can we identify a point in the development of humankind on earth where the human being has become a mortal being? If we can see through that point in a spiritual way, then we can also form imaginative ideas about how mankind will overcome death again." Johannes gestured to Philippe and looked at him expectantly.

"If you want to learn about the occult knowledge of humanity's past, you should read the 'An Outline of Occult Science' [3]. It is written at first sight, as a summarised and subsequently as a particularly concrete, objectively written history of world development and of the development of humanity. As a reader, you have to be prepared, let's say, to kindle the wood supplied as substance into a blazing fire yourself. You have to imagine that what is described is apparently experienced in the fire of the Spirit. But the author had to forgo this fiery glow to arrive at a description of what he had spiritually witnessed in comprehensible words – in such a way that the reader is not carried away but has to summon the necessary enthusiasm to transform the last vestiges of the Spirit knowledge given in this book (the words) within himself into the actual witnessing of the events themselves. There will not be many readers who understand that they have to read this book in this way – and even if they understand it, there will not be many who also find the courage and commitment to raise the contents to true Spirit knowledge. But the content is there, it is available to us. So, it is not the history of human development that we want to deal with in these weeks, but it is the future of human development. However, it is necessary to say something about history, because otherwise the vision of the future hangs in the air, whereas it is based on a similar situation in the past.

So, I refer to this book and hope that everyone has also studied and meditated on the passages concerned in preparation for the revelations we will be giving here.

Nevertheless, I would like to briefly outline that fundamental point in the past, which we must see as similar to that which we wish to describe for the future.

We have to imagine that during the development of the earth, man will develop the "I". The I is not meant to be egoistical, although it has partly become so. The "I" is meant here as a highly spiritual substance, which gives the ability to know that you are and also to control who you are and who you will become. The "I" is given to the developing human being during the development of the earth by the high hierarchy of the Exusiai (Potentates, Powers, Elohim). The soul, the

3 Rudolf Steiner 'Die Geheimwissenschaft im Umriss', GA 13. English translation: An Outline of Occult Science.

experiencing being of the human being, would reflect the development of the world unselfishly like a mirror, and the "I" would be there for a self-conscious contemplation of that reflection. There would be no personal contribution except in the contemplation of the reflection.

Our task in meditation is to imagine this as vividly as possible and to compare it with how we now, in the present development, experience our perception, the soul and the beholding "I".

In the development period between that time in the distant past and the development period in which we now find ourselves, a process has begun whereby this divine plan of the Exusiai has taken a different turn. This is also based on divine will, and we must always keep this awareness in our souls. The first sentences of the prologue of St John's Gospel clearly show that it is Christ Himself through whom all things were made, and that there is nothing that has not been made through Him. So, this rupture in the development, as set in motion by the Exusiai, is also a God-willed 'break'. There are seven great periods in the development of the Earth; that, which in occult language is called the Atlantean period, lies in the middle, i.e. the fourth. Around this, the periods are reflected, which is always the case in a series of seven: the fourth member is the middle one, around which the others are reflected.

We are living in the Post-Atlantean era and so the earlier period that keeps us in balance is the one which precedes Atlantis. This is called Lemuria in occult science. You can therefore say, with some reservation, that what takes place at the beginning of the Lemurian period will take place, in more perfect reflection, at the end of the Post-Atlantean period. The rupture described did indeed take place at the beginning of the Lemurian period and will therefore have to find its cure to some extent at the end of the post-Atlantic period. In all occult histories, in myths, sagas, religions, the Bible, you will find this great turning point in human development described. Usually, it is described as the Luciferian temptation, and if you take it in a symbolic sense, you could also call it that. But for a temptation to exist, the one who is tempted must in fact have the possibility of not being tempted either, of resisting the temptation. That is not how we should imagine it. We should imagine it as a spiritual effect that simply overcomes mankind, coming from a realm of beings that are more advanced than the human being himself and to which the human being cannot resist. So in fact it is not a matter of the human being, but a matter of these beings. They do something to the human being that makes it weak enough to be tempted. It was foreseen, as has been said, that the soul would be a completely unselfish mirror for the universe, with all that exists and happens in the universe, and that the self would behold this self-consciously. Now something is introduced into the soul, as a result of which it is no longer merely an unselfish mirror of the worldly realm, but to some extent develops self-interest in it. It also develops its own activity, its own possibilities of choice, its own insight.

You see, here lies the source of the freedom that is thus brought within the reach of humanity. But the price that is paid for this is that the soul acquires more affinity with the nature of desire than it actually should have, and that it mixes this desire nature with the process that would take place in the completely objective reflection: with the process of knowing. Thus, the "I", the actual spiritual being of the human being, is also involved in this decline.

The "I" has, as it were, a highly spiritual superior structure. It has three levels which it will make its own in the future, namely, the higher spiritual self-awareness with a full understanding of the true, beautiful and good... Secondly, a higher spiritual experience, an emotional life that is exclusively concerned with feeling and experiencing the highest values that exist in the cosmos. And finally, a high transcendental will which is not unformed, but which is as formed – but in a spiritual sense – as the human physical body. A wonderful sacred physical spiritual body is the upper tier of that which the human being will become in the future.

A part of the I, of the being that the human being received from the Exusiai, has now descended with it and it is immersed in self-interest. These egoistic impulses in the soul, right up to the highest area of the soul that is the I, have a degrading effect on the physical body and life body obtained on earth. Because of this destructive effect – because the egoism in fact drips into these high earthly being parts like poison – illness and finally death arise, and thus the human being becomes the "citizen of two worlds".

While at the beginning, there was still a possibility of remembering the purely spiritual life before birth and a glimpse of life after death, through this described process this consciousness too has darkened increasingly, until finally it has come to the point that in our time we by nature have no awareness of this at all, except possibly a belief. Only a few people still have a perception. This is why mankind has come so far in his development that the mirror of the soul no longer works, and that self-awareness seems to be completely connected to having a body. Therefore, the human being feels alone in himself, abandoned from God.

But therefore completely free.

An important part of occult science is the development of humanity from that point onwards. In order to be able to experience something of this, it is essential that we use our imagination as vividly as possible, to be able to behold how the high divine beings had foreseen this reflective function of the soul and the observing function of the self for the human being, on the one hand, and then – by imagining and experiencing this as strongly as possible – subsequently try to experience the transition to a human being, in which the physical has gradually become more compact and hardened by the forces of decomposition from within the soul, to bones, flesh and blood, containing a current which turns increasingly to the human – that is the cosmic intelligence – but which at the same time increasingly spiritualises itself.

This whole process of increasing egotism and densification makes us understand how, at a certain point, just before the densification becomes so strong that there seems to be no way back, the highest divine being incarnates in the human body, which has become dense, in order to reverse this process with all divine power. When you understand this, you will have a basis for seeing the onward progressing materialisation on the one hand and spiritualisation on the other, and for understanding the vision of the future. You yourselves must now ensure that the foundation of knowledge concerning the past is sufficiently present. I will then take the liberty of giving a specific daily task and assuming that a number of hours a day will be spent working hard, each by himself.

We have thus passed from a completely unselfish position in the universe, as a stage for all processes and beings in the cosmos, in which the self as observer would participate in the beholding of this reflection and at the same time would see itself reflected, to a state in which the self becomes active from within and is half participating in the egoistic drive, which will also play an increasing role in the process of knowing.

In the Egyptian cultural period, it was still the case that the person who had been initiated into the spiritual secrets had an awareness of the fact that his real spiritual being – the "I" – became visible on earth in a metamorphosis, namely in the physical appearance – and that what the person experienced as his inner self was a temporary flare-up of that luciferic part in the soul. In the Egyptian period it was still known that the actual higher self did not interfere with earthly existence and that it reflected it in the daily consciousness. This knowledge was gradually lost, and the human being awakened more and more with the I-consciousness on earth, became increasingly aware of the ability to think for himself, but thereby gradually lost the connection with the actual higher self, which is part of the whole spiritual world.

As we are now, from our natural constitution, here in the Occident, we have a strong intellectual development that is seen as a consequence of the physical development.

We bet on one horse and that is the physical body – unless there is an occult knowing. In ordinary natural science we know of no life, no soul and no spirit, and we see intelligence as a product and a quality of the brain. The better the brain formation, the more brilliant is the intelligence.

It is as if there are only living bones, muscles, organs, blood and brains, and as though the interplay of these causes the human being to have a vision, a hallucination of a being that he would be, an "I". Humans are believed to be able to form intelligent theories as the peculiar products of their brains... An initiate, however, knows that never in the development of mankind has the thinking of the human being, where he is working intelligently, been so spiritual as in our time. The content is not spiritual, but the intelligence itself has become purely spiritual in the course of human development, thanks to the impact of the Christ impulse. What we lack for the time being is an awareness of that spiritual element. That is not only a question of knowing it – because you can actually already know it once you have heard it – but experiencing it, living it and then learning to behold it in such a way that in the beholding of that spiritual element the capacity for higher knowing gradually arises. When you repeat it, it has no meaning. When you bring it to realisation, this is the step to true humanity of the future. It is this humanity that we want to talk about daily in these weeks.

I repeat once more: Let us experience the transition from selflessness to self-centredness in as differentiated and concrete a way as possible. You can only do that in meditation. And then let us try to consider how this fall into selfishness has led to a destructive effect of the soul on the body, causing illness and death. Let us experience how, on the other hand, this fall into selfishness has caused the body to become denser and denser, until it is so dense that it has spread like a veil over the spiritual world, through which we humans have found freedom on the one hand but have lost sight of the divine spirituality on the other. Only in this way it would be possible for what is described in the singularity and in transhumanism and posthumanism to become an objective. It is really only possible to think this when intelligence has completely lost sight of its true origin and then, out of a deep yet emerging desire for further development, begins to seek this development in technology. In this, after all, man clearly has a hand, whereas in the development of man's biological disposition, of course, this is far from being the case. You can increase and accelerate and perfect human knowledge with a device. But a transformation of the cognitive faculty as such remains impossible. From this arises the desire to create a relationship between the machine and the brain and perhaps even to fulfil the dream that the actual intelligent being of man can be taken over completely by a machine.

It is absolutely incomprehensible to me that one would not see the inconsistencies that lie in such a line of thought. But that does not mean that it is technically impossible. So, for the time being, we will take this vision of the future of the singularity seriously and try with all the power of mind to put into words how human intelligence, perception and willpower will eventually function when the biological body can no longer exist.

Study this described transition in Lemurian time intensively once more, meditate intensively. Then tomorrow we will try to describe the Christ Impulse in this light.

Then there is still opportunity now for additions and questions..."

Johannes said:
"Philippe, then we must imagine how our soul lived in complete surrender to the All, without any input or movement of its own, only consciousness. This is how a sense organ functions in our time, it only reflects. The whole soul then was like an infinitely differentiated sense organ."
"Without any materiality, yes."
"And the I was silent, without forming thoughts, it only watched. The luciferic impulse then gives rise to the desire to behold an outside world through the soul, not from an outsider's position. This then becomes the later sense function, through the body to the outside world. It is very beautifully represented in the myth of Persephone, who is seduced by Eros to pick the daffodil.... The self acquires a certain power of its own, but thereby loses 'paradise."
The Master said:
"In Eastern mysticism we seek the way back to this state. A complete surrender to 'what is' and a beholding of it, in which the observer and the observed must coincide. We refuse to acknowledge that the human being has to go through that selfishness to reach freedom. We see that selfishness as absolutely evil, and all ego urges must be renounced. From you, Johannes, I have learned how it is possible to go through the evil without losing one's true being, and then to step into the development, to the depth and with Christ to rise again... But it must not remain words, no religious attention alone, it must be worked on very hard. In fact, you must not utter the word 'Christ' at all, because it so easily becomes a phrase. You, Philippe, will succeed in teaching us how to speak of Him in realities rather than in phrases."
Beato said:
"We learn here, in this transition from paradise to earth, how the Evil One is the Good One. Lucifer calls us to come to ourselves, has brought us to this. But through that comes the possibility to take the development into our own hands, to come to know ourselves, and that will be the Holy Spirit in the future, when that 'Knowing Yourself' will be given back to our God by our own free will, without losing its own contribution."
Peter said:
"The soul has been like a zoo in primeval times, anima was animal.

We have been allowed to expel it, but it now stalks us from the outside. I experience the "I" as an impulse that always seeks harmony in the remaining animality. That is why I followed Johannes here, because at first, I experienced this from outside, coming from him. An animal is not selfish, albeit beastly. I am, though I am somewhat human already. It's very interesting, this..."

Raymond had listened with amazement. He obviously felt like a novice in the circle of people who were all well-informed about this occult science. He had prepared himself well. He had studied the relevant parts intensively but had not enjoyed them very much. In itself, he could not say that what he had read was implausible, but neither was he convinced that it had to be true. It seemed to be a summary of information and he now understood more clearly that it was only the wood that he had to kindle himself. When he thought back now to what he had read, it was like a complex of facts submerged in the semi-darkness of his consciousness. He was not able to experience anything.

Now he had heard exactly the same explanation from Philippe, although the use of words, with which Philippe formed his thoughts, was definitely different. He was now able to experience these thoughts to a far greater degree than when he had read them. It seemed as though Philippe's enthusiasm also ignited something in him so that a light began to shine, and warmth began to spread over these initially dark facts. The additions of the others brought more colour to what had been said... It was clear to him that each of the people present had a very clear direction in which he or she had taken in the presentation. What at first seemed to be a collection of facts piled up in a shady corner now became a colourfully impressive, indeed almost musical, palette. But with that, he lost the ability to remember anything at all. What he still remembered came from what he had previously read. He also regularly felt waves of criticism and even ridicule. He really didn't want to feel it, let alone think it, but it forced itself on him. Each time he pushed it away and assumed that it was not he himself who started these counter-movements.

He still had no idea what it must have been like in the past. What did the human being of that time look like? What skills did he really have, what was the corresponding primitive human being, known from evolution, compared to this human being who was drawn into egotism? In that sense, for him, it was still only a description and not the experience of a real event.

Meanwhile, the conversation continued. The youngest member of the group, Sophie, a girl of well under thirty, had the courage to speak and she said:

"It seems to me that musically this transition from unselfishness to selfishness is the transition from the one to the two.... First everything is unison, there is no differentiation, no discord and therefore no harmony. Now discord is born and with it every possible contradiction, it seems to me. So, it must be that because of this, the differentiation into two genders has taken place. There is a certain falseness in the tonal field - but we know from music that we can experience harmony thanks to the fact that there can also be disharmony."

Philippe nodded affirmatively.

Eva spoke up and said:

"It is clear that before this great moment in development, there could be no question of illness or death, whereas after that, it becomes a necessity that the physical sheath be taken off again and again. I know that the Greeks still had a clear notion of the effect of that egoistic soul - with of course also an unselfish part - on the fluid organism of the human being. The Greek physician hardly looked at the material physical body but could still sympathise with the penetration of the soul into the various qualities of the fluids. As a doctor, I have made a great effort to go back to that perception of the Greek doctor. It is much easier to feel how there is a thorn in the soul that is connected with egotism and how this is exposed to other influences later in the development of mankind, while the Christ impulse has already taken place..."

Philippe said:

"You mean that other counter-powers appear on the battlefield, working hard to tie the soul to the body?"

Eva nodded.

"As doctors, we are constantly engaged in these two processes. On the one hand, the soul's destructive effect, which has led to illness and death – and on the other hand, the tendency to chain the soul, which is after all a transcendental being, far too strongly to the material body..."

A silence fell. The other participants evidently did not feel called upon to go into this further, and after the silence had reached its lowest point, Johannes spoke up and said:

"When we deepen these first contents in meditation, it is important that we are not satisfied with the shadow nature of the thoughts. We must be aware that these past processes are still present in all liveliness in the true thought life of man, albeit in a reflection of these living thoughts, which gives them their shadow character. This is precisely a consequence of this luciferic influence, one might say: a very last consequence. You can suffer greatly from this, that what took place in the past in all its grandeur and vividness is now only *imaginable.* But it is precisely the experience of this incapacity that gradually makes it possible to find the way back to the original liveliness of thought, where thoughts are real events. That is, they do not *refer* to those events but *are* those events themselves.

It is important that we remember this – and on the other hand, there is nothing gained by force. So, when our thoughts retain the shadow character, we cannot do anything else in the first instance but perceive this inability, in order to move from the shadow character into true liveliness.

Then we will separate now and continue this work here tomorrow at precisely eleven o'clock."

Raymond and Els wanted to walk away, but Johannes stopped them and said:

"We still have the whole day to work on this theme. Shall we not have lunch together on the terrace?"

Raymond sighed and said:

"I'd love to, Johannes! I'm rather flabbergasted..."

Eva joined them and the four of them sat down on the terrace outside. Els said:

"We are beginners, Johannes! What do you want with us? We will never be able to keep up with it. It's like going to university as a child!"

Johannes burst out laughing.

"I can imagine that you feel like that, but in fact it's really different! Every person carries the contents that we are discussing here in his soul and in you two people we have recognised that possibility to learn to listen to them. This is not the same for all people."

"Let me say then," Raymond said, "that as a talented piano student, I have to learn to play Chopin's Ballade in G minor in the first year."

"That's a similar comparison," Johannes said. "Both studying at university and playing the Ballade in g-minor require a training of the physical body, which is a long and arduous process. What we are doing here now also requires training, of course, and that is also a long and laborious process, but that process is linked to the skill of thinking and not to the content of thinking. In fact, you can start at any point in the occult science as far as content is concerned. Your ability to absorb that content with a pure thinking activity is then decisive. That aptitude is not so much formed in the present life but comes from a more distant past – and of course we are able to perceive in people, how their aptitude in that area lies. If it is not there or if it is insufficient, then it is indeed as if you have to go to university like a pre-school child. Then you will absorb the university content in a toddler-like way. But that is not the case with either of you. I hope you didn't feel constantly out of place."

Raymond shook his head somewhat desperately and said:

"No, I haven't. You really give us a warm welcome. But I do suffer from annoying fits of temper, which I cannot consider to belong to my own judgment. That is one thing and the other is that, for the time being, it remains a science that proceeds entirely in the reflection, and the entrance to reality with a very thick gate with large locks and bolts, is inaccessible to me. In the rest of my scientific work everything is also shadow and there it doesn't bother me at all. But here it does. Because there is no foothold, and because as a human being one probably knows very well that this area is more alive than anything else in the world..."

"So, you have to learn to experience that powerlessness," Johannes said. 'That is the best medicine. For it is the physical reflection that is so strong that the reality behind it - or perhaps I should say, the reality before it - is totally unrewarding. Hidden indeed behind a thick gate..."

Eva asked:

"And how is it with you, Els?"

"Different. Of course, I have also read the preparatory texts and I have also read what Raymond calls summaries, but with me, it works differently. Since we were here last time, we have found a second way of thinking. We call it the 'other thinking'. One thinking is what we use in everyday life and in our work, and that 'other thinking' comes to mind when I read and study and meditate on spiritual science, or let me say, I think differently. I also notice it when I read a book like this. You cannot stay in the images, you have to move, so that you lift all those different terms that are there, as it were, out of their similarity. If you don't do that, it doesn't matter whether you are reading about a Spirit of Form or a Spirit of Movement. Then they are just different words. But at the same time, of course, you do know the difference between form and movement, and if you include that in your reading, then a certain mobility comes into your thinking. I have not known that before. It is like the difference between a film image and life itself. And indeed, when you sit here and listen to Philippe, his way of thinking - which he then expresses - helps you tremendously to get into that dynamic element. I think I can say that I really feel that my brain no longer participates in thinking, that the mirror no longer functions or works, is no longer reached and that I don't need it either because I am working on a completely different level of thinking. That is also a little bit scary because suddenly you yourself are a part of what you are thinking - whereas in ordinary thinking you can remain in your chair, so to speak, and then quietly wait for everything to happen to you. Probably we perceive this unconsciously in depth and we are also far more active there than we know, but we do not notice it. Now I do notice it and as I said, on the one hand it gives a feeling of blissful liberation, but on the other hand it is also a bit scary. As if you are saying goodbye to a part of this world. I don't think I would have understood a word of those texts if I hadn't climbed in and thought from the inside. Many words remain unattainable to a certain extent. Spirits of Form, Spirits of Movement, Spirits of Wisdom, Spirits of Will … that is possible. But when it is said: Spirits of the personality, or Fire Spirits, or Sons of Life. then it becomes a bit more difficult, then the power to think along wanes and it becomes incomprehensibly abstract."

Eva nodded and said:

"That is quite understandable, of course. In my study of spiritual science, I also studied for a long time before the words used and the concepts expressed with them took on anything substantial. You mention the spiritual beings of the angels, archangels and higher heavenly hierarchies. How should we, with our abstract reflective thinking, have direct contact with the reality of these beings? Of course, there can be no other way than to devote the necessary energy to that anyway…"

Johannes said:

"Yes, in that sense it is the kindergarten and the university. The difference is that in the unconscious you inherently have all these essential concepts but it is the constitution of the modern human being that shuts him out, as it were, from that gate with locks. Even if the locks were open, people would still not know where the hinges are and realise that the door is not only no longer closed but can also be opened."

Raymond sighed deeply and said:

"It's really hard for me not to get totally frustrated and run off! It seems like everyone, including Els, knows the rules of the game except me."

"That's not true at all," said Els, 'because just like me, you know that other thinking very well by now! It's just a question of finding the right application."

"You seem to have more talent for that…" Raymond grumbled.

"It is usually the case with you," said Els, "that when you have fully understood how something should be done, you then immediately take the lead. So, don't worry, it's just a question of patience."

Raymond burst out laughing and said:

"Well, you know, patience may be a fine thing, but it's not something I have."

Johannes had the last word and said:

"I suspect, my dear Raymond, that even your patience will be sufficient to grasp the change in thinking so that you may not be completely in the lead right away, but you will at least be able to keep up with us with the greatest of ease…"

In the evening at dinner, Raymond said to Els:

"I have spent the rest of today trying to put myself back in the state I was in before the luciferic attack. I have tried to be only a mirror and to do nothing but look at what the mirror reflects. But that is difficult! Only then do you notice how you constantly want to interfere in everything."

"Apparently that's the intention…" Els said.

"But we wanted to explore the transition from total selflessness to selfishness, so I tried to get in touch with a soul life in which there is no personal movement at all, only reflection and beholding and nothing else."

"How long did you keep that up?" asked Els.

"You can only keep it up for a few seconds and then you have to start all over again. I could imagine that a permanent state is perhaps something an Eastern master achieves. We here, in our culture, are of course so used to forming our own thoughts about everything and not being satisfied with not knowing anything, that we constantly meddle with everything, even internally, especially internally! In any case, I have seen that very clearly and I have seen and felt what it would be like if one were to leave all that behind."

"Would that be possible? Would it be possible to live in this day and age?"

"No, I don't think that can be a permanent state, but in exceptional moments it is something not to be forgotten. Another aspect is to perceive every detail of what changed after the impact. That is where one really needs the help of someone like Philippe or Johannes, who have not only studied all this, but have also learned to experience it themselves and to place it in the course of human history. When listening to Philippe, I feel that he has gone through all those human cultures with his consciousness and has felt how the luciferic influence has worked specifically in that period of culture. I must say that I am attracted to this. I would like to imitate it. That I could learn to move in the different successive cultures and then find out how the luciferic influence continues to work."

"You see?" Els said. "You're already starting to get ahead of yourself!"

"Not at all…" grumbled Raymond. "It's a big cycle of powerlessness. One wants to move into selflessness, and one only holds on for a few seconds. But in a way you are right. In those few seconds, a wealth of experiences is revealed. What did you do this afternoon?"

"I mainly read the work of the Master of the Occident. How he speaks in different ways about that point in the Bible called the Fall of Man I have never been able to agree with that, but the way it is described in, it becomes an inescapable truth. As a doctor I see, as Eva also expressed this morning, the effect on that miraculous body of the human being. That it can become diseased and that it must inexorably die, again and again and again... What we, as spiritually blind people, prefer not to think about – the fact that we have to die – is placed in a very special light here. You can understand that it is necessary, and you can also expect that it is temporary! That is, a time will come when we can continue to live fully consciously on earth, when we no longer have that earthly body, which we have to give back to the elements again and again..."

*

Philippe began to speak:

"I will stay with the same theme as yesterday once more, as I have received a number of questions regarding the separation in the sexes. I have spoken about this briefly, but I have not elaborated on it. The questions I received made it clear to me that if we want to outline the vision of the future as clearly as possible, it is important that we stop at this gender division. When you study what the Akasha Chronicle has to say about it, what we call the 'Fall' is not something that happened in a moment. It is a process that has taken a long time and in which not all participants in human genesis have undergone a change from a bi-sexual to a single-sex existence at the same time. We have to imagine that, during a transitional period, there were people who were bisexual, with, in addition, people who were asexual. It is very clear in the Akasha Chronicle that there are higher spiritual beings – that is, one level higher than human beings – in whom all that they deploy in terms of power is fully manifested. We call this gift love. Everything that you keep for yourself is not love; everything that you give outwardly is love. These beings come to wisdom through this revelation of love.

What I spoke of yesterday as the mirror of the soul, which has no activities of its own, we must here again imagine to a higher degree, namely, that the wisdom of the world holds a power of attraction, which is awakened precisely because everything that comes into consciousness immediately reveals itself to the outside world. There is, as it were, no secret inner concealed area in which something can be kept. This was the case yet with mankind on a lower level. As the human being immediately revealed everything he had to the outside world, as was the case for a time in bisexuality, no knowledge could come into being, no wisdom could be absorbed. The human being lived with the tree of love and life - but did not have the ability to take in the tree of knowledge. This is the image of the bi-sexual human being.

With the onset of development whereby the human being becomes either male or female, a complete change gradually occurs, such that a human being does become capable of absorbing wisdom. The Akasha Chronicle shows this as follows: The outer body has a limited design, concentrates, as it were, in one gender. This would result in a one-sidedness, were it not for the fact that with this outer one-sidedness, an inner life also ignited. The soul life becomes an inner consciousness and is marked by the opposite sex. So, when the body has a male appearance, the soul is female and vice versa. This would have been a total contradiction within mankind if there had not been a third possibility given to man, namely, that in this inner life there is always a communication of the soul with the spirit. The spirit now stands above the sexuality and cancels it completely. This creates spiritual equality within the entire human race. This spiritual equality means wisdom ... The soul, which is characterised by the opposite sex to the body, is fertilised with spirit, and this is the tree of knowledge from which the soul feeds. Therefore, in mankind, in every human being, in the hidden, namely in the inner self, there is a communion with the spirit. Love and procreation are shifted outward; procreation takes place through the power of sensual love. In the interior, in the hidden, that other fertilisation occurs: the fertilisation with the spirit. In that area the luciferic spirits are at play. The higher spiritual beings who are only love and have wisdom through love lead the human being to outwardly develop the love that for the time being can only be physical and reproduces itself with the blood. The tree of knowledge is the tree of the nervous system and in it hides the serpent who wants to give wisdom a purely personal character and separate it from the divine existence. On the other hand, the human being owes his ability to internalise and attain wisdom to these luciferic beings. To this very day, what we call knowledge, and what comes into being in ordinary human consciousness, is still given by Lucifer. We are at a turning point in our time, but we will talk about that later.

So today we must immerse ourselves in that passage in which we find a description in the notices from the Akasha Chronicle, and furthermore, through meditation, we must try to delve into the difference between the state of consciousness of those higher love beings that we call angels, who do not know any inner secret, but who consecrate all that they are and are capable of into the power of love. This love is consecrated, and through this consecrated love they are filled with wisdom. As human beings, we are not like that. But we are in the process of becoming like that, albeit with a different essence. The goal of earth development is that we reach that state of consciousness of the angels, of the love beings, in a human way. We do not have that state of consciousness yet. But we can make an attempt to imagine as concretely possible what this state of consciousness will be like.

And in contrast, we then imagine this division into genders, which simultaneously means a division between an outer and inner life for every human being, whereby the outer life is the school of love, and the inner life is the school of wisdom. In our case, it is not possible that love attracts wisdom. We have to prepare ourselves for a conscious conception with the spirit, through which wisdom will flow into us, and which we can increasingly let flow out consciously into the outer life. This outflow will then become decreasingly sensual and more and more a social gift.

That is the task for today, that we do not go home feeling satisfied with what we receive here together, but that we bring it into a spiritual fertilisation by meditating intensely on it."

Johannes said:

"There may still be questions in relation to this task that you are asking us, Philippe. Yesterday we had the opportunity to fulfil such a task for the first time and I assume that it was not easy for everyone. I think it would be good if those who wish to do so could give an account of it."

Elisabeth, Peter's wife, began to speak. She was an interesting character, with pale skin and reddish hair, intelligent green eyes and fine limbs. She was a mathematician by profession, and she worked together with the Master in this field of mathematics, attempting to breathe new life into the old teachings of Pythagoras. She said:

"I always pay very close attention in meditation to the realisation that I myself am the thinker, when I put a meditative content at the centre of consciousness, or when I try to formulate and solve a mathematical problem. Thus, I know exactly where my own contribution to thinking begins and ends. I have used this knowledge to make an attempt to be conscious without any input from myself. Of course, in meditation you always practice this, after you have become so active that the activity is perceptible. When you then do away with it, you are in fact in the same situation as you are when you directly try to be conscious without any input from yourself. But then I find it astonishing to see how little is actually left. Consciousness, yes, but that consciousness is empty. I can endure it for a few seconds, but then the void fills up again with my usual associative activity."

Philippe nodded and said:

"I understand that… But now it was not so much a question of establishing whether a certain skill had already been developed, but solely and exclusively an attempt to imagine what you would be like as a human being if there were no personal activity and you were a mirror for the universe in absolute silence, an equally absolute silent spectator of it."

Elisabeth nodded and said:

"Yes. What I want to say is, that you then have to conclude that you can't actually sustain that and that if that was to be a state of consciousness of the future, a great deal would have to happen after all."

"The problem is," Philippe said, "that we have to be aware that this is not the future of us. The higher spiritual beings wanted this as a possibility for man. But that would have developed without a luciferic influence. Now there is a luciferic influence and therefore the possibility of the future for mankind has become different. That is what we are aiming for from these weeks, that we will be able to develop an idea of that. So, yesterday's task was to imagine something that will not be realised in that way. What is the reason why it will not be realised? Because of the luciferic disposition, love becomes sexual and sensual outwardly, whereas wisdom is received inwardly in conception by the Spirit, thus giving up the separation in the sexes, but bringing about a completely different character to the receiving of wisdom. In the higher beings I have described, wisdom comes self-evidently as a result of love into the consciousness of those beings. This is not the case with the human being. Humans have to desire wisdom. He will not receive wisdom if he does not long for it. That is a very important characteristic of the human ability to attain knowledge. At the very depth of the soul lies an intense desire for wisdom..."

*

They joined Johannes and Eva for lunch again outside on the terrace. It was glorious summer weather, and one would have thought that it was a group on holiday having lunch there.

Raymond said:

"I hope you don't feel obliged to lunch with us here every day now! In any case, we are very honoured..."

Johannes laughed and said:

"Why shouldn't *we* feel honoured? No, look Raymond, I think it's important that we can sit together informally for another hour, because it's quite something for you, who have only been involved with this different view of the world for a few months, to be included in the centre of all this activity. I can imagine that after only two days you may feel that it is too much for you..."

Raymond shook his head and said:

"No! I must say I find it fascinating. Perhaps it would be different if it were only lectures. But now we are involved in a direct insight into the spiritual world, at least that's how it seems to me. Because there is also a task involved for ourselves, I found it more interesting today than yesterday. And yesterday I also found it very interesting! I am looking forward to imagining the next metamorphosis of consciousness and to comparing the three different forms: the reflective consciousness, the angelic consciousness and the single-sex consciousness, and then perhaps as a fourth reflection on what our own consciousness is like now, in this day and age."

Johannes' eyes lit up and he said:

"Look, here speaks the novice spiritual scientist. If you can take pleasure in exploring these inner states of soul and spirit, then you are in fact a spiritual scientist. Then I need not worry about your well-being. But the fact remains that I would not like it if you were present here as newcomers and did not receive any attention from us apart from that presence. So, we took into account that we would have lunch together and that we could talk to each other every day. After all, this does not always have to be about the theme. As we progress in this theme, the importance of your vision of the singularity and transhumanism and posthumanism will come up again. I don't think it's impossible that at some point we will ask you to give an evening speech on this subject. I don't know how you feel about that."

Raymond looked at him with wide eyes, but he said:

"I have no problem with that. I know that subject like the back of my hand, I feel completely at home with it... So, it doesn't even require any preparation. But whether a spiritualised crowd like yours wants to listen to it, that's another thing."

"Then they have to create an appetite, if they don't have one. I think it is of the utmost importance that we do not become unworldly here on this mountain, but that we remain alert to what is happening and developing in the world. I make sure of that myself by keeping up with a lot of literature, but not everyone can do that. Then a lecture like this would really be a gift to us."

"Well," said Raymond, "for me it would naturally be an honour to be allowed to do that. So, if you really would like it, let me know..."

Johannes turned to Els and said:

"How was today for you?"

Els looked ahead thoughtfully and then said:

"Overwhelming, I think. It's not so easy to remember the differences between those consciousnesses and certainly not to experience them... I still look at it more or less outwardly and will have to go and read about it soon to awaken my memories and will of course then also try to feel what the differences are meditatively. But I certainly cannot do it as Raymond describes it. For me it is more like a chapter of philosophy, in which you are presented with a content that is at first completely abstract and that you can only bring to life when you dive into the water, as it were, and start swimming. For the time being, that water is still undifferentiated, and I must first find the differentiation in order to be able to experience something in swimming other than the water around me…"

"Does it make you unhappy?" asked Johannes.

"No, it doesn't. But I don't feel that it's bearing fruits as I sense in Raymond. I am amazed at that! You will see that he turns out to be highly gifted in this respect too… Don't get me wrong, I admire that in him. I don't think there is a single fibre nor hint of jealousy in me and I also know that I have certain qualities that necessarily complement his. But I am amazed! Three months ago, I was in despair about his materialism and now look! You really don't think that's possible!"

Eva said:

"This is familiar to me, Els. We have been together for decades now, Johannes and I. I have never stopped marvelling at his wealth of spirit and his character. In the beginning all of this stood like a shimmering wall before me, and I had the feeling: How am I ever going to get in? But I managed to enter, that is, he just let me in. On my wanderings through his faculties, I pass from one wonder to another…"

Raymond said:

"The 'case of Johannes' seems to be rather different from the 'case of Raymond' to me. Three months ago, I may have been a total materialist, but I recognised Johannes in his spiritual life, which is unequalled by any Raymond."

"Well, well, well," said Johannes. "That's enough for today…"

Els and Raymond went for a walk in the park. In the distance they saw a dark figure approaching.

Raymond said:

"Oh dear, here comes the Master!"

Els laughed and said:

"We can hardly turn round, so let's just bump into him!"

They literally did, for the Master spread out his arms and said:

"Ah there we have our Raymond and Els! How are you, children?"

The children laughed and Raymond said:

"The children are doing quite well. We are both very happy to be here and to be experiencing this…"

"I tell you, Raymond," the master said, "I have never seen such a metamorphosis of a human being in my life as I see in you. The first time we spoke in that legendary conversation that made you so angry…"

Raymond made a dismissive gesture.

"No, no!" the Master said. "You were furious. In that conversation, I had a man before me, a young man with an indescribable pride of intellect – not incomprehensibly so, since he had an extraordinarily well-developed intellect – and with, shall we say, chakras that were tightly locked. Now it is a few months later, but when I see you now, I see the image of a young man with a modest attitude towards his high intellectual ability and I see chakras that have the tendency to open one by one. You are a very special boy, believe me!"

Raymond burst out laughing and said:

"Master! Don't feed my pride too much!"

He patted him on the arm, smiling, made a gesture towards Els and said:

"She's not bad either!" and walked on.

In the evening at dinner, Els asked Raymond:

"What have you done today with the task we were given?"

Raymond said:

"I tried to be an angel myself… You can see that you are not! You can't achieve that at all. Yet there is something inside that resembles it. But I understand that an angel doesn't have that 'inside' at all! When an angel has something like an inner consciousness, it must mean that he or she is together with all the angels, archangels and even higher beings. And when an angel thinks something, it doesn't take place internally, it reveals itself directly. You can only imagine it. It is impossible to reproduce it in inner life. And you can't do it externally at all. You can feel that the human being is not an angel, that at the most there is a certain resemblance or maybe even a unity with the angel, in a minute part of the consciousness, when you recognise something in truth…"

"Do you," Els asked, "not have anything at all in you that says: Who says that an angel is like that? Why should it be so, as Philippe says?"

"No," said Raymond. "Strange isn't it. There is nothing in me that doubts. I find it so obvious, that one could say: As a human being, you have something like an angel, you don't add anything to it yourself. You then have an inner feeling, in a glimpse you know: this is true and at the same time it is a revelation. I could never think it before, because I did not know it. But now that I have that knowledge, it is completely clear. Do you have any doubts, Els?"

"No, actually not…" Els said. "But I can talk myself into it, because you have the feeling that you shouldn't just accept things but test them or something. I can't just say: Yes, that's the way it is."

"I don't know why you can't say that! If you know something for sure? What's the difference with knowing for sure that a triangle is a triangle? You don't need any other knowledge for that, do you?"

"To know that, you need the knowledge of angles, lines and so on, don't you?"

"That may be…" Raymond said, "but that is the basic constituent knowledge. Of course, in the consciousness of an angel, you have that too: you know what you mean by consciousness, you know what you mean by wisdom, you know what you mean by love, by revelation, by inner, by outer - all those basic concepts are there, and the composite understanding of the consciousness of the angel is, as far as I'm concerned, clear, absolutely immediately."

"And if I were to say: 'Yes, but that is not an angel you describe, that is a seraph'?"

"Well," said Raymond, "as far as I am concerned that would be a question of names. I am not sure about that. Which spiritual being is that? I only know that a spiritual being can be imagined who has such consciousness, and that although Philippe did not use the word angel to describe it, it emerged from the whole composition of his discourse that it is the next level of the hierarchy. That this being is one step higher than the human being. I think I know that, which is why I say angel…"

Philippe resumed speaking at precisely eleven o'clock.

"Today I would like to discuss a third aspect of human development, as determined by the impact of egoism. Yesterday I described how the soul is fertilised internally by the Spirit. This higher spiritual being is to be regarded as the actual human being. In secret sciences it is described that the higher spiritual beings who are in control of human development on earth – these are the Exusiai, called the Elohim in the Bible - are the creators of the human higher self, with whom the soul can fertilise itself as a spirit. Today, the soul is still characterised by an animal process, though no longer as chaotic and wild as it was at the beginning of the Earth's development. It has been purified to a certain extent, since that which was most wild and chaotic in the soul has become externalised and now lives visibly in the environment as the animal realm... Yet the human soul still manifests animal tendencies. There is no question of the soul already possessing holiness. But now inwardly, the possibility of fertilisation with the higher human spirit arises, which in further development will be fully consciously within the reach of man as the "Spirit Self" or Manas, "Life Spirit" or Buddhi, and "Spirit Man" or Atman. In the distant future, the soul will have completely purified and sanctified itself, so that it lives exclusively in the non-egotistical true, beautiful and good. This will enter into the feeling, become the "Life Spirit" and finally enter into the will, to the physical body and become the "Spirit Man".

But because of the soaring egoism, this higher being does not yet come within reach of the human being. Very gradually, the soul is fertilised in wisdom with that higher being part. It is described as the most important characteristic of this being that it brings order out of chaos and peace out of conflict.

But this being still guides the development mainly from the background and does not manifest as a concrete presence yet. We have to imagine that in a long, long period of development, this higher part of the being, the higher "I", the actual individuality of the human being, will first bring complete peace to the restlessness of one's own astral body, so that within one's own soul all unrest and inner struggle will come to an end. When this has been achieved, only then will it be possible for this high spiritual human being to radiate into the environment and there unfold the peace and order-bringing power. As long as this higher being has not harmonised his or her soul this radiation to the outside world cannot take place.

There is a beautiful characteristic of this higher human being. This characteristic comes from the Jewish literature and reads as follows:

In you lives the Human Being
Who sees God face to face,
Who is eternal and is in the realm of the Seven Great Spirits.

It is above everything in you that is anger and fear.

It reigns with the powers of the upper world
And is served by the powers of the underworld.

It controls its own life and health and can do the same to others.

It cannot be surprised, it cannot be struck by any accident,
It cannot be confused and cannot be overcome.

It knows the being of the past, present and future.

It has the secret of the resurrection from the dead
And immortality in its possession.[4]

When we allow this to sink in, we have some idea in words of the highness and grandeur of that higher self, created for earth development, which has a resemblance to the deity itself.

We know, of course, that the inner egotism brought into the soul hinders or even makes the descent of this high human being impossible. Therefore, the way of this descent is not free. But it also creates the possibility for a person to come to an inner reflection and through that reflection to have the ability to learn to know and to bring about this higher self by self-awareness.

---

4 "In dir lebt das Menschenwesen...", to find in the work of Eliphas Levi, by Rudolf Steiner brought in a form with vocals and given to for instance Edith Maryon and Ita Wegman.

When we look at the development of mankind as it actually happened and of which we have records in various religious documents such as the writings of Mani and the Gatas of Zarathustra, the documents of the Egyptian traditions, the Old Testament, the ancient Chinese wisdom.... If we could study all these pre-Christian documents, we could see for ourselves how, in our Post-Atlantean age, development has passed through various cultural epochs and how there has been a loss of a primitive primordial society with the divine and, on the other hand, an ever-increasing refinement of sensory perception and the development of reason.

The human being withdraws more and more within the confines of his own body, begins to experience himself as an enclosed self, and thus gradually arrives at that opposition of self and world which we know.

The Luciferic impact has a meaning. It is the sense of the emergence of an inner life in which the impulse of freedom can gradually arise. On the other hand, this Luciferic impulse is an attack on the development of mankind as intended by God, and we must imagine how this Luciferic impulse could continue to act in such a way that the human being would indeed achieve freedom but cut himself off completely from everything else in the process, including God. For this to oppose, a second influence in the development of mankind must be established, and although in the religious sphere this is understood to mean that mankind's primal guilt is reconciled, we must learn to understand this differently, as symbolic imagination. For, as I have said before, something was *inflicted* on humanity without being able to do anything about it. And so, this second impact in the development of mankind becomes something that is also done to the human being, but which in fact is a redemption by the divine world itself for something that was done to him through no fault of his own.

You can thus understand why it is said: The coming of Christ on earth is in fact an event in the spiritual world. It is an event that must take place on earth but it is in fact making amends in the spiritual world. It is a matter of gods, not of men.

But the human being has a part in it, because he is the stage where all this takes place. You could also say that he is the one on whom all this is inflicted.

Let us set ourselves the task of immersing ourselves as intensely as possible in that high human being who is the bringer of peace, but who finds it difficult to gain access to the soul because of highly inflamed egotism..."

Marie, the Master's life companion asked:

"Then I should try to imagine all the possible ideal things that a human being is capable of and could be? And then try to identify with that being who has those possibilities and who would like to realise them in earthly existence? And then experience all that is in the way? As concretely as possible?"

Philippe nodded affirmatively.

"Or try to imagine very realistically that you could realise your ideals in the world without any problems?"

It was Chiara, Beato's wife, who asked. A somewhat quiet and shy Italian woman....

Peter added:

"Or that simply by your presence you would calm all minds and spread an atmosphere of harmony and love wherever you would go..."

"Or that you would radiate a natural healing power, so that your touch or your glance would already have a healing effect..."

Eva said this.

Johannes sighed deeply and said:

"All thought and felt and wanted, this... Yes, that could become a real representation of the true human being that surrounds us."

*

"Philippe and Angelique are joining us for lunch today," Johannes said as they walked outside.

Raymond nudged Els and said:

"Oh help! I want to vanish!"

Els whispered:

"Still a melancholic nerd then! What do you care?"

"You can't just sit at the table, with someone who is able to say things, which he says to us for an hour every day, can you?"

"You know him, don't you?" said Els. "We can even speak Dutch with him!"

"Well, there's no escaping it, of course..."

A little later the six of them sat in a shady corner of the terrace. Raymond thought, let me jump in at the deep end and he said:

"I am really very impressed by your erudition, sir!"

Philippe looked up in surprise and said:

"Since when am I a "sir" to you?"

Raymond burst out laughing and said:

"Surely you have to say 'sir' to someone who reveals such spiritual insights?"

"I warmly invite you..." Philippe smiled.

"Have you really seen all this yourself?"

Els held her breath... When Raymond overcame his shyness, he suddenly became very direct.

"No," said Philippe, "and actually yes. It works in a different way. Before I came into contact with this esoteric knowledge, I didn't see it all for myself. But by always actively thinking along with the various contents, an ability has arisen in me to let what I absorb through study in this field become a reality. Then I do indeed myself behold it in a certain sense, but in a secondary instance."

"Does that mean," asked Raymond, "that with the, shall we say, "other thinking" you absorb spiritual science and can then experience for yourself what comes out of it?"

"That is said too simplistically," said Philippe. "There is a whole inner path of development between the point of that active thinking and this real inner perception of spiritual facts. But that will probably become clear in the course of these days. The further we come in development, the more this description becomes a description of the inner path of development that I have taken and am still taking."

"The fact is," Raymond said, "that when I listen to you, I have a completely different experience than when you listen to someone giving a lecture. It is very clear to me that you are expressing your own inner experience. So, it is possible to have that experience through what is already there in the tradition..."

Philippe nodded.

"We don't have to see everything as new every time. That would be like becoming Euclid each time in mathematics. There you also make grateful use of what is there. As far as spiritual science is concerned, there is already a lot. But you are right, there is a very big difference between a lecture and giving a living testimony of what you have observed yourself - even if it is on the basis of what is already there. In my case I compare it to travelling. You can get a very good impression of a foreign country by studying a travel guide - but obviously that is quite a different experience than visiting the country itself. But the country is there and so are the descriptions. Of course, you do not have to recreate that country every time you visit it. So, it is with this land of spiritual science too.... But coming to an eventual beholding of a spiritual reality is far more than actively thinking about the content."

"In any case," Raymond said, "listening and watching you while you do so evokes tremendous respect in me - both for the person and for the spirit that appears - that it becomes somewhat difficult to sit down with someone like that and then just say 'you'. So, I wonder –" he looked at Angelique, "what it is like when you live with such a person..."

Angelique was a woman who looked as though she had stepped out of a fashion magazine. It was strange to see her at the side of this highly developed man, who was so quiet and modest. On the other hand, it was also a kind of stamp of quality printed on Philippe's person that this woman was his life companion. The striking thing about her was not so much her beauty - which she did have - but her perfect outer appearance, something you do not often see in people who are engaged in spirituality, as if they consider it excessive or sinful to be so concerned with outer physical care. This woman had not let herself be distracted by that and so she sat there as if she had stepped out of a fashion magazine. Perfectly made up, her hair was perfect even in the breeze, she wore fashionable clothes, the colours chosen with a sense of beauty. The way she sat down, her hand gestures, everything was nurtured and filled with beauty. At Raymond's question, she smiled at him kindly and said:

"You certainly can imagine how wonderful it is to live with such a person. He does not always speak from the spiritual world..."

"Is this easy for you to follow and participate in?" Philippe asked. Els felt addressed and said:

"The German is a hindrance, but I can follow it because you are not German. That makes it a lot more accessible. We also prepare intensively for these days by doing the exercises you give us. After the third day, you already have the feeling that you are being pulled along and something is starting to come alive. When we meet again tomorrow, the theme will continue in a certain way, as is already implied. So, I think it's going very well, and I don't have the feeling that it's too ambitious."

"Why is it that you, Philippe, do the talking and Johannes is a listener?"

"Maybe Johannes would like to answer that himself..." said Philippe.

Johannes nodded and said:

"I do not want to say that I have not awakened these contents in myself, but I see it as my task to teach this "other thinking" and its development. That which lies further on the path of development, as we experience it, I really see as Philippe's life theme - and he sees it that way himself. Of course, I could say that of myself as well. But it would not have that power that it has now."

"So then," Raymond said, "if you want to work with you, you have to be very good at knowing where your limits are and where the other person's limits are. You must be able not to want more than what you can set yourself as a task."

"It is not so," Johannes said, "that it would be more than I can do. It's not like that."

"I think I understand..." Raymond said. "It has something to do with the quality, and I suppose it has something to do with that very special quality of the individuality of one person or another. In any case, that is something I have come to understand far better after these three days. I am looking forward to immersing myself in this higher human being that we want to and may make our own in the course of the development."

"After all," said Philippe, "it's about developing a vision of the future and then a better understanding of what we have to do now. Johannes already asked you yesterday: we would really like to have a lecture from you, a lecture on the theme of the singularity and trans- and post-humanism. But I can't say exactly when I will come to the appropriate point. Can we ask you just in advance?"

"Yes," Raymond said. "If you were to say now: can you do that tonight, I will do that..."

The food had been brought, Philippe said a prayer and they started the meal.

"Imagine," Raymond later said to Els, "that you could come across someone like Philippe and not notice anything of what is going on in that man. An ordinary, somewhat quiet, pleasant man."

"Are you afraid of him?" Els asked somewhat surprised.

"Yes, maybe I am. What does this man see?"

"In you, you mean?"

"No... What he has in consciousness. Huge. The whole cosmos complete with development unfolds in that consciousness."

"Yes, that is indeed terrifying."

" But I am beginning to suspect that that is the purpose with us humans. That we develop our consciousness in such a way that the whole cosmos and everything connected with it can be shown and experienced on that stage. That is something different to the singularity, something other than filling the cosmos with technical information. That is completely the opposite. The 'brain' fills itself with the cosmos, instead of the cosmos with the brain... But it also burdens me. What a responsibility... And a man like Philippe, he carries it. All alone."

"He has Johannes,"

"Yes, but the consciousness is his. You have to be able to bear that. We want to unload everything into the device. He takes everything on himself. What is his purpose here? What else can he do but help others to gain insight and skills? That is love, Els...

The only place you also see this, Els, is in music. Maybe in earlier times it was also to be found in other areas, for example in religion, but maybe even in philosophy or in science... When you see a great musician performing, a pianist or a violinist or a singer, you feel the enormous skill right down to the fingertips or the voice control - but then completely differentiated according to what the composer has written. Then you see that he is totally filled with that composition and then performs it with his finely tuned physical instrument on any musical instrument, piano or violin or whatever. I see that with Philippe too. That man has such a virtuosity of thought that he can not only think the mundane trivialities of science, but with practised thinking he can think the spirit. It must almost be that the spirit then thinks with him.

That is the impression this makes on me, and I think it is something so unsurpassable, something I have never seen in any human being -

not even in Johannes - that when I have him sitting at my table, it is impossible to approach him as an ordinary person..."

Els said:

"I imagine that must be very irritating for him, because when he sits at the table like that, he naturally thinks with that high instrument of thought about the everyday triviality of sitting there and eating and so on."

"Of course, but when you have a great musician performing at your table, he doesn't play Beethoven or Chopin then either, but you know that he is capable of doing so and that makes such a person a personality, absolutely unique above all the ordinariness. I just want to say, I feel the same way about Philippe. I don't really understand that half the world is not sitting here, to witness that this man is here with us now bringing such things to us, in the way he does. There are twelve listeners here and of course there could be more. For there are probably about a hundred people here in the institute at the moment. You know what I mean, if it hadn't happened to rain in May, we wouldn't have come to this institute. And if you want to assume that coincidence does not exist, well, then it was our destiny to come here. But then, as far as I'm concerned, it was on the verge of being mistaken, wasn't it. It was then Johannes, of course, who spoke, but that was already impressive enough. So, I don't understand that this doesn't spread around, that people who go home, who have been here, don't say to everyone around them: You should also go there, to experience it is something unique!"

"Did we do that?" asked Els.

Raymond sighed deeply and said:

"No, we didn't do that either and we won't do that easily. Except in front of someone of whom you could hope wouldn't mock... I can't compare this - you understand - with a top sportsman. That's a completely different story. The only thing I can really compare it with is a top musician. Not with a composer, in our times, but still with a performing musician. If you then bring that into an inner comparison with artificial intelligence... My God, what a pitiful poverty! Quantitative perfection, yes, but qualitatively ... I don't want to say zero, but just a little bit more than zero..."

"How did you accomplish the task this afternoon?" asked Els.

"I tried to form a representation of that high human being that we were given in that verse. In fact, you can only say that you have nothing of the kind... But when you then imagine that you do have it, you experience the contrast with your ordinary self. You feel a tremendous increase in your power and control, in your insight, in your wisdom, but also in your knowing and doing, in the peace and harmony within yourself. You feel how you are partly fertilised by this high being at times; at a moment like this when we sit here together and talk about it, but also in the longing for peace, the opposite of the longing for discussion, the longing for mutual harmony and understanding. You feel that the actual human being is still far from becoming active through us on earth, but you do feel that it is true that a human being could actually become such a being, that it is the deepest motive of your existence, that I became aware of, very fleetingly and transiently…"

"Wonderful," said Els. "The way you can express that! It sounds as if it makes you quite happy!"

"That is actually true... Everyone knows those moments, for sure, but doesn't know where they come from. Now we will find a way to make those moments visible with awareness. 'What more can a person desire in life, than that God's nature reveals itself to him...?' I would like to metamorphose this sentence from our great Goethe: What can man desire more in life than that the spirit of man should manifest itself in him? I really believe, Els, when you look outside, around you, that you really can't find anything else there than what we find there with our science. A spiritless science. It seems to me that only man here on earth has spirituality with him. But oh woe! He does not know it and he does not want to know it! He wants the peace of the dead mind and pays for it with the unhappiness and the depression. And you Els? How are you doing?"

"I am of course scientifically specifically concerned with the human physical body. In my studies I never learnt what life is, or what the soul or spirit are... But now this verse about the human being! It gives hope that as a human being, you have the ability somewhere to heal, without using external means. To heal yourself and to be able to heal others as well. That eventually this could even go so far that you would learn to fathom the secret of death and resurrection. It seems to me that what you have put forward about the spiritual human being is related to this control of the forces of life and death, of health and disease. It is only a conjecture; it is by no means concrete. But I do believe that if as a physician one were to fill oneself with this saying over and over again, one would gain a courage to heal oneself and others that is unparalleled and unconquerable.

But if it were not for the sublime atmosphere in which we all live here, one would probably not see it that way, and one might even call it a dangerous deception. It is not the case at all that I assume that I could ever do that. But I can imagine with my whole being that it is possible.

Neither of us was brought up religiously, we hardly know the Bible. But even if you don't know the Bible, you know that in the Gospels it is said of Jesus that he could do these things. He could cure diseases by his presence and he could also raise people from the dead. That must have something to do with this. But again, I have to keep it completely separate from my medical studies and refresher courses and so on. Of course, it has no place there at all and no right of existence..."

"Ask Johannes and Eva about this, when we have a meal again tomorrow? Or also Philippe, when we speak to him again? But perhaps it will become clear in the course of time. What you are experiencing is very interesting of course, and I also find it very fascinating to see that a totally different aspect comes to the surface in you than in me, even though there is no contradiction."

Els nodded and sighed deeply.

"You mustn't think about how you are going to weave what we are now acquiring into your life back home in Amsterdam - me in practice, you at the university. And yet it is also very awful if two separate worlds remain. But perhaps it is still too early to have these concerns..."

Philippe gave his fourth lecture.

"Through long periods and cultural epochs the human being has developed further and further and has become remote from the original divine ideal. The body has become too material, the life body too rigid and hard, the soul too coarse and selfish, and the spirit is increasingly distancing itself from that human being incarnated on earth over and over.

If this tendency had continued, without any intervention from the spiritual world to reverse it, it would inevitably have led to a physical body completely devoted to the forces of death, and to a soul more and more bound up with it, until even the soul had become a mortal being. There is much to be said about the course of this development, but as I said, this time we are looking mainly to the future and the past appears only insofar as it provides a necessary foundation for understanding the future.

We know that a high cosmic being from the Trinity has taken it upon Himself to permeate the human incarnated being with His divine power and thereby liberate it from the downward line. In the spiritual world there is no death. There is only a state of changing consciousness. Just as a person enters a different state of consciousness when he goes to sleep, but is not dead, so in the spiritual world we must imagine the transition from one state to another.

For a spiritual being to know death, it must incarnate in a human body on earth. The high cosmic being we call Christ has chosen this path in order to turn the descending line of human development into a spiritual ascending line.

Yesterday we learned about the human being in the form of a verse.

This human being is a child of God, and it is not born of the blood, not born of the lust of the flesh, not born of sexuality. When we picture this reaching into the divine, into the Trinity, then we have some idea of the power that has reached into the physical human being in Christ. He turns the whole downward trend of development into an upward one. We must not imagine the material, but rather that the power of resurrection flows into all levels of the human being. When we speak of a physical resurrection body, it is a body without gravity, without particles of matter in it, without any material content and yet entirely a physical body.

This is the turning point in our deepest earthly existence, that the material aspect, the aspect of weight, the aspect of mortality of the physical body is overcome by Christ and transformed into a physical body that no longer carries any bones, flesh or blood, no nerve tissue, no muscles, no glands. But it retains all these functions in an ethereal sense, i.e. in an immaterial form.

It is a great task that we set ourselves today, in one day, to form an image of the physical material body and then make an attempt to imagine this purely as a thought-form that does exist, so real, that the human being could live on in it, without ever having to experience death.

The higher parts of the being will also go through this transformation one by one, in the course of time thanks to the Christ being. But today we will focus on the resurrection of the physical body, that is, that the sting of death has been pulled out of this physical body.

If you want to read hymns in praise of this resurrection, you should read Paul's letters in the New Testament. He had seen Christ in His resurrection body. That was the appearance of Christ at Damascus and he was well enough aware, as he was an initiate, to know that what he saw was really the physical body of Jesus of Nazareth, who had risen, who had stripped himself of all material weight and who revealed himself only as a physical body not filled with flesh and bones. Therefore, he was in a position to claim that he had seen the Risen One himself and he knew what that meant. This makes Paul's letters a significant document, even if they were partly written to the believers of the time and do not fit into our modern age - we should be able to leave that aside and read only what they have to say about this beholding of Christ in the resurrection body and its significance for mankind. Nor do we consider these letters as the starting point for our occult science. But we take them as confirmation that what is revealed in occult knowledge is also recognised by the Apostle.

I will quote some essential parts of these letters here for you.

What is important today, then, is that we should explore the comparison between the mortal body of flesh and blood and this resurrection body that is ultimately described so incredibly beautifully in the Apocalypse as the New Jerusalem, with all the power we can muster in our thinking and our experience!

The Letter of Paul to the Romans, Chapter 8

'Therefore, there is now no condemnation for those who are in Christ Jesus, because through Christ Jesus the law of the Spirit who gives life has set you free from the law of sin and death. For what the law was powerless to do because it was weakened by the flesh, God did by sending his own Son in the likeness of sinful flesh to be a sin offering. And so he condemned sin in the flesh, in order that the righteous requirement of the law might be fully met in us, who do not live according to the flesh but according to the Spirit.

Those who live according to the flesh have their minds set on what the flesh desires; but those who live in accordance with the Spirit have their minds set on what the Spirit desires. The mind governed by the flesh is death, but the mind governed by the Spirit is life and peace. The mind governed by the flesh is hostile to God; it does not submit to God's law, nor can it do so. Those who are in the realm of the flesh cannot please God.

You, however, are not in the realm of the flesh but are in the realm of the Spirit, if indeed the Spirit of God lives in you. And if anyone does not have the Spirit of Christ, they do not belong to Christ. But if Christ is in you, then even though your body is subject to death because of sin, the Spirit gives life because of righteousness. And if the Spirit of him who raised Jesus from the dead is living in you, he who raised Christ from the dead will also give life to your mortal bodies because of his Spirit who lives in you.

Therefore, brothers and sisters, we have an obligation—but it is not to the flesh, to live according to it. For if you live according to the flesh, you will die; but if by the Spirit you put to death the misdeeds of the body, you will live.

For those who are led by the Spirit of God are the children of God. The Spirit you received does not make you slaves, so that you live in fear again; rather, the Spirit you received brought about your adoption to sonship. And by him we cry, "Abba, Father." The Spirit himself testifies with our spirit that we are God's children. Now if we are children, then we are heirs—heirs of God and co-heirs with Christ, if indeed we share in his sufferings in order that we may also share in his glory.

Corinthians, Chapter 2:

'And so it was with me, brothers and sisters. When I came to you, I did not come with eloquence or human wisdom as I proclaimed to you the testimony about God. For I resolved to know nothing while I was with you except Jesus Christ and him crucified. I came to you in weakness with great fear and trembling. My message and my preaching were not with wise and persuasive words, but with a demonstration of the Spirit's power, so that your faith might not rest on human wisdom, but on God's power. We do, however, speak a message of wisdom among the mature, but not the wisdom of this age or of the rulers of this age, who are coming to nothing. No, we declare God's wisdom, a mystery that has been hidden and that God destined for our glory before time began. None of the rulers of this age understood it, for if they had, they would not have crucified the Lord of glory. However, as it is written:

"What no eye has seen,
what no ear has heard,
and what no human mind has conceived" —
the things God has prepared for those who love him —
these are the things God has revealed to us by his Spirit.

The Spirit searches all things, even the deep things of God. For who knows a person's thoughts except their own spirit within them? In the same way no one knows the thoughts of God except the Spirit of God. What we have received is not the spirit of the world, but the Spirit who is from God, so that we may understand what God has freely given us. This is what we speak, not in words taught us by human wisdom but in words taught by the Spirit, explaining spiritual realities with Spirit-taught words. The person without the Spirit does not accept the things that come from the Spirit of God but considers them foolishness, and cannot understand them because they are discerned only through the Spirit. The person with the Spirit makes judgments about all things, but such a person is not subject to merely human judgments, for,

"Who has known the mind of the Lord
so as to instruct him?"

But we have the mind of Christ.

Chapter 12 and 13
Verse 12 ff.

'Just as a body, though one, has many parts, but all its many parts form one body, so it is with Christ. For we were all baptized by] one Spirit so as to form one body—whether Jews or Gentiles, slave or free—and we were all given the one Spirit to drink. Even so the body is not made up of one part but of many.

Now if the foot should say, "Because I am not a hand, I do not belong to the body," it would not for that reason stop being part of the body. And if the ear should say, "Because I am not an eye, I do not belong to the body," it would not for that reason stop being part of the body. If the whole body were an eye, where would the sense of hearing be? If the whole body were an ear, where would the sense of smell be? But in fact God has placed the parts in the body, every one of them, just as he wanted them to be. If they were all one part, where would the body be? As it is, there are many parts, but one body.

The eye cannot say to the hand, "I don't need you!" And the head cannot say to the feet, "I don't need you!" On the contrary, those parts of the body that seem to be weaker are indispensable, and the parts that we think are less honorable we treat with special honor. And the parts that are unpresentable are treated with special modesty, while our presentable parts need no special treatment. But God has put the body together, giving greater honor to the parts that lacked it, so that there should be no division in the body, but that its parts should have equal concern for each other. If one part suffers, every part suffers with it; if one part is honored, every part rejoices with it.

Now you are the body of Christ, and each one of you is a part of it. And God has placed in the church first of all apostles, second prophets, third teachers, then miracles, then gifts of healing, of helping, of guidance, and of different kinds of tongues. Are all apostles? Are all prophets? Are all teachers? Do all work miracles? Do all have gifts of healing? Do all speak in tongues? Do all interpret? Now eagerly desire the greater gifts.

And yet I will show you the most excellent way.

On Love

If I speak in the tongues of men or of angels, but do not have love, I am only a resounding gong or a clanging cymbal. If I have the gift of prophecy and can fathom all mysteries and all knowledge, and if I have a faith that can move mountains, but do not have love, I am nothing. If I give all I possess to the poor and give over my body to hardship that I may boast,[b] but do not have love, I gain nothing.

Love is patient, love is kind. It does not envy, it does not boast, it is not proud. It does not dishonor others, it is not self-seeking, it is not easily angered, it keeps no record of wrongs Love does not delight in evil but rejoices with the truth. It always protects, always trusts, always hopes, always perseveres.

Love never fails. But where there are prophecies, they will cease; where there are tongues, they will be stilled; where there is knowledge, it will pass away. For we know in part and we prophesy in part, but when completeness comes, what is in part disappears. When I was a child, I talked like a child, I thought like a child, I reasoned like a child. When I became a man, I put the ways of childhood behind me. For now we see only a reflection as in a mirror; then we shall see face to face. Now I know in part; then I shall know fully, even as I am fully known.

And now these three remain: faith, hope and love. But the greatest of these is love."

It was quiet for a long time. When Philippe moved, Raymond felt brave and asked:

"We are not familiar with the Bible. Where can we read about Paul at Damascus? Is it in the Bible?"

"You can find it in Acts, 9, 1-31. I will read it:"

"Meanwhile, Saul was still breathing out murderous threats against the Lord's disciples. He went to the high priest and asked him for letters to the synagogues in Damascus, so that if he found any there who belonged to the Way, whether men or women, he might take them as prisoners to Jerusalem. As he neared Damascus on his journey, suddenly a light from heaven flashed around him. He fell to the ground and heard a voice say to him, "Saul, Saul, why do you persecute me?"

"Who are you, Lord?" Saul asked.

"I am Jesus, whom you are persecuting," he replied. "Now get up and go into the city, and you will be told what you must do."

The men traveling with Saul stood there speechless; they heard the sound but did not see anyone. Saul got up from the ground, but when he opened his eyes he could see nothing. So they led him by the hand into Damascus. For three days he was blind, and did not eat or drink anything.

In Damascus there was a disciple named Ananias. The Lord called to him in a vision, "Ananias!"

"Yes, Lord," he answered.

The Lord told him, "Go to the house of Judas on Straight Street and ask for a man from Tarsus named Saul, for he is praying. In a vision he has seen a man named Ananias come and place his hands on him to restore his sight."

"Lord," Ananias answered, "I have heard many reports about this man and all the harm he has done to your holy people in Jerusalem. And he has come here with authority from the chief priests to arrest all who call on your name."

But the Lord said to Ananias, "Go! This man is my chosen instrument to proclaim my name to the Gentiles and their kings and to the people of Israel. I will show him how much he must suffer for my name."

Then Ananias went to the house and entered it. Placing his hands on Saul, he said, "Brother Saul, the Lord—Jesus, who appeared to you on the road as you were coming here—has sent me so that you may see again and be filled with the Holy Spirit." Immediately, something like scales fell from Saul's eyes, and he could see again. He got up and was baptized, and after taking some food, he regained his strength.

Saul in Damascus and Jerusalem

'Saul spent several days with the disciples in Damascus. At once he began to preach in the synagogues that Jesus is the Son of God. All those who heard him were astonished and asked, "Isn't he the man who raised havoc in Jerusalem among those who call on this name? And hasn't he come here to take them as prisoners to the chief priests?" Yet Saul grew more and more powerful and baffled the Jews living in Damascus by proving that Jesus is the Messiah.

After many days had gone by, there was a conspiracy among the Jews to kill him, but Saul learned of their plan. Day and night they kept close watch on the city gates in order to kill him. But his followers took him by night and lowered him in a basket through an opening in the wall.

When he came to Jerusalem, he tried to join the disciples, but they were all afraid of him, not believing that he really was a disciple. But Barnabas took him and brought him to the apostles. He told them how Saul on his journey had seen the Lord and that the Lord had spoken to him, and how in Damascus he had preached fearlessly in the name of Jesus. So Saul stayed with them and moved about freely in Jerusalem, speaking boldly in the name of the Lord. He talked and debated with the Hellenistic Jews, but they tried to kill him. When the believers learned of this, they took him down to Caesarea and sent him off to Tarsus.

Then the church throughout Judea, Galilee and Samaria enjoyed a time of peace and was strengthened. Living in the fear of the Lord and encouraged by the Holy Spirit, it increased in numbers.

It is not my intention to make it a biblical hour..." said Philippe. "But again, there is no better confirmation to be found than these letters of Paul. The difference between the mortal body and the resurrection body. That is our theme today."

"I do feel some kinship with Paul..." Raymond said to Johannes at lunch. "It's really a kind of conversion I went through. Only I didn't have that apparition. It happened indirectly, through you, Johannes."

"I really want to fulfil that task, Raymond. I want to be a herald. It fills me with happiness that I could fulfil that function for you."

"For me, the Christ being is still an abstract concept. A name for a process, for a fact. I can't imagine much about it. Maybe that will change today, when I do the task later."

"That is how it is meant to be, Raymond, really; that you first understand completely as an image, without compulsion or content, that He exists and who He is. He will then, if He so desires, join that image and fill it to a reality.... It requires very hard work."

*

"It's a tough workout here!" said Els at dinner. "It's a good thing we didn't imagine going on holiday, because there isn't much time left for relaxation..."

"Today I certainly found the theme very intensive. That was clear from Philippe's emphasis: in one day! And for us it is an impossibility of course. Neither of us was brought up with Christianity and now here we are confronted with the fact that Christ is the center, the point of gravity, the culmination of the earth's development. As I said this afternoon, for the time being it remains a name."

Els said:

"Yet I also experience it as a great freedom that we were not brought up in a church and given specific dogmatic teachings, which would perhaps have made it far more difficult for us to accept what we are hearing here now. So far, there is a certain kind of logic in Philippe's argument. Not the usual logic, but an intelligibility that, if you remain in the train of thought and don't step out of it, allows you to clearly understand that the luciferian temptation had a catastrophic effect and that this had to be corrected by another, a higher divine-spiritual being here on earth. In this way I can accept what is taught in Christianity..."

"Yes, that is how it is... said Raymond. But in fact, when I try to find it within myself, I cannot confirm that this rise from the fall has already come about. I have a much stronger feeling that we, as humanity, are still in a further decline."

"Yes..." said Els. "But I think you should rather consider it as a possibility. If Christ had not come, then there would be no possibility for us to find and make that rise. Through his coming there is. He has brought this about in himself and has certainly brought about a change in the unconscious part of us humans. But now consciousness has to follow. That seems to me to be the theme for tomorrow or perhaps the day after; that we are placed in the present and then learn to experience exactly where we stand and how good can develop from there."

"Be that as it may," said Raymond, "in immersing myself in these two states that Philippe has indicated, the descending line and the ascending line, I have especially felt the weight of the physical body. Normally you do not have to deal with this. Apparently as a human being you have a possibility to ignore or alleviate that heaviness, I don't know exactly how that works. But when you really start to concentrate on the existing physical body as you carry it around, or as you are - which I had always thought - then you start to feel what an indescribable heaviness is in that body and how it pulls you down to earth. Suddenly I don't understand why science doesn't consider that at all. Perhaps there is still a pinch of Archimedes' law that is used... But how is it possible that your body, which weighs seventy to a hundred kilograms, is kept upright? What is that? I have felt how heavy it is and in contrast imagined that you would have that body, but it would not have that material heaviness. For the time being, this has remained completely unimaginable, except in that contrast. There, suddenly, the imponderable shines through. I suddenly understand that. If the physical body would not be material, then it would be unimaginable, then you wouldn't see it with your eyes, because you wouldn't have those either... I have read a few bits in the Gospel about the appearance of Christ after the resurrection. The remarkable thing is, that he apparently looks different, because they did not recognize him immediately. They recognize him by his movements and the way he does things. We have a Bible Day today, so can I read it to you? Luke, 24.

On the way to Emmaüs

'Now that same day two of them were going to a village called Emmaus, about seven miles[a] from Jerusalem. They were talking with each other about everything that had happened. As they talked and discussed these things with each other, Jesus himself came up and walked along with them; but they were kept from recognizing him.

He asked them, "What are you discussing together as you walk along?"

They stood still, their faces downcast. One of them, named Cleopas, asked him, "Are you the only one visiting Jerusalem who does not know the things that have happened there in these days?"

"What things?" he asked.

"About Jesus of Nazareth," they replied. "He was a prophet, powerful in word and deed before God and all the people. The chief priests and our rulers handed him over to be sentenced to death, and they crucified him; but we had hoped that he was the one who was going to redeem

Israel. And what is more, it is the third day since all this took place. In addition, some of our women amazed us. They went to the tomb early this morning but didn't find his body. They came and told us that they had seen a vision of angels, who said he was alive. Then some of our companions went to the tomb and found it just as the women had said, but they did not see Jesus." He said to them, "How foolish you are, and how slow to believe all that the prophets have spoken! Did not the Messiah have to suffer these things and then enter his glory?" And beginning with Moses and all the Prophets, he explained to them what was said in all the Scriptures concerning himself.

As they approached the village to which they were going, Jesus continued on as if he were going farther. But they urged him strongly, "Stay with us, for it is nearly evening; the day is almost over." So he went in to stay with them.

When he was at the table with them, he took bread, gave thanks, broke it and began to give it to them. Then their eyes were opened and they recognized him, and he disappeared from their sight. They asked each other, "Were not our hearts burning within us while he talked with us on the road and opened the Scriptures to us?"

They got up and returned at once to Jerusalem. There they found the Eleven and those with them, assembled together and saying, "It is true! The Lord has risen and has appeared to Simon." Then the two told what had happened on the way, and how Jesus was recognized by them when he broke the bread.

Jesus Appears to the Disciples

'While they were still talking about this, Jesus himself stood among them and said to them, "Peace be with you."

They were startled and frightened, thinking they saw a ghost. He said to them, "Why are you troubled, and why do doubts rise in your minds? Look at my hands and my feet. It is I myself! Touch me and see; a ghost does not have flesh and bones, as you see I have."

When he had said this, he showed them his hands and feet. And while they still did not believe it because of joy and amazement, he asked them, "Do you have anything here to eat?" They gave him a piece of broiled fish, and he took it and ate it in their presence.

'He said to them, "This is what I told you while I was still with you: Everything must be fulfilled that is written about me in the Law of Moses, the Prophets and the Psalms."

Then he opened their minds so they could understand the Scriptures. He told them, "This is what is written: The Messiah will suffer and rise from the dead on the third day, and repentance for the forgiveness of sins will be preached in his name to all nations, beginning at Jerusalem. You are witnesses of these things. I am going to send you what my Father has promised; but stay in the city until you have been clothed with power from on high.'

"That seems to me to be an indication of the manner of perception you have when you should be perceiving the immaterial body. When you came with the food, I tried to look at you in this way. Then, in fact, your whole beautiful visible appearance falls away, but another beautiful appearance takes its place; that is, the way you do things! I'll have to think it over, but maybe that's why I love you more rather than the colour of your hair or your white teeth..." said Raymond.

Els burst out laughing and said:

"Well, I would certainly hope so! After all, that really is the guarantee of permanence in love, even if I have become old and wrinkled. I may have slowed down in the way I do things, but it's still my way... So, it would be good if it were that, as a human being, which you appreciate above all!"

"I don't believe that we especially take note of it, but we could make a habit of it. To be more observant of the imponderables of the other human being. I am sure there is much more to this than just the way of doing things, but I came across it in the Gospel. Jesus is eating there with his disciples. So although he has no material physical body, he can still enjoy the meal together with them. What he eats is, of course, material. That is quite a puzzling thing.

We should dwell on this far longer and more deeply than we can now, in a day. But if we had more days, we would not do it. That is the curious thing. I am sure that if you stretched this 'learning curve', more could be done in it - but we would not. It is precisely the tense relationship between theme and time that makes it so intense. My experiences are mostly from the contrasts. That is why the way Philippe does it is very effective. He provides us with more developed contrast every day. Therefore, you have to differentiate and refine your images, otherwise there is nothing to experience. The real meaning must come from learning to imagine and live in these contrasts!"

Els laughed and said:

"Just wait a minute and a new spiritual teacher will be born..."

"Don't mock, Els!"

"This is not a mockery," she said. "I really mean it. It's amazing how you take this on, isn't it?"

"You too, don't you"' he asked in surprise.

"Yes, but differently. With you it's so differentiated, so delicate. In my case it's more about moral differences. I don't manage to form really clear, concrete ideas about them, but you do."

"Yes,' said Raymond, "but I have a to be conscious of the moral experiences involved. I'm sure I have them, but I can't access them that easily and I don't know what's more important... If I had had more of this quality of moral experience, I would never have pursued singularity for so long."

"No... But then we wouldn't have an expert in that field now either!"

"Let's go back to those experiences of weight for a moment. I then feel an almost unbearable heaviness of the physical body and have the impression that it could become so heavy that life is not compatible with it. Then life lets go and materiality falls apart according to natural law.

That was one aspect, and the other was that for a moment then - and I don't know if I can mention it now - I had an impression of something that would continue to exist. Something that is not life that has let go, that is not heavy disintegrating matter, but something that is as young and fresh as a baby's body, but at the same time as old and wise as the knowledge of an old man. And then completely limited to the body, but without material and without life. Yet something remains, it must be what Philippe was talking about, about the New Jerusalem... I have not had the time to read up on that. Maybe we can do that later. It will probably be an image and not a true-life description of the body.

That's great, Els, this is the best proof that what they are doing down there on that mountain is really true - we are just a bit higher up here, but where they are is high enough. It is the best proof that it is possible, on the basis of this morning's limited lecture, to come to these thoughts which I have now arrived at. Those thoughts also have an efficacy. They are not simply brilliant ideas that strike you, but you feel that they arise from that difficult proposition, which you began with and which then enters into another level or something similar at some point, through which the thoughts grasp spirit. You still think the thoughts then, you do not see them and yet it is a kind of seeing. But you can think those thoughts because they come from what you have already thought.

Just as from a rose bush the rose bud appears at a certain time by natural necessity and not suddenly a lily ... In a similar way, these thoughts necessarily give rise to new thoughts, new for us, not new in the great world order of course..."

"Yes..." said Els, "it's breathtaking."

Meanwhile it was Thursday and at precisely 11 o'clock they listened to Philippe.

"We must not imagine that through the coming of Christ man has been restored to the state he was in before the luciferic temptation. That would be a very great mistake in the assessment of the development of humanity. Nothing that takes place in it is meaningless or worthless; everything is imbued with a deep sense of purpose and has its rightful place and meaning in the development. It is only a question whether that which has arisen through the luciferic influence - namely, an independent inner life - can be shaped in such a way that it can come into contact with divine wisdom, so that this divine wisdom really becomes a part of the human being. This human being will then not be a mirror, but an active participant in the process of cosmic intelligence.

This is the development we see taking place after Christ. First of all, we can ask ourselves where Christ is after Ascension. If He had remained visible amongst men, freedom would not have been possible again - the human being would have had an immediate perception of the divine. Now the Holy Spirit is sent through Christ. Human beings can take this Spirit into themselves in freedom. The event is described and celebrated with the feast of Pentecost... It is an active spirit; it is a spirit that wants to be received actively. So, we see this process taking place gradually in mankind after Christ. Christ Himself lives on in *'soul form around the human being'* from that time onwards, connects with the becoming of the human being. And just as He incarnated on earth in a human body, so He is more or less 'ensouled' in an angel present around and within us. The human being is being given the intelligence to a greater and greater extent. This *does not mean* that the complete cosmic wisdom comes to man *as content*, but that the *intelligent functioning*, the intelligent activity, the intelligence in its activity, comes within reach of the human spirit, so that he gradually learns to deal with it and to use it to come to knowledge he himself.

You see this in post-Christian history. A man like Johannes Scotus Eriugena, in the ninth century, already tries to use intelligence independently in order to make divine wisdom his own. In scholasticism we see an extensive exercise of intelligence, a kind of gymnastics of reasoning, applied to revelation and the limits of knowing. It is a period of great and intensive thinking activity. When you think of a baby developing into a walking, running child, and you consider what that baby, that toddler, does in terms of physical exercise in order to finally have the body completely under control, then you have an example of what scholastics have done with thinking. Then it becomes habitual and thinking activity becomes increasingly vague. The skill has been acquired, and conscious practice of it fades into the background. The beginning of the new natural science comes into the foreground and there is a shift from thinking to sensory perception. A great advocate of this is Francis Bacon, who questions the significance of man's intelligence and substitutes it with the certainty of sensory perception. This becomes the hallmark of modern science. Active thinking relaxes and recedes into the background, but as sensory perception is exercised and thinking is mastered, an increasingly pure thinking develops within. Thinking becomes abstract, it becomes a possibility to think abstractly in general laws. And although its value is doubted - just think of Kant's philosophy - it actually develops into a purely spiritual element, which admittedly has a shadow existence, but which is a purely spiritual element.

In the 19th century there were people who noticed that point, who realised that everything that is perceived with the senses and thought in the inner self leads a purely spiritual existence there. If you could grasp that purely spiritual existence, and if you were able to free it from its abstract nature, you would be in the spiritual world.

But parallel to this, a harsh materialism emerges. A large part of humanity that is the bearer of the cultural age falls into materialism. That is, into the conviction that there is no soul, no spirit, and that existence is only material and transitory.

With these thoughts, people also die. In the spiritual world, especially where the deceased are close to the earth, a strong materialistic aversion to spirit spreads, and it is described in occult science that as a result the consciousness of the angel in whom Christ lives is darkened. You cannot call this a dying, but it is the equivalent in the realm of the etheric world of consciousness being eclipsed by materialism. This is then clarified and cleared up by the presence of Christ. Consciousness rises, and because consciousness rises, the possibility of partaking of this risen consciousness is distributed amongst humanity. It is the resurrection of Christ into the etheric world. This enables us to develop a different way of thinking than just the material way. It has directly to do with the fact that we do not have to lapse into the content of thinking alone, but that we can elevate ourselves to the thinking of the process of thinking. The more activity we can consciously put into our thinking, the stronger we make use of this resurrection possibility in the etheric world. While doing so, we connect with the Risen One.

It is very important that we try to experience two different states of consciousness side by side. The first state is that of passive thinking, in which the thinking follows what is given. With this we have characterised a state of consciousness as it was before Christianity. There, the spiritual world thought in us and we participated in it, but were not active in it. When we carry this passivity into our time, we are carried along on the disintegrating stream of material thoughts. We enter into analysis. We find it more and more difficult to synthesize and combine, and there is an increasing necessity for the combination of thoughts to be done by something other than ourselves. For this we can make use of everything that is observed in science, but also make use of what technology has to offer us; we simply surf along on the waves of what is there.

The other state of consciousness is the resurrected activity. Of course, we also use what is already there, but we elevate ourselves above what is given, by actively thinking the thoughts. That is an unpleasant activity at first, because the inner laziness rebels against it. You do not feel like it at all. But once you have experienced what happens in the inner world, when you are actively thinking the thoughts, the rebellion becomes superfluous. For you feel the power that emanates from it, which has a physically rejuvenating effect and gives you energy; it leads to a feeling of joy in the soul, and it gives rise to new original thoughts in the spirit.

This form of thinking has to be practised; it is not an innate talent. It is the beginning of what is ultimately the goal of earth development. That goal is that the human being, through his spiritual activity, makes all that the cosmos has to offer in terms of wisdom and beings and revelation and activity his own. When we stand in the world with passive thinking, the cosmos is abandoned from God. We really only see and hear with the senses and understand something of it with the mind.

It depends on mankind whether the cosmos will be deserted from God in reality to a greater and greater extent, or whether it will be permeated, interwoven and thought through with spirit.

It will be the human spirit that is allowed to renew the power, energy and knowledge of the distant past, so that the decaying earth and cosmos may gain new spiritual life.

Two forms of consciousness: a passive thinking, moving with the waves of existence; and an active thinking, which rises above them, because the will has decided to be present in every thought and in every combination of thoughts with full consciousness, will and experience."

Beato said:

"We must then imagine it in such a way that Christ united himself completely with materialistic thought, then penetrated it and gave it the power to rise to the spirit. Just as he incarnated in the body and thus identified himself with the state in which the body was, so he has now identified himself with the state in which thought was."

"That is right," said Philippe.

"And we bring ourselves close to that resurrection by activating thought. You feel, when you do so, that with the spirituality of will you irradiate the materialisation of thought, and so come to a spiritualisation of thought."

Els said:

"For us, for the time being, these are still conceptions. We try to fulfil the task every day and it is very clear to us that this is a developmental process, especially by experiencing the continuous opposites that go one step further. But it is still difficult to imagine that these images lead to real experiences."

Philippe nodded and said:

"That is precisely an indication of the materialisation of passive thinking. The life is out of it, the thoughts are just an illusion and what remains is an awareness that somewhere in you there is something that says yes or no to certain thoughts. That is what you can focus your investigation on again and again, for there lies the point of recognition of the truth. That recognition is not a dead process, but a fully living process of insight."

At lunch Raymond said:

"As Els said ... This is a really difficult point for us and we have to work our way through it. Yesterday it was not easy to believe in the resurrection of the body. Now something has come up that seems to lie far closer, and that is the distinction between dead and living thoughts. We can understand this to some extent, but when we have to think about this in connection with Christ, it is a very big leap for our thinking. Yesterday we had the Bible to support us. Today we have nothing but Philippe's words."

Johannes said:

"For me, this has been the great turning point in my life. I had doubts about everything, I was fascinated by death, which in fact lies unacceptably at the end of life's journey. A certain rhythm of a German-sounding poem kept coming to mind. I later found out that I had once read it in the library of my father, who was a freemason and also had some books on anthroposophy on his shelf, and that it had apparently made such an impression on me that the sound and the rhythm of the verse had worked its way through - only to come back to me when I was about forty years old as an unknown song. But the words, the meaning of that poem reflect exactly what Philippe said today. For me, that was the transition from the dead science of nature that medicine is, to a powerful will to seek life in science."

"What were those words, can you repeat them?"

"Certainly..." said Johannes. "I am imbued with them":

Christ once lived upon earth,
And the consequence of this life was,
That he hovers in the soul-form,
around the becoming of the human being.
He has united himself with the earth's spiritual part'.[5]

5 Rudolf Steiner, Theodora in the first Mysterydrama:
'Es lebte Christus einst auf Erden,
Und dieses Lebens Folge war,
Dass er in Seelenform umschwebt,
Der Menschen Werden.
Er hat sich mit der Erde Geistesteil vereint.'

Johannes continued:

"There are some lectures by the Master of the Occident on this theme. What we know about it is based on the revelations he has made, which we can then confirm through intensive inner research. You can do the latter, Raymond. And so, can you, Els. What Philippe pointed out in his last words, this remarkable and wonderful ability of the human being to recognise certain things as definitely true, you can include in your research today. So, not only the distinction between passive and active thinking, but with active thinking you can also try to become aware of how the sense of truth works. Once you have found it, divisive doubt has far less power. From your intellect you have to doubt what has been said here today. Yet you can search within yourself for the answer to the question: Is this true?"

Raymond said:

"I will certainly do that later. But before I do, I immediately feel the objection: How can you ever know that it is true, and if it is true why doesn't every person immediately feel: This is true! That would be the end of the discussion, the end of the different opinions and judgements..."

"For the time being, we have only reached the end of discussion in arithmetic. That's where the computer builds the certainty. The field of logic is in fact just as certain, but we are not used to dealing with it so precisely. Nor are we forced to do so by the compelling reality of number and its various applications. Yet, when you ask yourself the question: How should I know that this is true, that that is true? you would certainly find an answer to that question that you ask yourself. If you never ask that question, you will not find an answer either. And of course, it is important to have a solid ground underfoot, because the vision of the future is built on this ground from the perspective of occult science. If this ground should turn out to be a swamp or a shifting rock, there would be little point in the further development of knowledge."

"Surely it cannot mean," Raymond said, "that I am obliged to take all that Philippe has said today as true?"

"That is precisely what it does not mean! Nothing must be accepted; nothing must be rejected. The sense of truth must be sought. As long as you remain in your thoughts with all your opinions and judgements - which every person has - the sense of truth will be strongly influenced by it. If you think the thoughts purely as thoughts, without burdening them with yourself, while bringing all your will and feeling into them, only then will you have a chance of discovering the sense of truth. It does not lie in corresponding with the opinions already present in you, but it does lie in corresponding with your capacity for pure insight."

Raymond sighed deeply and said:

"I understand you Johannes... Then this should actually also be a task for today, namely, the distinction between connecting your judgement with your person and connecting your judgement with your true being – something like that."

Johannes smiled and said:

"It's nice to be dealing with someone who is so quick-witted..."

They took a walk around their home. Raymond said:

"The other day you said: it's breathtaking ... And I feel that now too, almost like a suffocation. Because insights are building up so quickly that you get the feeling: I don't have enough time to take things in."

Els squeezed his hand and said:

"Yes, of course I experience that too. But I believe that we must also remember that this is a life task. That here, now, in these weeks, a basic ground map is given to us that we will be able to walk the rest of our lives. I could imagine that those five different steps that we have taken so far could expand into five different worlds, eras, stages of humanity, beings, whereas now we are only receiving a condensed basic version of them."

"Perhaps that is precisely what is breathtaking. When you look into the abyss here, into the depths, only then do you realise how high you actually are. It is the same with these contents. As long as you go along with all the thinking, it goes well, but when doubt pulls you out of the process, then you look into the abyss, as it were, and realise how *high* you have climbed and how little power you actually have. You could also fall into the abyss.... Here it is so, that if you stay on the path and don't do anything risky, the chance that something will go wrong is minimal. That's how it seems to me with this spiritual walk as well Els. But I do feel that you should stay on the path and that doubt should only be translated into deeper research and not degenerate into light mockery, or reluctance, or fear. That would mean straying from the path and taking risks...”

“But you can’t just accept everything blindly, can you?”

“It is a different experience, isn’t it, when you think everything through with active thinking. Then it is certainly not blind. But we will look at it later. It’s not easy for me either, Els. Of course, every now and then a thought like: why on earth are you doing this, for heaven’s sake, just keep your feet on the ground! What do you have to look for so high? And at the same time, I know inwardly: it is not me who is saying that. So, keep in contact with yourself and step by step walk in self-awareness...”

At eleven o'clock sharp, everyone was present again for Philippe's lecture.

"We have now meditated on five opposites.

- The mirror of the soul with the "I" as observer versus the self-will that interferes with the soul.
- The division into genders and the emergence of an inner life versus the Angel that holds nothing inside but reveals everything directly.
- The descent of the "monad", of the higher human being and its characteristic as the bringer of peace, in contrast to the rise of egotism and the passion to fight.
- The human body coming to the point of decay versus the resurrection thanks to the Mystery of Golgotha.
- The resurrection of Christ in the ether world and active thinking versus dead passive dissociative thinking.

A sixth contrast follows today.

Apart from the transition to active thinking, it is also necessary to find a different attitude towards perception. We become aware of things outside of us through sense perception, and we become aware of them in such a way that at the same time we know that things really *are*. We are very familiar with the difference between an imaginative image and a sense image of what we call reality. Now, through the development that has taken place with mankind, our constitution has evolved in such a way that when we have a sense perception and therefore take it as something that exists, we do not have the certainty simultaneously that there is also a spiritual existence here. In other words, our sense perception creates the illusion that things are purely material and that there is no spirit. We can reflect intensively on this, and then find that we can naturally address ourselves and say: Yes, everything that is perceived with the senses is in fact also spiritual or is another form of what I carry within me as an inner concept. Philosophy will take you a long way in that area. If you supplement that with spiritual science, then at a certain moment in life you can come to the point where you at least know that what you have around you as the outside world is not spiritless. The senses themselves and the intellect that goes with them do not spontaneously give that spiritual insight. It is a matter of becoming aware of it thoroughly. Even when I have a vivid experience because of the beauty of the sunrise, or the budding of a rose, these experiences do not immediately give me proof that I have a spiritual world around me and within me. This will not change unless we first come to an intense experience of the exclusively material nature of our sense content. Only when I am fully aware of this will there be the possibility of developing a different habit concerning it. That is more than knowing that there is spirit in the world...

Yesterday we came to the conclusion that the spirit in the world is there insofar as the human being brings it back. That I experience the outside world as spiritless therefore is in a certain sense true. Only when I allow my own spirit to rule the perception with the senses do I experience the world thoughts that I absorb with the senses; life and spirit. The force of will, of activity in the stream of thought that I direct towards the senses makes them receptive to the sense perceptions *as world thoughts*, and these world thoughts do not live in the material, not in the liquid, not in the air, not in the warmth - but they live in the light, and in this way I can be aware that what I absorb with the senses as light are the world thoughts that weave into my spiritual will, making this whole a spirit-filled perception.

Yesterday we had the contrast of passive thinking - active thinking. Today we have the contrast of the material working of the senses in the subconscious will, with that of a consciously inflamed activity of the will to the senses, where these receivers of light bring this light as world thoughts into cooperation with the will. Then the world is filled with spirit, because we consciously makes his spirit available to the light of the world. Thus, it gradually becomes possible to perceive this light of the world as a purely spiritual element and no longer as a physical energetic manifestation. In the activity, we become aware of the perception of Christ in the etheric world."

Raymond spoke up and said:

"I really struggled with this concept of Christ in the etheric world yesterday. For me it is like a dogma, like something I have to accept as a dogma, and I did not succeed in relating my sense of truth to it immediately. In other words, I do not know if it is true. I am willing to accept it as a hypothesis, for the time being, but that is different from recognising it myself. I assume that in the past in church you would have said: I believe it or I don't believe it. That is not what we are doing here. What we are doing is: either I see it or I don't. And I don't know why you should acknowledge this. What was said about it is not illogical, but you could imagine a whole range of other explanations that could also sound logical. I think for example of Shamballah from Buddhism and there are surely many other terms and processes to be found in various religions by which you could explain the Fall of Man and the Redemption."

"That is not so..." Philippe objected. "You have to remain in the wholeness of the thoughts. If you don't, then you are right. Then you can find all kinds of other explanations for the Fall of Man and the Redemption. But when you have built up your thought process in the way I have done with you in the past few days, the transition from passive thinking to active thinking is part of it. And when you practice this within yourself, when you become aware of it, you will find that you need a certain power to really make yourself think actively. That force has to come from somewhere. It does not come from the body, that is quite clear. It comes from a place other than the body, and if you don't want to use names because you find them difficult, you should say: the force that enables me to think actively is on a par with everything I apparently do when I overcome a difficulty, a weakness, a laziness or whatever. This power of overcoming, if you imagine it infinitely magnified and strengthened, you will find a force that should be able to overcome even the utmost of passivity. That is death. If you do not look at what is physical but you look at thinking itself, at consciousness, then that is the same force that eliminates all cloudiness, all dullness, all drowsiness, all fogginess in consciousness and brings about a completely clear, strengthened consciousness with a corresponding thinking. I have spoken about that power and we are convinced here that that power does not come from a human being. That force is in fact contrary to everything that brings heaviness, materialism and dullness into the human being. This force must be a spiritual being in itself and if this force can work to the extreme, then it must be a divine spiritual being. It must be the creative Word itself, that force which brings life and joy to all that exists. Two thousand years ago it brought the resurrection, a resurrection of the body. Now it brings a resurrection of the etheric body."

Raymond leaned back and bowed his head. He said:

"Yes, if you explain it that way, then my sense of truth does indeed say yes immediately!"

"That I have also given that being a name is connected with the movement in which we find ourselves. Then it is about the fact that the being who was incarnated in Palestine in a human body, who was crucified, died, was buried and rose from the dead on the third day - that being is the same being who is now at work in us when we pass *from passive to active thinking*. That can become a reality in your life. Just as you know, when you say I, that you mean yourself and not someone else, so you recognise the essential quality of this resurrection power as Christ Himself."

"Good," said Raymond. "Then I have understood..."

There was silence for some time. Then Beato said:

"I would like to elaborate on today's account of perception and may perhaps relate a personal experience from my childhood. As you know, I grew up in the sublime South Tyrol, amidst vineyards and apple orchards. Every year, when the heat was over, the air was no longer completely clear and some veils seemed to come up that gave a translucent veil over the slopes and in the valley, only then did the sunlight really become perceptible. It was no longer as harsh and unforgiving as in summer, it became soft and full of richness, as it is every evening. In Bachs Passion of St. Matthew, it says so wonderfully, Am Abend, da es kühle ward ... In the evening, when it went cool....Thus, as a child, I experienced the coming autumn, the late summer, without really being aware of it, but therefore all the more intensely. And then I experienced, I saw and heard a living being in the light and I knew how to communicate with that living being. It is very gentle, very good-natured, very comforting. It caresses your eyes and gently permeates them. You hear it in the rustling of the wind and in the flowing of the mountain stream. You smell it in the slight decay of the plants and you taste it in the sweetness of the fruit.

I have grown up and I have seen many wretched things. My eyes have hardened and so have my ears... But the memory of that childhood in the late summer on the hills with the wine and the apples means that in every observation with my eyes and my ears I still hear the soft sound of he who spoke to me there. That has never left me, and of course I thank God that it is so. But I wanted to tell you about it because I heard exactly that in Philippe's words, which we have gracefully left as a child and what we now have to find anew as adults, as a new and fully conscious habit. In my case it is not difficult at all to realise that my friend, the child in the light, was Christ Himself in the etheric world. Why did he relate to me, to the little boy, who helped to pick grapes and apples... I do not know why he wanted to reveal himself to me, why he wanted to accompany me, and that can only fill me with gratitude and reverence.

I owe many of my successes during my operations to this, to the conversations with Him, that I can ask Him: What is the fate of this man? He almost always says: SAVE HIM OR HER! In fact, a NO from Him is only the case if fate has really worked in a totally irreversible way. I have seen many dying people come back to life on the operating table, after a conversation I had with Him, while my hands do their work as well as they always do..."

*

During lunch, Johannes had an animated conversation with Els about sensory perception, which was her theme after all. Raymond sat quietly. At one point, Johannes noticed this and said:

"Raymond, you are quiet today! Can you say something?"

Raymond smiled and said:

"I've been sent back to my room again. Didn't you notice?"

"It's just how you look at it..." said Johannes. "To me it has made more of an impression of a process of conviction using reason."

"Yes, it has," said Raymond. "But that's just it. I am used to my reasoning capacity being invincible, and here I have to repeatedly experience that this is not the case. It is humbling to me, the Germans say 'demütigend'. That expresses both sides so well. For it does humble me, but at the same time I experience it as humiliation."

"What nonsense!" Els couldn't help saying.

"Yes," said Raymond. "I know that, Els, that it is nonsense. When I look at it objectively, it's just that I couldn't think or speak of a specific naming spontaneously, that I considered it and that, after a reasonable correlation of thoughts, it became clear to me that the naming was most probably correct after all. And that it is not just the name, but it is really about the being that belongs to that name. And I am aware that because of the fact that the name has such an ecclesiastical connotation in our culture, I find it difficult to accept this just like that. At the same time, I also see the limitations of my mind in this. Of course, it is about how it is, and not how it affects my feelings. I know all that and yet I found it difficult. I have always experienced this here - with Johannes I actually experienced it the least - and it was a kind of spiritual wrath that then comes over me again, not from me, but from the other. A divine wrath that I am exposed to and that I have to deal with. Then I feel very small and very modest, I feel as though I have been punished and those are very unpleasant feelings! Then I have to come to terms with it. In the beginning, I also experienced this with you Johannes, in your lecture. But in personal contact it is not the case at all. You are a mediator for me towards the others. I have the feeling that I can turn to you with utmost confidence and that you always continue to see my other side, even when I start to drift..."

"Believe me," Johannes said, "it's exactly the same with Philippe. If you were sitting at the table with him now, you wouldn't have that feeling. But when he stands there as the representative of the Spirit, then of course he has to represent it and cannot spare you. I don't think you would want that either. How did you experience Beato's words?"

Raymond answered:

"I was fighting with my feelings, so perhaps I didn't absorb Beato's first few sentences very clearly. But who could remain closely connected with himself, when someone speaks like that? I couldn't either, I was not only captivated by what he said, but especially by how he said it, so that one can really experience it together with him. It is, of course, extremely moving to see how he lives it, that this Spirit Being, whose name I find so difficult to mention, assists him in his work, that he more or less consults with Him medically during an operation and then also receives the strength and the conviction from Him to bring about the utmost of technical achievements with all the love that he can summon - for I feel that he has it. It is fortunate for the unlucky person lying on the operating table that he meets this surgeon... I found the way he described his childhood experiences extremely moving, and I still carry that emotion in my heart."

Johannes said:

"Isn't this concrete effect, emanating from Beato's words, the best proof of the truth of the existence of this being and its name, Raymond?"

Raymond looked straight at him and said:

"I was already convinced of that, but my feelings were not really in favour of it and they have been completely cleared up by Beato. You are a wonderful group of people together. It seems as if all things are done without any direction and yet everything turns out to happen exactly when it is needed and to be exactly what is needed."

"You are right..." said Johannes. "We don't direct anything ourselves. It's not as if we came together yesterday and said to each other: I think Raymond is not quite on the right track so we have to take some measures tomorrow to get him back on it. We would not be able to do that, we would be disgusted by such an approach. We do what we can with all our might and then surrender to the course of events."

Raymond said:

"That is why it works. If one were to suspect, even be it unconsciously, that there was a human impulse behind it, the rebellion would only increase. It is precisely this innocence that makes everything harmonise so exquisitely. You can imagine from this that it must be so that everything that happens in human life has a deep meaning and that events have a wise coherence. That's a beautiful thought... But what I have actually lost somewhat is the task for today."

Els said:

"When you were sitting there just now, lost in thought, we discussed this at length. It is about developing a new habit in sensory perception. The task is to imagine this new habit and compare it with sensory perception as we normally experience it. We have been given the ability to perceive the *being* of things and the processes in space directly. However, in the course of development, we have lost the ability to experience this *being* as something divine and spiritual. In the new mode of sense perception, you yourself are active and this other standpoint would lead directly to experiencing the divine-spiritual *being* of things and processes through the wisdom that lives in light. That very thing would then be Christ in the etheric world."

"You express it wonderfully well again..." Raymond said without mockery.

Johannes smiled and said:

"Yes, Raymond, that Els of yours is not just anybody."

'You don't say," said Raymond. "There have been times over the past few months when I have thought, "She is my spiritual teacher; I am an infant in that area myself. She sees the spiritual meaning behind everything I know."

Eva looked at him with her heavenly blue eyes and said:

"Raymond! You can't be serious!"

"That she would be my teacher?"

"No, that might be possible... But that you would be an infant! That is really not true! I've been listening to you for days now and I think it's really excellent, the way you can take the content and summarise it and transform it into an exercise. So, you really shouldn't say that!"

"Good, good! Another reprimand!"

Eva said:

"Well, that is the advantage of an upbringing that was full of reprimands, that I have become totally immune to them. I have had a lot of trouble finding and defining my own position within myself. But now no one can undermine that position, not even Johannes..."

Raymond looked at her thoughtfully. One of the most beautiful women he had ever seen. Not the beauty of a film star, not the beauty of Angelique who had walked out of a fashion magazine, but the beauty of a real person in a woman's body. A woman who had worked herself up above the workings of her gender, which she had apparently enjoyed in her youth. Els was much more naturally confident in herself. This gave him food for thought, this was also a contrast. One could probably develop certain feelings from this with regard to a future two-sexuality, in which the human being would no longer be a woman or a man, but would have united both in harmony. Els had some of that and maybe he had some of that too. They did not have such a strong male-female division of roles and that was not an outward thing ... It was strange that this should occur to him in the middle of a conversation at the lunch table. He wanted to park the thought until later and then think about it...

"I have a completely different feeling towards Eva and Johannes than I do towards any other friend we have ever had," said Raymond later when he was with Els. "In a friendship you always have the feeling that it has something to do with *possession*. You have that friendship, but you can also lose it. You interact with each other and that can also come to an end. Somehow, this does not play a part at all when dealing with Johannes and Eva."

"Maybe you shouldn't call it a friendship then," Els said.

"Yes, because I realise that what I feel for these two people and the way I behave towards them - and they towards us - is actually what you look for in a friendship with people and in fact never find. So, it is a heightened friendship."

"That is, of course, because this friendship is built on being engaged in the spiritual sciences together and does not stem from the ordinary sympathies that you have when you enter into a friendship."

"Yes, it must be. Therefore, the fear of losing a friendship cannot sustain itself. Because you would lose it only if you lost spiritual coherence. That is an impossibility. It is entirely up to you and there can never be a disagreement if you don't want one. It is a strangely free feeling. I feel completely acknowledged by these two people, but also totally not claimed. And again, and again I hear the words of Goethe: "What more can a human achieve in life ..." and I would like to add to that now: than that he finds true spiritual friendship! I remember reading something by Thomas Aquinas, who said that friendship rests on a like-minded will. That seems to be a true characteristic of this friendship to me. But the word friendship is actually inadequate, because there we have all the connotations of ordinary friendship and this is something that goes far beyond them."

Els said:

"There is no envy involved either. When I see Philippe talking to Johannes, or Johannes talking to Beato or the Master - it would be ridiculous to have feelings of envy about that. This is also due to the fact that in such a conversation with Johannes and Eva you are completely satisfied. Of course, you would like to continue the conversation and it is never enough in fact.... But you are not left with the normal feelings of negligence or of something not being addressed or the doubt whether you have been properly understood and so on and so forth."

"We get enough impulses here," Raymond said, "to write a whole bookcase full of books about it. Even the subject of friendship, through the example of Johannes and Eva's relationship with each other, evokes a world of thoughts in me that are known but not yet thought of in this life."

'What you say there is strange...' said Els.

Johannes and Philippe sat together in the study. They had used a day of rest to go over the preceding days again, before they could really begin to discuss the vision of the future. Philippe said.

"When one starts to speak about these things, they always turn out differently from the way they were originally intended. I know from experience that what actually comes about is always better than what you had planned. That is the direct inspiration that takes effect. But there is a very curious phenomenon, which I told you about at the beginning of course, and that is that a kind of threshold appears, which rises by the hour, which you have to cross in order to be able to say something sensible about the future. As far as thinking is concerned, you can still rely on the past, and when considering the past, you can rely on thinking in reverse. But as far as the future is concerned you have to find the willpower, with which you can visualize the possible future scenario. Is this not the right moment to ask Raymond to give his lecture on singularity and posthumanism? I think it would be a good idea to do that for the general public. Then we can really make our way into the future."

Johannes looked at him with a smile and said:

"It's as if you're going to hold back a little before you can start to describe the future..."

Philippe nodded and said:

"It is really difficult, Johannes. I don't know if you have done what is necessary to visualize what will happen in the future. After all, this is how John's Apocalypse begins, which is also a vision of the future. It is quite a different thing to contemplate the unfulfilled future or to look at the completely fulfilled past."

Johannes nodded and said:

"Yes, I have tried that myself and experienced how difficult it is. Fear is perhaps the most important emotion that stands in the way. Not so much fear of the possible disasters that lie hidden in the future, but a far greater fear of failing, of seeing things wrongly, of ending up in fantasy instead of in the sensible view of the future."

"And do you," asked Philippe, "have any concrete results from your research?"

"I haven't gone that far..." said Johannes. "I may not be able to go that far, because I want to put my mind completely at the service of your mind. But if you think it would be good to make my own investigations from day to day, then of course I shall do so."

Philippe sighed and said:

"I can think of no greater support from your mind's power than that you should be wholly involved in imagining the future. I will not ask you about your results in advance of my lectures, but I would like to ask you about your additions and similarities and also other visions afterwards every day."

"Good!" said Johannes. "Of course, I also feel a reluctance to making concrete statements about this. You see, in the work of the Master of the Occident, the part in which he speaks about the history of the development of mankind is much more elaborate than the few remarks he makes about the future. I suppose that had he lived longer, the time would have come when he would have spoken about the future of the world and of mankind.

But we cannot do otherwise than give all that we have, and when we have given it all and it can *stand* there firmly in these difficult times, then it will also be possible for what *stands* there to take root, grow and flourish..."

"So, we will ask Raymond to lecture on the singularity and posthumanism first. And when he has done that – I assume that can be done this evening – we will really start our journey into the future. I hope that the tone and the choice of words with which I speak will also succeed in transforming into a future form. But I can only prepare myself meditatively and then hope that the divine inspiration will be such that not only the content will change from the past to the future but also the way I speak. After all, the flow of time reverses and we must make an effort to read what is coming towards us in it. We cannot look back, we can only go along with that which is humanity in us with trust, which will gradually become the entire divine spiritual permeation of the cosmos. I do not want to say: if all goes well, with every statement – however I feel that I would like to say that. In contrast to *fear*, which is the emotion of the future, I want to try to develop true willpower, which is also called *hope* – a remarkable openness to the future, which is not a certainty, because you can only have this when you have a firm foundation in the past, but which is an entirely different quality, which is not so easy to describe as with the word hope!

So, I will describe the positive development, balanced, of course, by the negative counter-movement, but I will assume that the positive development will actually come about and that it will literally prevail. It is, Johannes, as if you stand richly filled before a total void, and that you cannot use anything from that rich fullness to contemplate the emptiness. You know that you have to enter into an inner reversal of your capacity to know, through which that emptiness turns out to be a fullness. It is a different way of seeing, but you must also understand how that which comes from the past must become conscious to man as the past, which will fill the cosmos with spirit with a great movement through mankind, in which having a physical body will gradually become a burden for man, until this burden is finally allowed to be released and a new human existence on earth will begin, in which we must find completely different images from those to which we are accustomed."

Johannes nodded and said:

"Yes, Philippe, I feel the enormous activity that is necessary to gain and express this knowledge of the future, and I completely understand that you are reluctant to do so, although these words from ordinary life are actually unusable for the state you are in now.

All right, let us hear from the other spirit of the future first. I assume that Raymond is now ready to refer to his own inspiration rather than being directly inspired by this spirit. And then we will start our actual task tomorrow…"

*

Els sat in the first row in the large hall. She felt completely out of touch with reality. A few months ago, she and Raymond had entered this hall for the first time and had seen some people in the front row who were apparently in charge of this spiritual institute. One of them had given a talk, and that was Johannes. Now, only a few months later, she was actually sitting in the front row among those people, and the one who was going to give the lecture was Raymond, her lover, who could give a lecture on artificial intelligence on the spur of the moment in an environment where the subject was a foreigner...

Raymond waited in the side room until it was exactly eight o'clock. Els was probably more nervous than he was. He never seemed to have any trouble speaking in public. Maybe it was because of his great intellectual self-confidence, maybe it was because of his mastery of the subject...

The clock struck eight, the door opened, Raymond entered and began his speech, without paper or notes. He took into account that he was speaking to a group of people, most of whom had no knowledge of artificial intelligence at all and who were most likely - without being precisely informed – fierce opponents.

Quietly, he spoke:

"I have been asked to give an introductory lecture tonight on the subject of artificial intelligence. It is a subject that has only become known to people who are not scientifically involved since the 1990s. I remember, for example, how my father pronounced these two words for the first time with great astonishment and said: What do you imagine that is! I was in secondary school at the time, extremely interested in computer technology and very well aware of what artificial intelligence was and should be. I don't think there is a person alive today in our Western culture who does not know what artificial intelligence is. We all make grateful use of it as soon as we take out our smartphone and put it to whatever use. It is an extremely intelligent device – that is why it is called 'smart', it is smart and it uses the cleverness of artificial intelligence. But the applicability of this intelligence, which is not handled by the human brain but by a machine, already goes far beyond what we know about it in everyday life.

From the beginning there have been two clearly distinct currents of scientists, scientists who see artificial intelligence, as we know it now, namely as a useful support for our own intelligence, enabling us to have certain difficult processes carried out by a device, just as we have the washing done by the washing machine and no longer stand scrubbing on a washboard or cooking in a tub on the fire and turning the washing through a wringer to remove as much of the water as possible.

So, there is a group of scientists who see artificial intelligence in that area, but the other group talks about a hard artificial intelligence, and they have very different views on its meaning and significance, especially its significance for the future. They mainly focus on the enormous speed and perfection with which a machine, thanks to a calculation program, can perform certain thought processes. They see this in contrast to the laborious operations of the human brain, and they have a specific vision of the future from the outset that is supported by the way in which this artificial intelligence develops in the course of time.

So, the proponents of hard artificial intelligence are convinced that mechanical intelligence will win by far in the end rather than biological intelligence and that the small advantages that biological intelligence has when compared to artificial intelligence will be developed in an artificial way. I want to talk about that hard artificial intelligence tonight. Developments in science are often far ahead of their applications, which then eventually take place in the world. When I talk about my father who, in the nineties of the last century, did not know the concept of artificial intelligence at all and could not really imagine anything about it either, we have to realize that people were already working intensely on this computer intelligence in the sixties and that at a certain moment in the American chip company Intel one of its founders – Gordon Moore – established that the development of the transistors with which the computer intelligence is performed was advancing at a tremendous rate. He put that into a formula and a graph. The law is this: The number of transistors in an integrated circuit doubles every year due to technological progress. Later, he adjusted this to a term of two years. This means exponential growth. Perhaps you know what that means. In 2006, the same Gordon Moore announced that his law would not last forever, and in 2011 there was a revision, because it was found that there were fundamental physical barriers. But the growth continues. The group of hard artificial intelligence still sees this exponential growth, i.e., a curve that at first still looks like very calm growth, but at a certain moment an acceleration occurs, such that the line almost runs straight up, i.e. increases to infinity in a very short time. If you put this against time in a graph, this would mean that around 2040 this transition will occur in an almost straight upwards line. That has become a showpiece of the proponents of hard artificial intelligence. The cost factor would also shrink exponentially, so it would become cheaper and cheaper.

They have all kinds of reasons to believe that not only the technology will progress quickly to provide an explosion of possibilities, but that the data processing, the calculation methods, the speed with which all this takes place, will also grow exponentially.

We have not reached that 'explosive development' yet and we can still keep up with what the artificial intelligence is doing with our biological intelligence. We are able to refine the artificial intelligence in such a way with our biological intelligence that self-learning machines are created, developed, programmed in such a way that they can learn from their mistakes or their imperfections and improve their performance in the next procedure. If this were to escalate as well, it would mean that man, with his biological intelligence, may have given rise to these self-learning processes, but that, when they explode, as it were, biological intelligence will no longer be able to accomplish what artificial intelligence is capable of in any way.

You could say that this would give any sane person goose bumps. When you really grasp it, it is an extraordinarily exciting prospect, whether experienced positively or negatively.

The representatives of soft artificial intelligence do not believe in such an outburst. They believe that there will be limiting factors. Proponents of hard intelligence are convinced that this is a process that humanity should really long for, because this will be the next step in evolution.

Until now we have had biological evolution. Homo sapiens invents artificial intelligence and knows how to programme it in such a way that a new type of intelligence will emerge from it, with which the biological human being can either be fertilized or have this intelligence built in, or the biological human being can have his being technically contracted into a formula, into an *algorithm*, and this algorithm can then be inserted into a computer, enriching the human being with the artificial intelligence. These are truly futuristic images, which you come across when you delve into this vision, which has been given the name: *Singularity*.

Of course, over time we have become accustomed to using standards anyway. In the past a doctor had knowledge regarding diagnostics and therapy and that doctor could make free use of his knowledge, as it were, when a patient was sitting across from him or her. It depended on many factors which examinations were agreed upon, whether a referral was necessary, whether immediate therapy could be given, or whether therapy was not necessary at all. Nowadays, the procedure is completely standardized. If you find this, you have to do that, in that and that order, and it is a kind of branched system: if you find this, you have to continue with that and if you find that, then continue there. Therapy: that is the first-choice medicine, if there are reasons not to give it - those reasons are listed - then that is the second-choice medicine and so on. As a doctor, you must write down every step so that, if something goes wrong, you can always show that you have thought and acted exactly according to the protocol. It is, of course, obvious to think that a computer can do this better. It is not disturbed by unsought intuitions or ideas, it simply follows the protocol and is much more precise, faster, more thorough and more reliable than the biological brain. This is the way people think, and when you empathize with them, only then do you begin to understand that medicine, where it has been an art, lies precisely in those moments of unsought intuitions, of impulses, the whole area that lies outside standardized work. Of course, this still takes place, but there is an effort to limit it as much as possible and one can imagine that one might be tempted to see this as entirely desirable.

In the circles of hard artificial intelligence, human intelligence is seen as obscure, as awkward, difficult, slow, not exact, disturbed by personal impulses, and so on. And yet we know very well that with human intelligence one accomplishes certain thinking and understanding processes that a computer cannot. Therefore, despite all the contempt for the human brain, there is also a great respect for it. This is expressed in the fact that certain projects are in the process of mapping the human brain in terms of its function. This is not only the cerebrum, but also the cerebellum, the midbrain and the whole area of physiological functions. We try to record all the functions of the human brain millimetre by millimetre, and then test this in the computer, where we try to simulate the brain according to these patterns. In this way, it is hoped that the remarkable phenomenon that the human brain seems to have, namely doing certain things *at the same time*, can ultimately be imitated in the computer or supercomputer.

This research on the human brain is actually still in its infancy, but the proponents of artificial intelligence already see great progress in this. I wonder how many people are aware of the fact that here in Switzerland, in Lausanne, a blue brain project is under way, in which similar research into the human brain is being carried out – not in humans, of course, but in laboratory animals; in people with neurological disorders, attempts are being made to carry out research in the brain at the same time as investigating the disease, but the bulk of brain research is based on research in mammals. In Europe, all scientific centres now have a section for this brain research, subsidized by the EU, a project that has been given the name of the Human Brain Project, in which attempts are being made to actually map the human brain – albeit on the basis of research that is still largely conducted on animals.

You, who are looking for spiritual science, will probably be surprised by the fact that, from research on animal brains, something is thought to be concluded for human brains, because you know that a human being is a completely different creature than an animal, that a human being has the spirit on earth and the animal does not, and that in the human brain one finds an organ that is adapted to that specific human spiritual quality. It is precisely this that disappears, as it were, when you carry out your research on laboratory animals. But science does not think like that. The human being is an animal form, and one can therefore examine certain parts of the organ that have a resemblance to the human organ very successfully and then draw conclusions.

So, on the one hand, there is the flight of development of artificial intelligence, on the other hand, a laborious but steadily growing knowledge of the function of the brain. The proponents, or those who believe that hard artificial intelligence will prevail, imagine that what the human brain has as an advantage above artificial intelligence will become known, that it will be able to be added to artificial intelligence, and that because of the perfection with which artificial intelligence can work, there will be an unprecedented exponential growth of possibilities.

Now the aim is to beam this data, which is being collected with the help of all this research and technical development, into the cosmos later on, as it were. At the moment, this can only be done partially, because the speed with which the data can expand is still too slow. It is imagined that in the future, due to the exponential growth of possibilities, it will also become possible to spread data through the cosmos at a speed greater than that of light and even, one might say, to penetrate other solar systems through certain openings at the edge of our cosmos. This is a futuristic vision, but it does exist.

In physics, we know the phenomenon of singularity. One speaks of it when a certain state is reached in which all physical laws cease to apply. Then one speaks of a singularity. Something similar is expected for the explosion of artificial intelligence, in which man with his limp brain will not be able to keep up, unless he has linked himself to this exploding artificial intelligence.

I believe that the most dangerous thing we can do is to declare this vision of the future to be exclusively science fiction. That there is a certain unwarranted optimism on the part of hard artificial intelligence seems obvious. When we work with smart technology, we are all too often confronted with the impossibilities. And anyone who pays attention will be able to see, in the things that go wrong, how superior the human mental – I do not say biological – intellect actually is. But then this human intelligence has to be used more and more consciously. For technology is an apparatus and that apparatus can be programmed to work even faster, even more perfectly, even more comprehensively. If humans simply leaves human intelligence for what it inherently is, then it is possible that the singularity will prevail. Personally, I do not see that happening in 2040, but we are on our way. There are many inhibiting factors, fortunately, but the human being itself must become the greatest inhibitor, so that what is developed in artificial intelligence is used solely for the benefit of human development – as the proponents of soft artificial intelligence rightly see. We must – this is my opinion – first of all take this raging technical development seriously and try to think along with what is hoped to be accomplished in hard artificial intelligence. On the other hand, we must also be able to put this into perspective and actively look for ways to make this development of artificial intelligence completely uninteresting, by developing a purely human spiritual intelligence. I can only point to that, as I have not developed it yet myself. But I do stand here as an example of someone who, as young as I am, has believed in the singularity for decades and who, after spending a few weeks here in the mountains, has realized what a real singularity could be."

Raymond nodded, thanked the audience for their attention and sat down on a chair in the front row.

Johannes came forward and said:

"Thank you, Dr Raymond Veenman! I would like to tell you, my dear listeners, that in September the speaker will be taking up his teaching duties at the University of Amsterdam in the subject of ‘Humanities and Artificial Intelligence’. So, we have been extremely privileged to listen to such a prominent expert in this field!”

Philippe was never plagued by nervousness before a lecture. He had always prepared himself in such a way that he felt completely absorbed in what he was going to say – at least in an all-encompassing intuition that developed as he was speaking.

This was also the case now, although there was an accompanying unsteadiness as to the certainty of the intuition, because he was now going to speak about the future, as it would take place in the best sense of human development. He felt doubts rising again and again as to whether the development will indeed proceed in the best sense? He knew all too well that the powers and forces in the world development that do not want this best sense of human development, brought about this doubt in him. He knew therefore that he had to fight this doubt with all the power and strength of his human being and so he went to the meeting in the institute with strength.

He concentrated on his intuition and began to speak:

"Johannes and I had a preliminary discussion yesterday and I pointed out that in the unfolding of a vision of the future, which in fact will be a modern Apocalypse, it is continuously the doubt that arises, that tries to dismiss this vision of the future as unfeasible. On the one hand, one feels the great power of those beings in the spiritual world who want to lead us back to an immaterial existence, admittedly with an egoism, but not with a clear-thinking self-consciousness; on the other hand, there is the power that only wants the dense materialism to be recognized and that hopes to seduce mankind to such an extent that it will move away from all spiritual wealth.

When you try to stand in the middle of this and try to receive the vision of the future, you feel the doubt rising up in you from both sides. This is in fact a concise characterization of this modern Apocalypse, which seeks to describe how human beings will participate in the building of the Holy City, the New Jerusalem, which will not be built from the base upwards, from earthly forces, but will be built from heavenly forces – but will therefore be no less solid and reliable. For this, both one doubt and another must be laid to rest again and again in different ranks.

It will now be my task to describe that whole process. We listened to

Raymond's lecture last night and received a good summary once again of what is also regarded as a vision of the future for mankind, which is then called transhumanism to posthumanism. That vision points to a being that will have evolved from the human being and that will have been enriched with artificial intelligence or that will no longer need a biological entity at all and will fully develop in the field of technology – whereby it remains a mystery, for the time being, who will operate that technology. But we leave that vision of the future aside, except insofar as it has stimulated us to arrive at a *spiritual* vision of the future.

The beginning of the future human being that will have a posthuman form, in the sense of no longer being in the earthly physical body that we know, will include the transformation of the human being as it is now into the new human being. This begins in our time, and it is hardly visible yet. Here the doubt immediately arises as to whether a non-visible beginning will have the opportunity to develop, whether it will be possible for this very fine beginning to grow and flourish, instead of being trampled under the big footsteps of the robots.

I say: this transformation begins in our time. How does it begin? In the Old Testament, Jerusalem was seen as the city built from everything the earth has to offer. Jerusalem was seen as an outwardly built form of that which the human being carries as a divine building, as a physical body. Both body and city were seen as composed of *earthly substance*. This point of view continued until the coming of Christ, who gave a new impulse to physicality. This impulse no longer comes from the earth but from the Kingdom of Heaven; it comes, as it were, from above. The impulse has been given and the human being, in a slow development, must become mature enough to shape body and city in a new way with the help of forces and substances that do not come from the earth, but may be taken from the *Kingdom of Heaven*.

This process can already be started consciously by humanity now. There have been some forerunners, especially in the 19th century, but the human being who has taken up this conscious transformation of the body as completely as is possible in our time is our beloved Master of the Occident, Rudolf Steiner.

In his early work on the theory of knowledge, he explains, as it were – though not explicitly – how one, as a modern human being, can arrive at a disposition of the Spirit Man, that is, of the spiritual physical body.

Every human being has the germ within him, thanks to the Mystery of Golgotha, but this germ must be planted in the right spiritual soil in order to grow and blossom, in order to finally become that great spiritual city in which all people can participate, the New Jerusalem.

What exactly is this seed that was given by the young Rudolf Steiner at the end of the 19th century?

Perhaps the early essay on the only possible refutation of atomism is the clearest indication of where to look for this seed.

In natural scientific thought we have the atom, which is said to be the basis of all matter. It is explained very clearly in this essay that the atom can be used as a model, but that it is completely wrong to forget that it is a model and to assume that the atom really exists, although it has no material existence. It is pointed out here that something either has an existence in the realm of the senses, in the material world, or, if it does not, you are dealing with a concept or an idea. Everything that is conceivable must be conceivable either *as existing* in the realm of the *senses* or as a *concept* or an *idea*. When at the end of the 19th century the atom was said to be something that does not exist, that has no material existence, but which is not a concept either, then this is a total impossibility. And when you come to realize that in the time since then physics and chemistry have based themselves increasingly on the model of the atom – and you meditate on it – then you see a structure of thought coming into being, which in no way relates to anything that exists. *No sense reality, no idea reality*. Thus, in fact, the seed of the resurrection body has been extirpated from the perceptible reality.

The theory of knowledge that Rudolf Steiner then brings is intended to make this germ conceivable again.

This is the beginning in our time of that great reversal, in which the form of the human being will no longer be visible from the earth, no longer from below, but increasingly from above and will become visible there too – albeit in a different way.

The doubt that arises here has to do with the fact that the form from below, the body and the buildings on earth, are solid and visible, while that very first tender bud that has to come from above seems to be a feather, blown away in the wind of the universe...

But that is precisely the difficulty of new beginnings... We must find the point, in an area that is purely spiritualized and that is really completely pure, in which there are no mistakes and no selfishness, where the false character that is inherent in thought, in intelligence and therefore also in the spiritual principle, is overcome. We must find the point, which is not an appearance, but which actually represents a being. That is the task of the very beginning. Then we will find a point-like being, but it is a being, and it is a spiritual being, because it is found in a spiritual appearance. It will depend on our effort and endeavour whether that point of being receives the right attention, allowing it to gradually grow beyond itself. That point of being is the point which in occult language is called in the spiritual human being, the Spirit Man. This Spirit Man is equal to the resurrection body, but we still carry only a germ, namely a point within us. Here lies the turning point of development.

Previously, everything came from below and from outside, here everything comes from above and from within. Through the inner commitment in meditation and in the development of the pure sense-free thinking, which is able to think of one's own human being, the "I", through that commitment an inner experienced spiritual body comes into being, consisting of the risen thinking body. This newly formed thinking body becomes a body and this body becomes ensouled. The spirit being of the human being is looked upon by the beings in the spiritual world. This perception is the ensoulment. This new body of the human being experiences itself through the beholding by the higher spirit world. We can try to imagine this in meditation. If we are already on the way to strengthening this "I"-point in pure thinking in such a way that it becomes an experience of being, we can also experience more and more truly that we are ensouled by being beholded. We too are beholding...

In ordinary life, this is known in the love that one human being has for another, because of the excellent qualities that the lover perceives in the beloved. The lover beholds the excellence in the beloved and the beloved feels loved precisely because of that, because he or she feels that perception. It is another way of knowing oneself. You do not look at yourself through your own eyes, but through the eyes of someone who loves you. In self-knowledge you see your lower being; in the love of a fellow human being you will never experience that, but you will always experience your excellence through the eyes of someone else.

We can immerse ourselves in this and will then experience how the present physical body no longer plays a role. It is sitting in the chair, lying on the bed, but the spirit person is in no way involved with this body anymore and has completely elevated himself to soul and spirit.

However tender and incipient this may be, we can still taste its greatness.

I repeat again: Thinking has completely freed itself from thinking of sensory content; it thinks purely in the idea, and there it strengthens itself through the use of willpower in such a way that it gradually experiences that willpower in thinking. Thus, the experience of thinking changes from the experience of a phantom idea to the experience of a 'real being' idea. And the bearer of this, which becomes conscious through the constant effort of will, is the individual Self, the I, as impulse of will. Because this impulse of will appears in the pure sphere of thought, the concept of the self is also a pure concept in thought and at the same time a pure will.

Therein lies the powerful beginning of the unfolding of the whole human being in the non-sensory thinking body that is a *resurrection body*. It has torn itself away from material existence and can now consciously experience itself and can experience all knowledge that this self unfolds in itself as a Spirit-Man. It is a spiritual process that proceeds entirely in intuition. Willing and feeling appear in thinking and bring the experience of being into this thinking. Through practice, it then becomes possible to stay in this spirit person for a long time and experience how it is the spiritual new ground of existence there. The spirit body is brought to life in a spiritual way; indeed, it is as if it were a spiritual breath that passes through this body, through which inspiration comes about. Finally, it is the supreme spiritual enthusiasm that ignites the spiritual individuality...

I cannot possibly be satisfied with my words, for I am trying to express something for which there are no words, even the capacity of thought falls short of expressing these experiences, these perceptions. Therefore, I try to describe what can be described from different angles, but it remains extremely limited.

We must therefore try to imagine – and some of us have already realized this – that the purely sense free perceived thought as a will, as a whole human being in the spiritual sense, breaks free from material existence, has a form there, has life, has consciousness. Instead of an environment with sensory content, a world of beings flows towards this new human being. In the *beholding* of these world beings lies the new consciousness content.

For the time being, this remains a shadowy life in a sense, because we have to become used to the completely different position with regard to content. We have to look outwards and see, and we have to look reverse and see. But it is the very first tender beginning; there is a long developmental path between this first appearance of the New Jerusalem and the city that has come to full bloom, in which the content will shine more brightly than nature can ever achieve. In which the new body will have more skills than those of the highest scientist, the most skillful artist or the most thorough craftsman..."

Raymond said:

"I would still like to maintain the comparison with the trans- and post-humanism of the vision of singularity and the question is the following: The people who envision singularity in the future imagine that there will be artificial intelligence instead of brain intelligence, with all its speed, perfection and, in a certain sense, purity, because it is not distracted by personal emotions. One imagines that the element that we already know today, namely the wireless distribution of data, will become, as it were, a substitute mind-element, to which every human being will have access, but without the use of devices, not an iPhone in your hand or a PC on your desk, but built into your physical being, or the information of the physical being uploaded into the computer. In a way, the film series The Matrix is an impotent attempt to portray something similar. I call it an impotent attempt because it is still based far too much on what we know at the moment and therefore does not take the singularity into account, that moment when the situation will change completely. The consciousness of mankind will then be a consciousness *in* artificial intelligence and the supporting element will be the electromagnetic field, which will then be transported through air and light. We are already being prepared for this. In fact, we do our exercises every day – even if we are not aware of it – because we are becoming increasingly used to asking the device all our questions, becoming at home in the World Wide Web, in which both objective and coloured information is stored, news and fake news, fact and fiction. We surf the waves of this web with a certain frivolity, getting more and more used to the fact that the content of consciousness coincides with the content spread in the electromagnetic field by air and light. It is all still in its infancy. Every human being has quite a bit of his own consciousness and only a part of 'www-consciousness', but we are becoming more and more used to exchanging our own memory for the memory on a device.

How do you see this in relation to the thinking body, ensouled by the world's thoughts and beings?"

Philippe nodded and said:

"You very accurately describe the greatest countermovement to what I have tried to discuss before. While it lies on our path to initiate and bring our own thinking into culture, our *own thinking creativity*, we are tempted to make less and less use of it and allow ourselves to be flooded with information from the world wide web. When we develop a thinking body and feel witnessed by the spiritual world, the wisdom of the world comes to us in full, and we can develop in such a way that we ask the right questions and receive the corresponding answers in the beholding. Then, we would have an increasingly rich and more detailed knowledge at our disposal, without artificial intelligence.

There are already people known who had an extensive wisdom at their disposal on the basis of natural ability. An interesting figure is *Friedrich Eckstein* (Mac Eck) from Steiner's time in Vienna, of whom it is said that he knew so much that the encyclopaedia came out of the cupboard to consult him when the encyclopaedia could not answer the questions.

These answers were very detailed, down to percentages and numbers. We see something similar with Rudolf Steiner, but then in a spiritualised sense. We know that at one time there were some young students at a lecture who wanted to put him to the test and asked him questions about totally unknown tropical plants of which they only knew the name. Rudolf Steiner knew exactly how to answer the questions about those plants most aptly. With Rudolf Steiner we are dealing with someone who had a natural access to world wisdom, but who had to make all this wisdom his own by means of an extreme discipline with his *I*. That is our example. However, most of us, or perhaps all of us, no longer have that natural aptitude which enables us to read the chronicle in which all wisdom is written.

Another example, who goes even further than the two people described, is the Count of Saint Germain, a century earlier, in the 18th century, of whom it is known that he possessed certain techniques to make profound changes right down to matter, right down to substance. It has also been reported that he was present in several places at the same time and also that after his recorded death he visited several people, who reported this. It seems that this individuality possessed an immortal body, which became invisible after death, but with which he could make himself visible again if he so wished. Such magic strikes us rational people as complete nonsense and is only tolerated in children's stories – which are then gladly read by adults – think of Harry Potter. But we will have to get used to thinking, imagining, accepting these supernatural phenomenon and relating them to a spiritual vision of the human future, in which, of course, there are always precursors."

Raymond nodded and said:

"Indeed, it is not easy to accept such facts as true. But can you put the two visions side by side again? That is, can you counter what I have just described as the concept of the singularity with what you have just said in your lecture?"

Philippe smiled, sighed deeply and said:

"I will try.

As human beings, we are a step above the processes of nature, thanks to our capacity for pure thought. The body participates in nature to a certain extent, but not wholly so, but the element of knowledge in us is, insofar as it is not concerned with nature, a supernatural element. And this supernatural element is as much above nature as the electromagnetic field is below nature. So, you have to imagine: Nature in the centre in this respect, towards the spiritual, towards a purely sense free spiritual thinking, as far above nature as the electromagnetic field belongs to sub-nature.

Artificial intelligence with all its fabulous possibilities extends entirely into that sub-natural field of electromagnetism. The more we surrender to it, the more strongly we are banished into the sub-natural, while we are under the illusion that we are in a realm of thought that corresponds to supernatural thought. We have to free ourselves with a jolt from nature into the supernatural thinking, but we are easily sucked down into the sub-natural thinking. This sub-natural thinking is the kingdom of Lucifer and Ahriman. They are infinitely wiser and more intelligent than we are. Lucifer has grandiose power as wisdom and beauty and Ahriman possesses the intelligence as it functions in artificial intelligence, but on an infinitely, say, singularly enhanced level. We can, as thinking people, allow ourselves to be led down into the electromagnetic field of thought, then be absorbed and carried away in it and be endowed with a shining Ahrimanic intelligence and a diabolical fantasy. Or we can climb to the top of Olympus with difficulty and attempt to find the thinking element in the pure etheric heights of which I have just spoken. Spiritualised thinking as a body of thought, which, as a soul, takes in the thoughts of the world. And as I have just described it, it is not only the world-thoughts, but in the process, we even behold with the world-beings, we speak with the world-revelation, and we think with the world-thoughts."

Raymond had listened breathlessly and when Philippe had finished, he nodded and said:

"Thank you very much!"

Phillipe said:

"Johannes, maybe you have some additional thoughts?"

Johannes looked immersed in thought and said:

"I was deeply moved and touched by the manner in which you described this first stage in the direction of human existence without a physical body."

"But Johannes, you would have surely described it slightly differently in your own way? Perhaps I could ask you to do so?"

Johannes nodded and said:

"The question that arose in me was: We have now received an experience of the pure etheric thought-life, as it can be realised in the thought-body while it is being thought. The question that then arises within me is: Where is the specifically personal individual emotional life? Is it left behind with the body in the chair or in the bed, or does something of it remain?"

"And that's what I have to respond to?" said Philippe. "Don't you want to do so, Johannes?"

"Yes..." said Johannes. "This very personal individual emotional life is elevated to a pure experience, and when you were speaking, I could experience this and perceive that becoming aware of that which ensouls the thinking body, is precisely this personal individual experience. Otherwise, there would be nothing left of you. But the pure Christian element specifically is this very fine, delicate, artistic experience, the awareness that you are being observed and, in this glimpse, you sense – that is to say, feel, experience – the richness of the qualities and of the other conditions, although that sounds too sober. But I think for instance of the categories *suffering* and *active*, of *being in space* or *passing in time*... These perceptions, but then not as thought processes, but as *experiences*, as feelings, are then the expressions of the person. Whoever has some experience in the field of occult knowledge knows that everything that is gained in this way is infinitely, indescribably richer, more powerful, more effective, more real in us than everyday knowledge. However, when you try to describe this new form of inner being, you cannot avoid the danger that this description works as the description of a shadow area. It therefore seems to me that the emphasis on the emotional life, as activated by the power of thought, is of great importance. Of course, we then think of a poet like *Novalis*, who in his poem '*When numbers, figures, no more hold key*... indicates a future in which science will be transformed into love. And also, in his fairy tale *'Eros and Fable'*, a wonderfully sensitive world appears, which one could experience as a romanticised vision of the future. Although this does not strike one as representing what will really be, these conjectures, this premonition of Novalis, are extraordinarily instructive for those of us who are looking for a future human existence in which the sobriety of cerebral thinking will have fallen away, while the *exactitude* of the scientific method of thinking – in a metamorphosis – will have been retained."

Raymond responded by saying;

"As a novice, I don't want to do all the talking, but I hope that my early experiences will contribute to the development of this vision of the future. I have listened to Philippe and now to Johannes and I have the impression that what Johannes describes is possibly a later phase in the development than what Philippe described. At least, if I may relate this to myself, I notice that it is less difficult for me to think in the purest thoughts, than to make the transition to a more magical fairy-tale experience. I can imagine – but this remains an impression – that this also becomes 'personal'. You also observe it in the development of the virtual realm of thought, in all possible magical surrealistic representations, which are then also used for games. There, everything, however enchanting, is nevertheless extremely rigid. What Johannes describes strikes me as the feelings of the life processes themselves. But again, as far as I am concerned, they are further removed from my current thinking than the image of a thought body."

After a silence, Beato spoke and said:

"It seems important to me, however, to emphasise from the very beginning that the first thing to be developed is the *will in thinking*, through which thinking becomes a body, but then to immediately include perception. Not yet in a Novalis-like way perhaps, but in a discipline *to experience* every intensified thought *with the feeling*. When you introduce the will into thinking, it occurs as a self-evident effect. But maybe we would not be able to pay attention to it, not enough, and therefore I would like to ask, Philippe, if you would consider this aspect of feeling, which Johannes has brought to our attention, to be the focus of attention tomorrow."

Philippe nodded and said:

"I will certainly do that! Science, that has become a deed, becomes art, but not art as we know it in our earthly existence, but art based on a super-sensible primal image. In the course of our development, we humans will return to this, enriched by the whole human development, as it has been, and it will go even further than that. Tomorrow, then, I shall concentrate on the experience that arises when thinking becomes a body, which takes in the world thoughts as its soul."

During lunch Raymond said:

"What I find so impressive is that what emerges in this discussion becomes so real. If you were to read it in a book, you would just take it in as content. But now that 13 of us are sitting together and Philippe or Johannes is speaking – it becomes so real, so intense, that you could almost say that a joint body of thought has already been established. It is as if we are allowed to have a share in this body that we do not yet have ourselves, because it is being discussed in a group of people, some of whom have developed this thinking body. Do you think, Johannes, that this is so?"

Johannes nodded and said:

"Yes, it is. But you do have a lot of potential Raymond… You could imagine that there would also be someone there who, let's say like a Judas, would withdraw from the entire thing and judge from the outside that it's all nonsense."

"You took a risk," said Raymond, "by asking us to join you... You couldn't possibly know that I wouldn't be such a Judas, could you?"

"Oh yes..." smiled Johannes. "Then you underestimate our powers of discernment, which go a bit further than just listening to people's words."

"Does that mean," asked Raymond frankly, "that you also know who we are? Who we have been in previous incarnations?"

"It could mean that, yes," said Johannes, and he said it in such a way that it was clear that no further questions could be asked....

Later Els said to Raymond:

"It's incredible how you change! Of course, you are still the same, but something is becoming visible and gives you a strength and certainty that you never had before. When you sit there at the table with your friends and ask your questions, you really are one of them and they see you in the same way..."

"And you, dear Els?"

"It doesn't matter to me how I appear, or what people think of me. I am completely satisfied and happy with the fact that I can be there, that I can understand what is being said, that it feels like something personal, that I have no doubts at all. And besides, I am so proud of you ... I really don't need anything else, Raymond!"

"I do have my moments of doubt ... Then I think: Are we completely normal? We have been entirely freed from all triviality, we are dealing with a subject that has nothing to do with our current existence, at least so it seems, we are in a group of people who all see something in it that is justified – they are not little boys and girls, that is clear. But then the feeling of doubt surfaces anyway."

"That probably can't be helped. You have served a very different master for decades. Of course, he doesn't just turn around and leave quietly. He will certainly try to get you back, even though we know very well that it will not happen. And what do you do with your doubt?"

"Look at it and let it pass. I try not to address it at all, and experience shows that it then subsides, because the certainty of what we are learning here is so great and still growing that I am well aware that any doubt is a fleeting thing..."

Philippe began to speak:

"I have studied the feelings associated with the birth of the thinking body. There are, as is well known, several possibilities and ways of giving birth to this thinking body.

In the first instance, the birth of the thinking body means an awakening to the etheric body, which we, in our Western culture, no longer perceive at all. All wisdom and all thoughts live in this etheric body, but we only know its reflections, which we have thanks to our physical body. And we know the inner motives in the desires and wishes and in all the emotions. Now the brain's reflections of thoughts are devoid of emotion. They do express feelings, but they are not sensitive themselves. The characteristic of the etheric body is precisely its high sensitivity, its tender, gentle, sublime sensitivity. As soon as the thinking body is born, the thoughts are no longer insensitive, no longer abstract, but highly living sensitive beings. So it cannot be possible that this thinking body is only a will-thinking structure, without feeling, for the characteristic of this thinking body is precisely feeling. Now, of course, there is always the question of the best path to take in order to gain access, as it were, as directly as possible to this sensitive thinking body, which is primarily an awareness of the etheric body. On the one hand, it is necessary to do thinking exercises using a sense-free, pure thinking, preferably in philosophy. On the other hand, a religious intensification is a benefit, when this is possible. Through intense religious contemplation, the etheric body is directly activated. My experience is that being as intensely absorbed as possible by the Gospel of St. John, thinking again and again and again about the chapters in the Gospel, finally leads to an emotional world joining the thoughts.

You can also put it this way: The activity of thinking gives the body of thought a certain substantial solidity, which is based on the will in thinking. You could call this *the Grail*, an absolutely reliable, dependable receiver of the world thoughts. But those world thoughts stream into the vessel as a feeling. This is the same feeling that arises when one works through the Gospel according to St. John meditatively over and over again. But that means that the new-born thinking body, the Holy Grail, is animated by the World Thoughts of the Holy Spirit, which are *love itself.* You feel how, above and beyond your body, you are a newborn human being, born of water and spirit – as the Lord says to Nicodemus when they speak of the rebirth. *Water* is life, the etheric body; the *spirit* is the Holy Spirit, these are the world-thoughts. This is not the appearance that man will have far, far later, when he no longer needs to incarnate in an earthly body. We will speak about that later. I am now describing the preliminary steps that we can take now of our own free will at the beginning of this new development. But then the thoughts are nothing like our present abstract thoughts or our emotionally driven thoughts. Indeed, they then become more like the thoughts and images from Goethe's fairy tale or from the already mentioned fairy tale of Eros and Fable by Novalis. Through that veil of beauty, we must then learn to contemplate the true meaning of those images, which is in fact directly given, but to which we are entirely unaccustomed. There is a great longing for abstract reasoning in the modern earthly soul, and it may be retained only as a quality, but not used. It is good that the soul has a rational skeleton, but it must otherwise refrain from using it."

"May I ask something?" asked Raymond.

Philippe nodded invitingly.

"What you tell us, you say in the rational forms of the intellect. You do not speak in fairy tale images."

"In order to convey what wants to be said, you always have to use the present forms of thought. They are not really adapted to what the Spirit has to say, but the time is past when we could teach in images. This is still true for the little child, but not for the adult. It is a task in itself to 'translate' what comes into consciousness as tender sensitive knowledge into the intellectual forms. But there is no other way..."

"That delicate, sensitive beauty... is there a comparison with experiencing music?"

"No. There is no known experience that you could take as an example. Although in all artistic pursuits, those experiences are the fundamental ground. But we cannot access that without initiation."

"Forgive me for interrupting your lecture…"

Philippe shook his head and continued:

"For us the task is to learn to live in the body of water and spirit, to be able to remain in it for a long time. Then it will also be possible to direct the thinking body towards the physical and let it be shaped in such a way that it becomes a transcendental stable form which no longer needs flesh and bones, but which can live in the elements."

"What is the effect of this rebirth, as you have described it today, on the rest of nature?" the Master asked.

"You know better than anyone that as soon as you become conscious in the ether body, there is not such a surrounding by the skin there as in the physical body. You are far less enclosed in yourself than you are used to in physical existence. You flow, as it were, with great rivers, with small streams, you pause in puddles and lakes, and then you are gently carried out to an outgoing stream. That is the stream of thought-life and when the human being knows how to breathe new life into himself, thanks to the vitalisation that becomes possible through the resurrection of Christ in the etheric world, this vitalisation also flows into the great etheric world and enlivens the whole of nature as a consequence. Just as a flame of a candle illuminates total darkness, just as a drop of tincture colours a large quantity of clear water, so new life streams into the great etheric world when even one human being carries a vitalised etheric body through consciousness, through which nature can recover from all the assaults that man is otherwise continually inflicting upon it.

But we are still speaking about the beginning. In our time, such enlightenment, an awareness of the etheric body, can only be achieved when the person concerned engages in self-education. Not only thinking practice is needed, meditation is needed, religious intensification is needed, but also a deeply penetrating will to change one's own temperament and character. When we look into the distant future, when mankind will have reached the point of being able to exist on earth *without* a physical body, then this does not only apply to the highly developed souls, but it is valid in principle for the whole of mankind and we will still have great difficulty in imagining what that will be like. But a slow build-up towards it will create clarity for us. Even though a large part of humanity in future – not all – will not have to experience the phenomenon of death, it is still true that we must take the lead now through the path of sanctification and inner activity. Everything that is present on earth is transformed by us into concepts, and because we want to do this fully consciously, with our free will as the objective, this commitment is equal to love. Wisdom and love are the pillars on which the development towards the future rests. The thinking activity we perform can be considered, in as far as it is concerned with understanding, an activity of wisdom. But the conscious penetration with will, through which *the thinking body* arises that *takes in the world thoughts as sensitive*, is love. This experience of the enlivened etheric body occurs as a point at first, in the place of the third eye, but with continued practice this point gradually expands over the whole body, occupies the place of the entire body, although the intensity is greatest in the upper pole and it remains perceptible downward, but fades and seems less finely differentiated.

What follows is the exercise of learning to live in this body, that is, to contemplate it. There is no other content than the bliss of the flowing, ever-moving, formative, religiously infused ether body, but ordinary consciousness pulls at us and we easily fall back. Meditation takes on a completely different meaning. We are no longer meditating a thought *content*, but we are meditating the thinking *body* itself. But it can take a very long time before the meditating soul can take this seriously. This activity is a world of trials and tribulations. Doubt arises continuously as to whether this is a sensible activity.

When it was still a matter of thought *contents*, we had the feeling that we were doing something sensible. Now there is nothing left of that, and it is a moving, forming, sensitive world, which does bring contentment, but in which certain points arise that either obscure our attention, or create thoughts in us that cause us to doubt our own activity.

Tomorrow I want to begin the presentation of the state of development that follows this described state.

And now I would like to ask if Johannes has any instructions or additions."

Johannes nodded and spoke:

"Yes, certainly. I wanted to point out another image from the Apocalypse, that of the Angel with the book.[6] The Angel has a face like that of the sun; the legs, pillars of fire, stand on the sea and on the earth. The pillar on the sea is seen as the pillar of strength... The pillar on the

6 From the Apocalypse of John, Chapter 10

land as the pillar of wisdom. And the sun shining above is love. He has a book in his left hand, which is the ether world with all its contents of thought. The human being, John, has to eat this, it has to come into consciousness, and it will not only taste sweet, but also be bitter in the stomach. I wanted to mention this because it is not only wisdom and love, but also strength. Strength is Elias, wisdom is Moses. They come back in us in the way that Philippe has just described. It is the will, the strength, that transforms love into wisdom. That is how Philippe described it, of course, but it is very moving to see in this image what he described. "

The Master said:

"May I make one more personal addition?"

"Always!" said Philippe with a smile.

"What we have heard in the last few days has evoked strong memories in me of my first meeting with Johannes. I had severe pneumonia, had been brought to hospital unconscious, and Johannes was sitting by my bedside when I regained consciousness. At that moment I was not thinking at all, and I saw Johannes as an immensely expanded sacred coloured aura, multicoloured, and yet infinitely calm. Later on, the memory of that image became clearer and clearer, took more shape, and I began to see, whenever I met him, that his thinking was shaped like a diamond with a multitude of facets, but liquid, not hard like a diamond, but flowing and yet at the same time full of shape and colour.

I came to Europe from the East. I was born clairvoyant and, in the monastery, where I was brought up that clairvoyance was schooled and shaped according to a rigorous doctrine. The core of this doctrine is the primordial idea that man has lost his clarity of vision through the development of thought. When a way is sought to regain or preserve clairvoyance, the innate tendency to want to think through everything must be overcome. This was achieved in us through a discipline of memory. We were brought up in such a way that our thinking capacity was used entirely to practice memorisation and not to think for ourselves. So, I learned that we have to consider thinking as a kind of opponent and that it has to be brought under control with iron discipline, so that it can be turned off, so that you can be a human being without constantly involving thinking.

That is how I came to Europe, to the Occident, where the culture of that thinking, which we regard as an adversary, reigns supreme. For years I taught overcoming thinking in the institute where we are now.

Then came Johannes, and I proved to be honest enough to recognise that where I saw thinking as an opponent in everyone else, I saw it as a holy, flowing, multicoloured diamond in him. I did not immediately recognise that this was his thinking, and I also tried to convince him that he had to learn to switch off thinking, in favour of pure perception, which then becomes clear vision. So that means that I tried to convince him that he should ignore the already developed thinking body, perhaps even throw it away.

That this had to lead to a temporary break, of course, is very clear in retrospect. What I am actually trying to say with this personal recollection is that what Philippe described as the development of the thinking body, which takes in the thoughts of the world as soul, becomes symbolised, or put into an image, or becomes an imagination of a liquified diamond, which is formed in an infinite multitude of colourful facets, which never become rigid or stiff, which are always in motion. I have understood very clearly that a new initiation, a new clairvoyance, is possible, which begins *precisely* with that element that we want to get rid of in the East, by trying to side-line rational thinking. Here in the Occident this intellectual thinking is not to be sidetracked, but on the contrary it is to be intensified, I now understand that very well. I understand that thinking, which is basically a luciferic element, is to be developed in such a way that it becomes a thinking of the Holy Spirit. And the Holy Spirit reveals itself to clear discernment as a liquid diamond with an infinite multitude of colourful facets."

Philippe nodded and said:

"That is exactly how it is experienced in the initiation. When you have developed the thinking sufficiently, so that the two-leafed lotus flower has developed as the third eye and its power extends over the whole human being, so that the fire that burns in the depths of the human being can rise sacredly and purely without danger, then *this sacred fire* joins the two-leafed lotus flower and becomes the *beholding* of thinking. At the moment that this takes place, the first holy form of the future New Jerusalem develops – and that form is the liquid diamond with an infinite multitude of colourful facets!"

They were having lunch with Johannes and Philippe. Raymond felt such a deep respect for the two of them that he could hardly bear to sit at a table outside like this. He would have preferred to remain silent, but he felt that something was expected of him. He asked:

"Why are you both our hosts today?"

"Eva had to attend to some matters at the clinic and Philippe wanted to be with us informally."

"Do you understand that I often feel totally out of touch with reality? As if I have already died, or something like that. What was 'normal' in our lives doesn't utter a word, instead the spirit speaks a wonderful language..."

"That is one of the reasons why we have lunch together every day. The other reason is companionship. But we completely understand that it is not easy, and I think it is brave of you, Raymond, to take it all in."

"I have no problem taking it all at face value – at least, when not over-come by doubt. But I don't know how this will find a place in my life in Amsterdam. Just imagine, I am there with dozens of rational thinking people, who have no sympathy for this, it would not occur to them – just as it has never occurred to me. Now I am stuck with it. And what do you think of our feeling towards you? What kind of people are you? The actual 'aliens'? Extra-terrestrial sages? Or is this in every human being, if only they are willing to look at it?"

"It's a bit of both, isn't it? We bring the Spirit to earth, that is a fact. But we don't reveal anything that wouldn't be attainable for everyone. What do you say, Els?"

"I completely understand how Raymond feels, I do too in a certain sense, but I don't allow it to happen, because I know it's pointless. Or more clearly said: our presence would lose its meaning if I allowed it. We have dived into the depths, but it turns out that we can swim after all, without having learned to do so consciously. Every day something grows, there is more than yesterday. What it is exactly, I cannot say, I hope it is the thinking body..."

"That's also true...' sighed Raymond. "I haven't learned to be reverent ... I'm making up for that now."

"But," said Philippe, "how do you cope with these matters when you have no doubts, in the positive moments?"

Raymond smiled and said:

"Fortunately, there are more of those than moments of doubt. Doubt arises especially when I compare the contents here with those that I occupy myself with and also have to occupy myself with in daily life. Then I don't last out for long, but most of the time I completely surrender to what is entirely new that is presented here, and I am also very impressed by the way you portray this content. A greater contrast with singularity and transhumanism is not possible in fact, although the subject seems to be identical. In the vision of singularity, you have to grow accustomed to completely surrendering your intelligence to a system that knows everything better. Here it is exactly the opposite, namely that as a human being you have to let everything that creation has to offer flow through you, through your capacity of knowing. While artificial intelligence hopes to spread the artificial intelligence through the cosmos and even beyond, in our vision here the human being himself will become the source of cosmic intelligence because he will let the original cosmic intelligence flow through him or rather process and rework it. When you deepen that understanding in yourself, then the differentiation becomes clear, even though the word 'differentiation' does not indicate the difference at all – it is indescribable, and I can feel the fire of enthusiasm for what the human being actually is igniting in me – whereas in the study of artificial intelligence a detached coolness arises and the enthusiasm for that vision lies in a completely different realm. With artificial intelligence you have to remain detached, because it does not concern your own intelligence, but the intelligence that has been generated by human intelligence but is increasingly going its own way. I feel that my emotional life, as I am now, is too weak and too small to fully perceive this difference. But I am aware of something of it and it makes me hang onto your every word, Philippe. I find it indescribably fascinating, and I look forward to the descriptions of the human being as he will be when flesh and bones are no longer needed. I hope that the gradual transition to that state will be described as clearly and, I might add, as rationally as the development so far. One question that still arises in my mind is, of course: How do these men – you – get their knowledge, there is no university where you could study this as a subject?"

Philippe looked at him slightly surprised and said:

"I thought the answer to that question was a foregone conclusion.

The whole development I have described is in fact the evolution of mankind. Every human being participates in it, some are only more developed than others, no matter how this may contradict our equalising ideals. In the very development itself lies the study of that subject. If you were to decide to take this meditative path, you would increasingly experience that every step you take in that development is also an enrichment of your knowledge and ability."

"It is difficult to grasp how such a total transformation of the phenomenon of study comes about. I must say that in the last few months I have already experienced to some extent that I am changing as a result of this knowledge and that my change means an increase in my insight. So, in fact your astonishment is justified, this question will answer itself if I pay attention."

Philippe asked:

"Do you also meditate?"

Raymond nodded and said:

"Yes, we retreat for about an hour every evening to repeat, reflect on and explore the contents of the morning and, if possible, experience them. Since we came here in the spring, we have not abandoned this new habit of deep exploration. For the time being, our meditation consists only of deepening, and we have not yet meditated in the way that I understand you do systematically, by focusing the whole attention on a small content and not letting it go."

Raymond felt painfully how this conversation remained on the surface, while he felt the need to convey, to put into words, the depth that he really experienced, what these daily talks brought him in terms of life-changing insights and feelings. He shook off his discontent and spoke freely:

"I would really like to say that these days here, Philippe's lectures, the words of the others, touch me extremely deeply, and my whole life is transformed by them. I have no words to express the feelings of gratitude and reverence that have arisen in me since I have known you. I can only compare them to the feelings of love I have for Els and the feelings I have when I make or listen to music, but in fact the latter feelings are infinitely weak compared to what I am experiencing here. You would like to go out into the world and proclaim everywhere that people have to come here to *find their lives again*. But at the same time, you know that such a journey is pointless ... It has to happen more or less by itself, just as we came here more or less by ourselves. And I also believe that a person has to have a certain maturity to be sensitive to what you have to offer here. But in answer to your question, Philippe, I wanted to say how grateful I am to be able to experience this."

Raymond was very quiet that afternoon and evening... Finally, when they were sitting together on the sofa, Els said:

"What is the matter Raymond?"

He took her hand and said:

"I am having difficulties with my feelings. They don't fit in me or my soul or I don't know where. They are so vast and I am so small, something like that.... You would want to go to church and kneel before the altar, or before a crucifix. But I have to work with that inwardly, don't I? I don't know these feelings of reverence and fulfilment. Do you?"

Els shook her head.

"No, neither do I. I tend to think that things are exaggerated. And now it can't be 'exaggerated' enough. We are the generation of 'just being normal' and only going crazy in the pub or at festivals. The more earnest, the dumber and more boring. And now it's the seriousness that makes the feelings so intense..."

"Yes, we are excluding ourselves from the 'community', that much is clear. But it does not concern me at the moment. Right now, I'm dealing with overwhelming feelings that make me aware of my inability to bear them."

Philippe began to speak:

"We have now spoken at length about the spiritualisation of thinking, the coming to life of thinking, which, when it is not cultivated, is a dead shadowy thinking, which has no substance, and is without reality. We have spoken of the fact that thinking can be transformed in such a way, that we could speak of the birth of a thinking body. That *thinking body* is then so clearly present that it can be constantly perceived as though you were perceiving something which exists with your senses. Of course, when you are not meditating, it escapes your perception, but a time comes and a time will come, when that thought body has such endurance that it is a perceptible body outside of meditation, too, in which you can live.

Now we move on to the first step in the future. Just as thinking can be brought to life in our time, in a next phase – and this phase is also being prepared for now – it will become possible for the *spoken word* to come to life, so that it becomes a perceptible spiritual revelation, which will have a different quality than thinking itself.

The human being will be increasingly gifted with the *living word*, not only as a living concept, but increasingly as a living reality that can be spoken. Initially, this will still require the physical voice to make this speech audible, but we already have an example in eurythmy of how the word can be perceived through certain movements that have become visible. We must try to imagine as vividly as possible how, in the future, movements that are now produced by the larynx and the speech organs in the air will become possible without the use of the speech organs, albeit with the use of – let us say – a transcendental larynx, but no longer physically audible to the senses, but experienced as movements in the air. We are familiar with Rudolf Steiner's book *Occult Science*. In it he describes the first form of Saturn existence, which preceded the development of the earth. In that Saturn existence the predisposition for the physical body was given, and it is described as a *warmth substance*, which was highly differentiated, so that in that differentiation the structure of the physical body was expressed, as it were.

We must then imagine something similar for the future, for the living word, which will not be spoken in the warmth, but in the air. The movements, the forms made in the air by the spoken word, as expressed in eurythmy, will become the living word perceptible to every human being in the future.

We learn to flow like water in the thinking body. The typical earthly stable rest does not occur there; everything is always in motion, in a meaningful movement.

The word, when it is enlivened, becomes sensitive movement of the air current. You can only try to grasp this by going into meditation and imagining these details as vividly as possible. It has been described for the sixth cultural period that Maitreya Buddha will really become Buddha, he is now still a Boddhisatva, a Buddha on his way, and that this Buddha will work through the *living active word*. In our time, it is still so that the word itself is not active when it is spoken. It is accompanied by thoughts and emotions. When you think of the emotional orators of the 20th century – I am of course thinking of Hitler and Churchill – you can see, as it were, that it is not the word itself that grips people, seduces them or whatever else a speech can bring about. It is not the word, but the meaning and especially the emotion that determine the effectiveness of the speech. We should *not* imagine this with the living wordartist who will become the Maitreya Buddha. He will only use the reality living in the spoken word itself. We have completely lost that in our time, we have nothing left of it. We speak automatically and we speak what we think, or we think according to what we speak. But the word itself has lost its meaning. I have often referred to Plato's significant dialogue which bears the name of the person who is speaking there in particular – that is Kratylos (Cratylus), who expresses that he knows the original meaning of the word. When you go into nature and you see a natural object, it reveals itself in its sensory perceptibility. However, the object also has a name. Kratylos (Cratylus) still had the sacred awareness of the fact that the name is an essential form of the object transformed into the word. When you look at a plant and you are familiar with the primal idea of the metamorphosis of the plant, as Goethe presented it, then you know that all the different phases in which the plant grows and blossoms are expressions of the same primal idea but brought into a metamorphosis each time. Thus, even the scent that the plant may release can be seen as a spiritualised, etherealised expression of the plant's primal idea. Kratylos (Cratylus) knew that the word is an *even more spiritualised metamorphosis* of the plant's primal idea. When you pronounce the name, you are actually in direct contact with this primal idea. Only the awareness of it has become increasingly vague. It had already disappeared in Socrates' time – as this dialogue shows – and it is no longer even conceivable in our time.

But when we look to the future, we may assume that this highest metamorphosis of the primal idea – the concept may be even higher, but in a certain respect it is not – will again become perceptible in eurythmic movement of the element we know as air.

Air is already almost imperceptible to us. We still perceive something of it in the sense of our breathing. A singer has more awareness of it; when a wind blows and the air is moved vigorously, we also become more conscious of it; but we lose ourselves to a greater extent in the phenomenon of the wind than in perceiving the air. But a time will come when those very gentle air movements that we know through speech – even if we do not consciously know them – will regain their effect as speech perception, as awareness of the living divine word that has formed and continues to form everything.

I cannot but repeat over and over again – in the hope that by rephrasing I am enabling access to this unspoken but perceptible higher living word.

So, we imagine that we will still have a larynx, but it will be less physical than it is now. It is a flexible sculptured organ that is able to bring the element of air in motion. The movements that are then introduced into the air become audible not only to the fellow human being, but to all fellow spiritual beings in a higher sense. The word spoken in this way does not work through underlying thought, nor through emotions, movement of the mind, wish or will, but works as pure revelation of the primal idea. We should actually see eurythmy performances very regularly and then try to hear, without the word being spoken physically, what is being said there in the movement. This is a preparation for the pure living word, the pure Logos, spoken in the future, where the meaning is no longer the profane, but always the actual primal idea expressed through the objects, which has become the Name. Then, in the future, the common name will steadily disappear, and the movement of air will increasingly become the true essential communication.

The word we now speak lives for us in consciousness in a complicated process of thoughts, willpower in speech and the transformation of the thoughts into the word. The very complicated physical process of speaking itself takes place beyond our conscious perception. We live in thoughts and in the physical production of speech, we experience the activity of the speech organs in particular, as well as the breathing associated with it. But our awareness does not extend to the movement of air and the forms that are created there in a highly artistic way – and which are actually the point. Thinking back to the very beginning of the Earth's development, to the transition from liquid to solid, we can form a clearer picture of how the Logos, the creative word of the world, worked in the air formation, how it transferred the air forms to water and how the formation of the water finally condensed into physical earthly forms. We have completely emancipated ourselves from this with our human word, we now possess the power of words ourselves and our task now is to see how that which forms the word in the air can be perceived and finally brought under control, so that it becomes a creative tool again.

I always like to use the word "rose" because it is similar in all languages. If we now pronounce the word "rose" with our humanised speech, we really have to make an effort to perceive an effective form and the ensouled force in this word. Since we are not able to reach directly into the elements with our consciousness, we can work the other way round, in such a way that we *barely* utter the word rose, whereby we can become aware of the transcendental powers of the word. This seems to me to be the first task in this new area of the future human being, to speak a word, a proverb, perhaps the first words of the Prologue of St John's Gospel –preferably in Latin – as intensively as possible within ourselves, without moving the larynx and the speech organs, but not too far away from them either, so that speech is indeed given, but not to the movement of the physical body. Then we can hope to catch a glimpse of that future *Word which will be spoken with spirit power as revelation,* and which will be active in the element of air."

Johannes said:

"May I still go back to the liquid diamond? I know that you will return to this in a later phase, because now in our time it is more a question of a liquid diamond, which is still far from being colourful.

But still, given the fact that we have to immerse ourselves in the good creative word and that we also have to develop an awareness of the activities in the etheric world of that word, I would like to see the etheric aspect of the liquid diamond explained a little further, whereby the transition to the colourful aspect of it is the transition to the perception in the astral light."

Philippe looked at Johannes and said somewhat wearily:

"Would you like to do that Johannes?"

Johannes nodded, remained silent for some time in contemplation and then began to speak:

"If we want to imagine mankind in the future, we have to develop a differentiated perception of the different layers in which we as humans are more or less at home on earth and also in the super sensible world. On earth it is about the four elements: earth, water, air and fire. We know the pure earth element now mainly as hard and tangible, perceptible to the physical senses. This will change in the future and the earth element will be active mainly as a densifying activity.

We experience thinking as flowing, like water, which is the etheric element in itself. But in the form, we know it on earth, it is the water, the liquid I should say.

The word is spoken in air. And the deed, the love, takes place in warmth. Insofar as the element of warmth penetrates thinking to a greater degree, the element of thinking also gradually becomes an element of warmth. But as we now know thinking, "I"-less as it is, it is certainly not warm and it renounces, as it were, its origin in love.

But there is a *quinta essentia*, a fifth essence, and that fifth essence is *threefold*. This is the pure ether, which consists of a light ether, a sound or chemical ether, and the life ether.

It is known that thinking also has a light aspect, that light shines every moment when an insight is born. Then the light falls as it were on the dark world of concepts and by practicing this you can become increasingly aware that thinking of insights has a light aspect and, in this sense, it is also at home in the light ether.

Pure thinking also lives in this area of light ether, but this light ether is interwoven with astral light. The astral light is in fact a higher field and its substance, the substance of which it consists, is sympathy and antipathy, lust and sorrow. So, it is not woven truth, but rather *woven feeling*.

It is of course immediately clear that perception in astral light is determined by the degree of purity of the perceptive soul. If it is still driven by its own lust and suffering, it cannot see the reality in the astral light, and everything is coloured by its own subjectivity.

But when we speak of a liquid diamond with many colourful facets, we are speaking of beholding in the astral light. In this astral world we also find the penetration of sound ether or chemical ether and life ether. Over and above this, there are a number of strata of the astral world, which originate in a purer area.

When we find access to the astral light through the development of pure thinking, we enter the astral world, as it were, from above. That is, from the area in the cosmos where we locate the sun.

Through *pure thinking* we had heightened our development in thought to such a degree – even though it was dark and colourless – that it reaches *up to Saturn*, where it receives the element of warmth. Then it descends and enters the astral world from above, finds the perception in the astral light from above, and with sufficient practice there arises that perception which Philippe described as the Holy Grail receiving the Substance, the divine viaticum. Then the Grail is inverted, that is, the vessel comes from above and the light streams into it as it were from below as astral light.

The entirety of this could be called the liquid diamond with many facets.

The Word comes from a far higher region, which is cosmically still above the sun, in the sphere we know as Mars, but also this word has a reflection from above in the astral world. And just as thinking in the astral world is connected with light ether that is passing through it, the word has a connection with sound ether that is at home in the astral world.

It is not easy to get used to these interconnected relationships when you are not able to elevate yourself to these differentiated levels, even if it is only by way of thinking.

We will discuss this in more detail when we have come to the point in our reflections where we can describe the functioning or the life of a body-free human being on earth. How does such a human being live? We can only understand this when we put these preparatory exercises concerning the seven-foldness of the astral world into practice and then we can say that the lower three layers; *light-ether, sound-ether, and life-ether – are irradiated by astral light*, then we enter the area of the astral world, which is in the region of the moon, then Mercury, then Venus and above that we find this very pure substance, which contains no personal sympathy or antipathy, but which is exquisitely sensitive, that is the Akasha Chronicle. That is the region of the Sun. It is there that everything takes on its spiritual form, so that everything passes, as it were, from the formless to the formed. We may place our formed thinking body in that region."

Johannes was silent, aware of the inadequacy of his words.

Raymond asked:

"It is in itself a kind of assault on the conceptual intellect that we are undergoing here. For I must now imagine that my thinking, which I know only as mirrored by the brain, is actually weaving and flowing in the etheric world. At the same time, I have to think that it is conscious from the highest cosmic sphere and that it has its substance in the Akasha Chronicle. That is quite a task Johannes, that you are challenging us with!"

Johannes nodded and said:

"I know... And our present thinking and speaking is so inadequate. But the advantage is that it only becomes a reality for the listener when he himself becomes inwardly active. When you think all this through this evening in your meditative contemplation, you will find that the one does not exclude the other, and that in this world the conclusions are far broader than in our intellectual world of concepts. It is precisely because of the effort you have to make to think through and feel the different meanings of, for example, thinking, that what we call the thinking body, which has as its purest substance the Substance of the Akasha Chronicle, ultimately comes into being. But that is also, as it were, the great history book of humanity. It has two sides: On the one side it is formed, it receives the formed idea, and on the other side it is unformed and transforms that which is unformed into formed idea, making it conceivable for beings living on earth."

"Then I have another question,' said Raymond. 'If I am to imagine these things as exactly as possible tonight, I still need to know what the astral light is precisely?'

"There is an exercise for that,' said Johannes. "And that is, that you imagine yourself in utter darkness, where there is no light at all, inky darkness. A light can rise in it, and that light is you. You yourself can become light, and that light which you can become is the astral light."

Beato asked:

"To what extent are these elements which you describe, and which of course we all know thoroughly, comparable to the five elements as described by the prophet Mani?[7] Through those five elements, can you see clearly the densification, the materialisation on the one hand, and the spiritualisation and sanctification on the other?"

Philippe gave the answer and said:

"We will certainly come to that! I believe that we cannot understand the future earthly form of man if we do not include this Manichean wisdom."

Beato thanked him and a deep silence fell.

---

7 Roland van Vliet, Der Manichäismus: Geschichte und Zukunft einer frühchristlichen Kirche, Urachhaus

Philippe spoke:

"Yesterday I spoke about the living word that is active right down to the elements, but that will continue to grow in strength. I would like to emphasise once more that, as far as spiritual development is concerned, the development of the thinking body is necessary in order to arrive at this living word. But when we consider this emergence of the creative human word as a general human achievement, which will be the case in the future for a large part of humanity, then we must also look at the activity of the word in the etheric. We have found that the thinking body is developed through a consciousness of the etheric, but that it will acquire a bodily aspect through its connection with the resurrection body. Johannes has added that the substance is the pure spirit substance of the Akasha.

That we are able to develop this living thinking in our time – without going to a school or an initiation institute – we owe to the resurrection of Christ into the etheric world and to the Master of the Occident who described this school of thought.

The engagement of the "I" in thinking has to do with *warmth*. The "I" lives in the warmth and in so far as this "I" penetrates the thinking, the thinking also has to do with warmth, although it is a cool element by nature in our time.

Now we have occupied ourselves looking forward to the next stage of development, which will be the living, creative, *human word*. Just as thinking is related to light and therefore to the *light ether*, so this word is related to sound, is based entirely on sound and therefore there is the connection with the *sound ether*.

So, the *word* lives in the sound ether. All our speech sounds live in the sound ether and just as the sound has a formative work even in the substance, so the creative sound ether word has an even higher formative work than the work of the thinking body. It comes to us from the worlds above the astral world, but we only find it there after death, when we have already ascended high and have cast off all earthly ties.

But the human being on earth will receive more and more of it, until it will be so far that reproduction on earth will come about directly through the creative Word.

These are thoughts that are so high and holy that reverence for them cannot be great enough. We must not actually think these thoughts with our brains. Of course, we must always begin in such a way, but we must not remain in this thinking mind and simply ponder these thoughts. In meditation, we must reverently raise them up to their true level, even though our little soul may not be able to reach them. Then this small soul can still experience how little it is capable of thinking and feeling this greatness. Therefore, we cannot go on from here unless we exalt the given contents in meditation with all our strength.

In the beginning of our era there was the Mystery of Golgotha. Thanks to that event, the decaying physical body of the human being was brought into a resurrection, through which it carries within it the possibility of being a physical body, *without*, let us say, flesh and bones.

In the 19th century, a materialisation of the etheric body – that is, of thoughts – and the resurrection from it by Christ into the etheric world took place. Thanks to this event, we have the possibility of finding, in the etheric body, which is becoming more and more hardened and materialised, the point in thinking from which a resurrection is possible, through which we can develop the thinking body that, as a soul, takes in the world-thoughts. Not, therefore, the material thought as soul, but the world-thoughts as soul.

We must then imagine that in the next cultural period – the sixth – a *third resurrection* of Christ will take place, namely the resurrection of Christ *in the soul*. Only then will it really be possible for the word, which has become so dead and pragmatic and desirous, to rise to become the underlying creative, sounding, living World-Word.

Maitreya Buddha will be an example of this. He will show the people how the word can sound in such a way that it brings forth good from itself. It is not so much the content that will be used, but the living, formative good Word itself. This will be the great example for mankind, leading them to direct their attention to the resurrection of Christ in the soul world. Not in the elemental world, not in the etheric world, but in the world above. That is the astral world, that is the world of the soul, where sympathy and antipathy live, lust and suffering. When there will be people who will *speak* the good in imitation of the Maitreya Buddha, it will bring about a great unifying effect in humanity. But we must point out to ourselves time and again that it is no longer the content that will matter so much, but the Word will work in such a way that it will have a metamorphosing effect on the soul.

In our time we do speak of brotherhood. But we do not know it at all in reality. Then, in that time when the spoken word will ascend, the brotherhood among the people will really be *spoken out*. The earth-atmosphere will be filled with this *good spoken Word* in all the sounds that the Word is capable of.

But in the meantime, the other development will have continued. When we have a sense of reality, we are at present engaged in a hard struggle with artificial intelligence. The advocates of hard artificial intelligence imagine, as we have heard from Raymond, that this intelligence can be developed in such a way that it will fill the entire cosmos. You could feel a sense of desperation. We do not despair, because we are aware of the fact that a small number of people who develop the thinking body and the related unfolding of the etheric thinking will have enough effect to completely radiate that artificial intelligence away.

As the rising sun makes the night disappear, so will etheric thinking, which is fulfilled with the resurrection power of Christ, be the sun through which the darkness of technology will not be able to unfold its power. It will be there, and it will accomplish great things, but it will remain powerless, although it will develop to a greater extent.

While humanity is actually striving for spiritualisation, on the other hand, in the electromagnetic and nuclear energy field, in connection with artificial intelligence, a more far-reaching under-sensual development is taking place.

That which is physical in living nature will be supplanted by this hardened sub-nature. With our sensory eyes we see the decay of nature and the increasing emergence of technical structures with great sorrow. These technical structures actually give rise to a sensualisation in the direction of the subconscious.

Mankind can lapse into this, and it is sad that part of humanity actually does. It cannot be helped that this awakens in us a powerful impulse to do *everything possible*, far into the future, to bring these people to reason in the first place and then to speak to them with goodness in the next phase. After all, it is an Apocalypse in which we live. There is a division between spirit and matter – and spirit makes use of a different matter from that which is becoming increasingly under-sensual. So, we must not think that the spirit would not use matter, but it will be the primordial matter that the spirit will shape according to its idea and word.

Beneath this, in the sub-natural, it is technology that gives form and that leads to an ever-increasing hardening, until it comes to the point that this sub-natural nature can no longer produce bodies in which human beings could incarnate.

We do not yet have the external creative, sounding word of the world, which still belongs to the divine-spiritual world. But we can prepare ourselves for this, and we do this, as I said yesterday, by seeking the word within in meditation where it expresses itself purely spiritually, namely where it is about to set larynx and speech organs in motion, but where we consciously restrain ourselves from doing so.

The forces that unfold there are a forerunner of this creative, good, active, living Word of the World, which will later become available to us and which will be active right down to the elements. The wind will become a force that gives form, filled with goodness, which will touch our fellow man, stirring him, making him want to bring that which has touched him into manifestation. We can receive a preview of this and our speech and the use of words will *therefore* change as a result. It will contain more and more spirit and progressively less emotion."

"Do you have any additions, Johannes?" added Philippe with a smile.

"Yes, I would like to connect with what I said yesterday regarding the astral world. When in the future we will no longer have a physical body as we have now, the etheric-astral part will remain of the perception with the senses in interaction with the elements. We have not reached the point of discussing that yet, but I think it is right to discuss perception in the astral world, as it is now a reality for a number of us and of which we can say that it is an extension of the development of the thinking body, of living resurrected thinking, the liquid diamond with many colourful facets.

But it does not always remain this multifaceted phenomenon, and I would like to say something about this.

When you get to know yourself as the creator of the astral light, you experience very clearly that this light *emanates from you*. It is comparable to the development of thinking, only now it is not only an impulse of will, but this impulse also starts to become light, to become luminous. You should not want to be in *opposition* to it, but to immerse yourself in it, go along with it. That is obvious, because you are the one who uses that light, to go along with the activities that occur in that light. And then it comes to the point of *identifying* with it completely. That is what you have to learn: to become completely absorbed in everything that happens there.

In everyday life we know this kind of inner movement in *love*. When one, as a doctor, has a consultation or makes a visit to the ward, then it is only love that makes it possible to become immersed in the suffering of his fellow man. When there is no love, the distance between oneself and the other person remains like an abyss.

This is an example of what we have to learn from within in the astral light and then we will notice that a moment comes when we no longer have the impression that the light is emanating from us, but that there is, as it were, an *inversion* and the light comes to us. That is the moment when one really enters the astral world. There everything turns around, even time turns around, time becomes a reverse flow in the astral world. But that which comes from outside still comes from us, and in that which comes from us the higher beings of the astral world settle increasingly, as it were. The more we are able to unite with them, the more we get to know them, and they also want to reveal themselves because what we surrender to completely – so strongly that it is as if we *are* that revelation – we can also, as it were, learn to interpret in that evolving revelation. We know all these processes from the development of thought, but we now *let go completely of all our own contents* and we merge totally into that which is movement and formation and revelation and activity and being in the astral world, which is recognisable to us because we identify with it. The knowledge of the other then coincides with self-knowledge.

The light can still be invisible white light for a while, as it were, but the surrender to it makes it colourful. Of course, this colourfulness is not the way one sees colours in the outer world with the senses, but to a greater extent the way colours are when one perceives them without sensory perception. These colours in the astral light are infinitely stronger and richer than the colours in the sensory world. In the imagination we have only a shadow of them. The colours in the astral world are also reversed, they are the complementary colours. So, if we want to judge what we see, what we behold, what we sense through surrender, we will be mistaken if we take the concepts of the outer world, and that applies to everything. That makes reading in the astral light something that has to become a new habit. But that reading can also be postponed for a long time. At first, we have to become at home in that unusual *surrender* and in sensing certain features in surrender, which remind us of the sense impressions of the physical world."

On this day Philippe spoke and said:

"We have now gathered a number of components to finally develop a vision of the future for the human being who lives on earth but no longer needs a body. I already told Beato, when he asked about the elements as described by Mani, that we need these as the cornerstones to be able to arrive at this vision of the future.

Mani was an early Christian prophet, who worked mainly in the East and who established a Christian religious movement that reached from, let's say, ocean to ocean. From the ocean between Siberia and Japan to the ocean that borders France and Spain.

But outer Christianity did not accept this movement and we have only fragments of the Manichaean teachings. But added to the occult knowledge that exists, they give enough insight into that teaching to highlight certain parts of it that are of great importance for the vision of the future.

Mani described five sacred elements; the earth element was not included. He described *water, wind, light, air* and *fire* – and I would like to suggest that today, and later each of us individually, engage in an in-depth study of these five sacred elements. These five elements recur in different manifestations, namely as soul manifestation, as thought manifestation, as spiritual manifestation – the "I"-element – and also as bodily manifestation, with in each case the degeneration into evil.

In fact, Mani sees the emergence of the physical body, as we know it, as a victory by evil, through which the five sacred elements have become too condensed.

We must first immerse ourselves meditatively in the *condensation of water.*

We can reach a point imaginatively in which we can imagine how the muscle system came into being as a result of the condensation of water. It has the flexibility of water and gives form to the body, with the forming ability of liquid. But it is a highly developed material form, which makes the body as solid and tangible but also mortal as it is.

The second element is *pure wind.*

This has become a nervous system, and we can imagine that whatever lives in the moving air, that is the wind, with an astral function - also in the form of thoughts – that this has condensed into a system through which the human being, incarnated in a physical body, can experience those astral movements. That is the nervous system. The whole sensory world of thoughts and experiences has condensed into a nervous system. We can think of the imagination of the earthly paradise, in which Lucifer has hidden himself in the tree of life, making it the tree of knowledge. Then we see the condensation of the pure element of wind in that tree.

The third element is *light.* Light is connected to the sun and the sun gives that rhythmic expansion and contraction that we know as summer and winter, with autumn and spring in between. That is a great rhythmic circulation, which has condensed into the circulation of blood in the human body. The blood itself carries what a human being takes with him to earth in the form of sunshine, that is his 'I'. The blood rises and sets again, rises and sets again, both in its circulation and in the creation and decay of the blood substance itself. We have to deepen meditatively into the condensation of light as a pure element into blood, circulating in the vessels of the human body.

The fourth element is the element of *gentle air.* It is, as it were, the element that, when there is movement, is wind, but the wind is not air. Wind is the movement, the force of movement. The air itself is moved by it. It is an element which in itself knows stasis and which, when it becomes dense and compacted, becomes the most densified thing that the human body carries within it, namely the skeleton.

It may not seem so obvious at first – air and skeleton – but when you consider it in depth, you find that connection with great certainty. In the esoteric hours we have been given a substantial indication in the sixth hour.

Du sinnest in dem Lüftewehen	You think in the weaving of the air
Nur in Gedächtnis-Bilderformen;	Only in memory-image forms;
Ergreife wollend Lüftewesen,	Seize the air beings willingly,

Es wird die eigne Seele dich	And your own soul will threaten you
Als kalterstarrter Stein bedrohn;	As a cold and rigid stone;
Doch deiner Selbstheit Kälte-Tod,	But the cold death of thy self,
Er muß dem Geistesfeuer weichen.	It must give way to the fire of the spirit.

Finally, we have the *element of fire*. Later, when we start to form imaginations of man on earth without a body, we will ask ourselves: How then, without a body, without a skin, does man manage to not merge completely into the environment?

Here, in the teachings of the sacred elements of Mani, we find a clue, when we learn that fire, when it becomes condensed into a body, becomes skin. At this point you would like to make a sketch, as it were, of a person without a body. You would like to make his circumference fiery! We have to meditate on this in order to experience how the element of fire – which is not fire, of course, but a transcendental fire – how, when it is too condensed, it becomes *skin*.

It is possible that what I am about to say may seem like too much theory. But we need this theory as building blocks for the future human being, and it is of course possible for everyone to let what seems to be theory turn into a living reality through meditation on their own life's path.

After we have experienced the condensation of the five sacred elements, we can experience their spiritualisation. Tomorrow, I will then describe the evil degeneration of the four branches of these five elements.

When we seek to rise to the soul level from the basis of the five sacred elements, we become familiar with the metamorphosis of the elements into the soul. Of course, in the end we have to understand the whole process in reverse, as coming from the spirit and increasingly condensing into the elements, but once we have come to know these elements through and through as what is closest to us physically, then we have to bring them *into* an *ensoulment* and a *spiritualisation*.

The water is a specific soul characteristic that you could read, as it were, when you look at the constantly flowing water with a higher consciousness. Then a certain mood comes into the soul, which is best expressed with the word *patience.*

The ever-flowing water is the *patience...*

When you place the element of *pure wind* before higher consciousness, that is, when you concentrate on the phenomenon of pure wind and try to unite it with your whole humanity without any further thought, your soul changes into a certain soul-quality which will be the same quality in all people who can accomplish this objectively. When you want to give that quality a name, when that quality reveals itself in a name, then this is *faith.*

Then we pass on to *the light* and in the same way we want to absorb this light with our higher consciousness in such a way that our soul enters into a very particular state. You can imagine that there are different words to express this state. Can the soul as a *soul* reach a higher sphere than the light? If it is completely light, then the best word to express this light-ness of the soul is *perfection.*

Then comes the element of the *gentle air.* We know this gentle air best when we think of a soft summer evening. The sun sets, the light fades and the air is gentle, not only in temperature but also in quality. We present this gentle air to our higher consciousness and we rest in it for a while and feel how our whole soul becomes a gentle air. There is only *one* word to express this and that is *love.*

Finally, we have the fire. *The fire* is not a burning object, but it is the fire of enthusiasm, where the soul opens itself to the spirit, to the Holy Spirit. The whole soul becomes flaming enthusiasm. We present this to our higher consciousness and for some time we fill our whole soul with this fire of enthusiasm. The Holy Spirit descends, and the soul finds its destiny and becomes *wisdom.*

Then we bring these ensouled elements further into a *spiritualised form.*

We go back to *the water* again and present the flowing ever-moving spirit to our higher consciousness and rest there for some time. The water has become spirit, and we feel that the movement of spirit in this liquid – as if it were liquid – is entirely congruent with what we call *contemplation*, a systematic, deliberate ongoing movement of thoughts.

Then we go to the *pure wind*... We feel the wind as breath, as Pneuma, as spirit, which becomes *thought*. One would like to ask the Muses, the arts, to paint, sing, dance, speak and poeticise these wondrous metamorphoses of soul and spirit... But we must do so in our individual meditative composure.

Then we go to *the light,* and we imagine what the light in the spirit is, what it means when the spirit is enlightened. When we offer this image to our full consciousness in meditation, we ourselves experience the similarity with what is working in us as the *intellect*. It is not the intellect, but the much higher being of the Prudentia, that is the intelligence.

Then we move on to the *gentle air*. What is the spirit when it manifests itself, allows itself to be experienced as gentle air? In it, peace and quiet reign, nothing moves, nothing compels, it is the nurturing life itself that is spiritualised. The Greek word for it is *Nous*. In German we say Vernunft, in English Reason, the latter word no longer quite corresponds to what Nous actually means, but it is related to it.

Finally, the spirit itself catches fire with enthusiasm and something becomes possible that in fact is only possible with *fire*. We introduce the flaming spirit to our higher consciousness and experience that all spiritual metamorphosis ultimately culminates in the absolute realisation of meaning, and that is the *resolution to take action*.

As the highest level, we find the metamorphosis in the five elements *of the I*, or of the spiritual individuality.

When the I has found complete harmony with the I as ever-flowing water, with the fluidity that is not hindered by senseless resistances, then the I metamorphoses into

Then the I takes the form of the pure wind, which is the will in the Pneuma, but then the I changes into *strength.*

If the I becomes light in such a way that it is no longer hindered by darkness, it reveals its own *light nature.*

The metamorphosis of the I into gentle air, or the metamorphosis of gentle air through soul and spirit to the I, fills it entirely with *life.*

And when the I catches fire, becomes inflamed, then it starts to smell and spreads a *holy fragrance.*

Tomorrow, I will go into the metamorphosis towards evil, of the five holy and pure elements. We have already experienced the condensation into a body, we will then delve into the evil elements, the evil soul metamorphosis and the evil spirit metamorphosis.

I would like to ask you to immerse yourselves today in these elements and their metamorphoses, their different spheres, as vividly as you can, for we really want to come to a vision of the future for mankind as he is capable of becoming when he no longer has a body and no longer has a gender, when he reaches the state he was in before the Fall in Lemuria, but through this long period of trials has developed a higher consciousness.

Evil is still far from being conquered, but certain aspects of it are thoroughly understood and have therefore become powerless. We want to develop this into a vision of the future, but in order to do this I need your active cooperation."

He looked at Johannes and said:

"Johannes?"

Johannes nodded and said:

"I feel some reluctance to add anything here, because the way you have enabled us to experience Mani's teaching in a sketch is vast and impressive. I don't want to interrupt unless I can do so in a way that is complementary to it..."

Philippe nodded and waited.

Johannes said:

"I spoke about the astral light yesterday and today I want to add that there is a division in this astral body, in this astral light.

We have felt that what Philippe has just said with regard to the elements, soul, spirit and the self, is thoroughly Christian. Mani was an early Christian prophet and had to position himself as an incarnation of the Holy Spirit himself, that is, that the astral light as a being was incarnated and expressed through him.

When we have a rich meditative experience, then at a certain point we have that gracious experience, that in the powerful body of thought comes an activity in which you know: This is the Lord Himself. The Lord who has entered into me. It is the greatest, most powerful, purest protection against all possible influences that could make initiation something dangerous.

Today I would like to add that in the astral light one can also see and experience evil, and that it does not always do this in its own form, but here too portrays itself in an inverted nature than it really is. It can present itself to us as holy and good, while it is not.

But since the Mystery of Golgotha, Christ lives in the earth-atmosphere, lives in the astral world of the earth-atmosphere as the Astral Light itself. There are two worlds of astral light: *the old one*, which you might call the pagan astral light, and *the new one*, which, when you absorb it, can rightly say: Not I, but Christ in me!

It is in this sense that Paul's statement is to be understood; it is no longer the old astral light that speaks through him, but the new, Christ Himself, who surrounds our souls in the soul world. The good holy elements of Mani are *His* elements. When we are fulfilled with them, we will never fear danger during initiation. We can permeate our entire being with His Light, His Life, His Power, His Beauty and His Sacred Fragrance!"

Raymond sat upright and asked:

"I hope you don't mind me asking questions almost every day, but you will understand that it is all new to us and that we would like to participate very intensively. I listened with great interest to the description of the five elements and their different parts. It was a lot because it is also a summary, of course, but you, Philippe, do it in such a way that it touches one's heart. But I do wonder ... we have *one* day for that.

How should we do that, how should we try to summarise 4 times five elements in such a way that it is not simply a memorisation, but that you can actually experience it yourself, that there are correspondences between for example the flowing water and patience, that we are not just grabbing at straws, but that you can also experience it through and through?"

Philippe nodded and said:

"That may be too much to ask, when you have only had a short experience of the power of meditation in depth, to experience more than a more or less logical assignment of one thing to another in this multiplicity. You should actually try to imagine the element, which is being talked about, as vividly as possible, as if you were *in it*, not in a specific sensory memory, but in a general familiarity with the element. We all know flowing water, we all know pure wind, light, gentle air and fire.

You first have to experience this intensely, and then when you have taken the experience of experiencing the element of water to the extreme, for example, you can possibly experience its resemblance to patience and consideration. You should do it this way for all five elements, and then the art of the matter is always to be satisfied with the results you have at that moment, which are simply appropriate to the state of development you are in. You cannot want more than is possible - but you should not be satisfied with less than is possible! This is an art we have to master, and it doesn't matter if you are new here or have been here for 20 years. Because even if you've been here for 20 years, you have your limitations and your accomplishments."

"Ah yes," said Raymond, "you can always feel the inner laziness surfacing anyway, so that you don't feel like putting in so much effort..." He was silent.

The Master spoke up and said:

"As an Oriental, I feel particularly at home in experiencing these elements, and as an Oriental initiate, wanting to bring that initiation here to the West, I always gave a great deal of attention to experiencing the elements and experiencing the sense impressions in general. When, as a Westerner, you have grown up at a desk with a monitor in front of your face, that rich world of the senses is no longer the first thing you experience. You have to reclaim that, as it were, with force. And I have understood in the course of the years here that this cannot be done directly with sensory perception, but that it has to be done where you show your strength, specifically in thinking itself.

As we are working here now, we have reached a point where sensory perception is going to undergo a metamorphosis and become important in a new way. I wanted to ask you again, Johannes: We have noticed a difference in our developmental paths in the past. It has become very clear that you had to look for that particular point in thinking, and through that you have reached an increased intensity of sensory perception. Can you tell us again exactly how this transformation takes place?"

"Yes," said Johannes, "what you mean is that in the development of mankind there is a middle point in a certain sense – you could also call it a low point – where man's thinking has become so abstract that it can function entirely outside all sensory perception and that it carries within itself logic, rationality. A person who has developed this because it is a cultural factor, dreams just as well in half-sleep as during the day, when associative thinking sinks, as it were, into the senses and is immersed there in a semi-consciousness. This dream state occurs in images, and there was a time in the development of mankind when this was the generally prevailing state of consciousness, an image-consciousness, but without self-consciousness. Here in Europe, in the West, we no longer have image-consciousness, but object-consciousness, and that object-consciousness is entirely self-conscious.

What we are going to describe as the future development of mankind is the development towards a new image-consciousness, an imaginative consciousness, but in a self-consciousness, an elevated consciousness. We are on the way there. We have not yet reached that point in the general human development by a long shot, but there are individuals who have already reached it.

What Philippe presented to us today, when he described the elements and the layers in the soul, in the mental realm of thought and in the I, is an extraordinarily intensive and effective exercise for acquiring this self-aware image consciousness. Of course, it still remains a beginning, we can hardly imagine what this future consciousness will be like in its perfect development. Have I hereby answered your question?"

The Master smiled and said:

"Perfect, Johannes, as always..."

Philippe began to speak and said:

"It is a shortcoming in this development of a future vision of the human being that we cannot share our inner experiences from day to day. We have to do it on our own initiative and move on to the next step on the following day. There is no other way possible, because we would have to spend too much time in this exchange. So, I will continue with my explanation, without asking about your experiences.

It will certainly *not* be the case that when in the sixth, seventh and eighth millennium death will have been conquered - as well as birth - that evil will also have been conquered. The human being will still live on earth, but no longer in a body as solid and mortal as it is now. It will be the elements in which he will live, just as it is the case now with the angels, the archangels and the primal forces – they too live on earth.

It will be quite a task to describe what this elemental body of man will be like then. You cannot even say: What it will look like.... But evil will still be present in all its might and power, trying to achieve what it wants to achieve.

The prophet Mani impressively described the degeneration of the elements, and once again I am faced with the problem that when I want to discuss this, I only have simple words available, which you will have to ignite later with the fire of your enthusiasm, so to speak, so that they become the realities actually meant by these words.

Let us imagine the pure flowing water once more. That pure flowing water takes on an intensified material aspect, it wants, as it were, to penetrate the whole atmosphere, not remaining in a flowing form alone, but also becoming vapour and mist. Everything that was clear becomes misty, foggy and shrouded in a *dirty mist*. And where it touches the tangible area, it is *mud*.

Then we will once again consider the element of the pure blowing wind and try to imagine what that wind is like in its pure graciousness. Through the influence of evil this wind is seized and whipped up into a blazing *storm*.

Then we immerse ourselves in the light that illuminates everything, in which there is not a single point of darkness, and in contrast we imagine evil, which is *pitch-black darkness.* You have to dare to use the powers of imagination to the utmost!

Next, we deepen the element of gentle air and imagine how that gentle air is seized by evil and becomes *stinking*, impenetrable suffocating *smoke.*

Finally, the phenomenon of fire remains, and I have always said: that is not blaze! *Conflagration* is the variation of the fire given by an evil influence.

Thus, we have five evil elements:

Mist and mud, blazing storm, darkness, smoke and conflagration.

These are the fallen elements and in these fallen elements, evil can become active.

When we think about the soul, each one of us can think of the opposites of the soul:

Patience turns into wrath; faith into disbelief; perfection into desire; love into hate; and wisdom into stupidity.

Evil, here, of course, is pre-eminently the Ahrimanic *condensing* dark force, which is also closely associated with death. The Luciferic side is to be sought far more in the area where the good elements strive for *too much liberation*, so that control by the self in the spirit is in danger of being lost. This is a side of evil that is not so clearly defined in Manichaeism.

But we have now built up a wealth of building blocks, having thought through the past, the present and part of the future of human development, and we can now confidently begin to envisage the human being as he will be when the mortal body is no longer needed.

*

Today we are going to embark on the beholding of the human being as he will be in the future. The starting point for us has been the current vision of transhumanism and posthumanism, a new type of being that will succeed the human being from evolution, so that he is the creator of the being that will come after him. In this, we become aware of precisely that which will be reality in a specialised form, not excluding the technical mechanical, electromagnetic variant that will also be a reality.

We have been preparing for a fortnight by imagining the history of human development from the past to the present and then becoming aware of a number of building blocks that we need to be able to access the beholding of the future human being.

I will speak in the form of perceptions and concepts, for only in this way can what is being contemplated be mutually conveyed. You yourselves must then enliven these perceptions and put the concepts into practice, so that you yourselves can come to a vision of the future.

So, I will always use the wording 'we imagine', but that does not mean that I am talking about speculations.

We only have limited information from the work of the Master of the Occident that can help us to arrive at this vision.

At three places[8] there is spoken of the future time, which will mirror the moment in Lemuria when procreation became gendered. This sexual reproduction will come to an end. A time will come when the human body of the woman will no longer have sufficient vitality to be fertile from puberty onwards, so that fertility will be completely lost and that the human being will reach a state where he will no longer have that solid mortal body that we are familiar with and that is so dear to us.

We must thus begin to imagine that from the sixth, seventh millennium onwards, when we want to be active on earth and thus incarnate, we will start to develop that activity on earth without the physical body known to us. For this I needed the elements of Mani, in order to be able to reach a thorough conception of life on earth without the physical body known to us with muscles, nerves, blood circulation, organs, bones and skin. We will then have ascended to a *transcendental* physical body.

8 "Again, in the seventh millennium, a time will come when their bodily nature will be capable of development only until the fourteenth year of life. Then, women will cease to be fertile; an entirely different form of living on earth will come about." (GA 204, S.240/241, English translation on rsarchive.org).

GA 196, S.59/60, GA 196, l S. 90 ff., GA 175, p. 245

This is difficult to imagine, because we are used to regarding everything that is physical as a material earthly body and we now have to grow accustomed to imagining a physical body that no longer contains this dense hardened earth element.

We are familiar with the portrayal of the resurrection, the third day after death on Golgotha. In this picture the Lord's physical body, after it had been vacated by Him and laid in the grave – while He descended into hell in order to, let us say, put things right there – was already in such a loose state of material connectivity that an earthquake was sufficient to cause all material substance, all matter of substance including the skeleton, to disintegrate. But there still remained something invisible, which was the actual physical body, but without tangible, visible matter in it, which could rightly be called a Phantom. It was imperceptible to the senses, but still a physical body.

We shall have a similar body then, and that body will not be confined to one place in the same way as the solid material body enclosed by the skin is on earth at present. This is where our first difficulty arises in the perception. We feel enclosed in our I, thanks to the fact that we can mirror this I on earth by means of a self-contained physical body, which you can, as it were, bump into and thus become aware of.

We know, for example, that when one hand touches the other, self-awareness arises. That has to do with the direct perception of touch.

Now we have to imagine a physicality that no longer has this, that is no longer as bound to a place as our present physical body. It can be universal, but it can also contract. That which every soul and spirit experiences after death – namely, that it expands to encompass the whole cosmos – will become, let us say, a normal characteristic of the human being living on earth at that time. He will be able to be everywhere at once, both in the region of the elements and the earthly region and also in the astral and spiritual spheres above.

He will also be able to contract with that body in space in one specific place, and to contract in such a way that he becomes perceptible in a self-contained concentration.

Let us imagine that not all people pass into this spiritual earthly existence at the same time, then the people still living on earth with a biological body will still be able to perceive these other earthly citizens from time to time, namely when that individuality decides to compress itself in such a way that it becomes perceptible with the senses.

This phantom, this transcendental physical body, can still express itself physically, but not in flesh, bones, nerves, organs, blood circulation and skin, but in those five sacred elements that we know from the Manichean doctrine.

The human being will have a self-consciousness and will orientate himself to the transcendental physical body and will also be able to express himself by means of this physical body, whereby the mobility of this body, the physical movement, could extend to liquid, to water.

If you, as a still physical-sensory human being, stand at the sea, then it might occur that a human movement suddenly becomes visible in the water. Not the wave movement of ebb and flow, of rain and wind, but a meaningful deliberate movement, where the meaning is transferred by the movements in the air – that is the pure wind.

Thus, the physical-sensory person at the beach sees a sudden meaningful movement in the play of the waves created in the water by the wind, and the light will move simultaneously in a magnificently majestic way, entirely in harmony with the light shining from outside as sunlight.

The air plays the role of an encompassing strengthening envelopment and the light that shimmers in this elemental body is connected to a radiant fiery enclosure of this being that shows itself in a physical way, but in an ever-moving meaningful form.

It is very debatable whether this could still be seen with physical sensory eyes.... It is quite possible, that it is not the case either. But we have to build a bridge between what we are now and what we will become.

Of course, I am very aware – when I say this – that it is not easy for everyone to accept that the muscle-bone-nerve-blood-skin form will be lost and that this elemental body will take its place. But that is connected with the very weakness of our thoughts and our words, which makes it very difficult for me to bring about a more direct representation of what I do perceive spititually. As soon as I articulate it, it becomes a shadow and coincides with our present representations of liquid, wind, light, air and fire – whereas we should try to imagine these five in a grandiose manifestation and not only in black and white, but in a rich ethereal play of colours.

The human being, as a self-conscious being, will be able to handle this transcendental physical body completely. The distance which now exists between our inner existence and our external form and maneuverability, the activity, the capacity to act, will cease to exist and what is innermost will also be able to express itself immediately without hindrance in this soft sacred transcendental physical body.

We must be well aware that the formation of the thinking body, with which we are so actively working in our time, is the basis for the creation of this Elemental Body. We are now familiar with how the thinking body works in communication with the ether body and the astral body. But then, in future, the "I"-nature of the thinking body will make it possible to extend its activity into the elements. That would mean that, when the physical body expands to encompass the cosmos, it will also encompass the entire wisdom of the cosmos, and that the "I" will be able to make a choice from that cosmic wisdom and bring it into action far down to the elements, which will then find its expression in the physical elemental body."

Philippe was silent.

Beato said:

"It will take considerable effort on our part to find the meaning of being human on earth, when you are no longer working with flesh and bones. After all, it is my daily work and I feel the pure Christian element and the intense compassion for the suffering of the wounded. How can you imagine that this is also effective, when the physical body is no longer there? What kind of activity is still meaningful on earth then?"

Peter said:

"The question is also how that which we call art will occur on earth.... When there will be no more museums and concert halls...."

"And," Eva said, "what then is love, when one cloud covers another…?"

Philippe smiled and said:

"You see, this first portrayal already raises several questions. I can only continue my reflections and hope that they will touch on your questions one by one...

For today, the most important task is the first imagination of the body that manifests itself in the elements of the sea; that we make it an imagination, even if in the future the sea might not be there at all or might manifest itself in a completely different form..."

Johannes said:

"You have described, as it were, an encounter between a human standing on the beach, while using the possible physical sensory perceptions in the elements, meeting a new human.

It is also possible to form a picture of two bodies of elements meeting, or deliberately alienating themselves from each other. When you know perception in the astral world, as the initiate is aware of in our time, then you know that your spiritual encounters are brought about through strong imaginative power, making yourself completely one with beings and processes in the astral world. These are the encounters that you have and that you are only *able* to have when your imaginative power is strong enough. Otherwise, there is no medium in which the encounter with you can take place.

This will become a completely new communication with this future human being – you will certainly describe this – and you can imagine that this can be a meeting in the elements. Not only in the soul and spirit as we know it now on earth – and physically in sexual intercourse – but as it always is in the world after death, namely that by imagining very strongly you evoke that which you seek.

It is possible to imagine, for example, that two individualities, both of which have a phantom body that is active right through the elements, can unite completely with each other, that one metamorphoses into the other and assumes exactly the same form as the other, so that the one gets to know the other and the other the one, completely according to that body. But that you can also, as a kind of necessary state of rest, retire entirely within yourself. That you light the fire of your skin, as it were, as in a burning egg, you withdraw within in order to reflect on yourself and reinforce your self-consciousness..."

Phillipe took the floor again at exactly eleven o'clock:

"The difficulty I have is that I can only describe one aspect each time and that the bigger picture then hopefully becomes visible and tangible from these aspects. Because when I look back at what I said yesterday, I immediately see the shortcomings. For it would be quite incorrect to have gained the impression from this that the new physical body of the human being, which no longer needs to go through birth and death, would consist solely of elemental functioning. Of course, it is also not the case that in the sixth, seventh millennium the resurrection body, as it is described as the New Jerusalem, is already built in its full perfection.

However, we must assume this and then see how that, which is then available to us as a physical body, will be built further, refined and made independent in the course of the aeons until the end of the earth's development, but also 'communalized' into that great New Jerusalem which will then descend from heaven."

From The Revelation of John, 21 and 22

"Then one of the seven angels who had the seven bowls full of the seven last troubles came to me, saying, "Come with me, and I will show you the bride, the wife of the Lamb." And the angel carried me away by the Spirit to a very large and high mountain. He showed me the holy city, Jerusalem, coming down out of heaven from God. It was shining with the glory of God and was bright like a very expensive jewel, like a jasper, clear as crystal. The city had a great high wall with twelve gates with twelve angels at the gates, and on each gate was written the name of one of the twelve tribes of Israel. There were three gates on the east, three on the north, three on the south, and three on the west. The walls of the city were built on twelve foundation stones, and on the stones were written the names of the twelve apostles of the Lamb. The angel who talked with me had a measuring rod made of gold to measure the city, its gates, and its wall. The city was built in a square, and its length was equal to its width. The angel measured the city with the rod. The city was 1,500 miles long, 1,500 miles wide, and 1,500 miles high. The angel also measured the wall. It was 216 feet high, by human measurements, which the angel was using. The wall was made of jasper, and the city was made of pure gold, as pure as glass. The foundation stones of the city walls were decorated with every kind of jewel. The first foundation was jasper, the second was sapphire, the third was chalcedony, the fourth was emerald, the fifth was onyx, the sixth was carnelian, the seventh was chrysolite, the eighth was beryl, the ninth was topaz, the tenth was chrysoprase, the eleventh was jacinth, and the twelfth was amethyst. The twelve gates were twelve pearls, each gate having been made from a single pearl. And the street of the city was made of pure gold as clear as glass.

I did not see a temple in the city, because the Lord God Almighty and the Lamb are the city's temple. The city does not need the sun or the moon to shine on it, because the glory of God is its light, and the Lamb is the city's lamp. By its light the people of the world will walk, and the kings of the earth will bring their glory into it. The city's gates will never be shut on any day, because there is no night there. The glory and the honor of the nations will be brought into it. Nothing unclean and no one who does shameful things or tells lies will ever go into it. Only those whose names are written in the Lamb's book of life will enter the city.

Then the angel showed me the river of the water of life. It was shining like crystal and was flowing from the throne of God and of the Lamb down the middle of the street of the city. The tree of life was on each side of the river. It produces fruit twelve times a year, once each month. The leaves of the tree are for the healing of all the nations. Nothing that God judges guilty will be in that city. The throne of God and of the Lamb will be there, and God's servants will worship him. They will see his face, and his name will be written on their foreheads. There will never be night again. They will not need the light of a lamp or the light of the sun, because the Lord God will give them light. And they will rule as kings forever and ever."

"It is the bride of the Lamb; it is not the Lamb himself. In occult science, matter has always been regarded as the maternal, the female, and in this sense the physical body as it will be in the next ages as the New Jerusalem for mankind, where all the individual bodies together will form one great body, is a feminine quality, the bride of the Lamb. It is just as richly organised and multifaceted a being as the biological physical body; only the processes that really are connected with the purely material aspects are no longer to be found in it. Here we have to think of the glandular workings and the secretions, but also the digestive processes.

It will be a completely purified physical body that no longer contains any matter, but that is material, a substance other than matter. That will be available to the human being.

It is of the utmost importance that we become intensely and accurately aware of this. In Jewish conviction one has always seen the earth as the source of all raw materials for the physical body, but also for building the city and for building the temple.

A time will come when the earth will be exhausted in that respect and the human bodies will no longer be able to reproduce themselves.

That is the moment of the beginning of the descending of the New Jerusalem, which will not take place from the earth below, but which will descend from above from the spirit-soul area.

It will take on a physical structure, and that structure is described as an image in the Bible text I have just read, which again we must understand as a first impression and an imaginative expression of what the resurrection body will be.

But the lowest physical form in which this resurrection body can be visible is the elements, and when Christ Jesus appears to his apostles, after the resurrection, and then eats with them, and when Thomas can put his hand into the wounds, then we must regard this as such a condensing into the earth element, but coming from above, that Christ is present with the apostles as a physical appearance.

We now succeed somewhat in strengthening, condensing and enlivening the shadow existence of representation and understanding, so that it acquires a realistic character. In future, we must imagine that this same area, the thinking body, has the potential to expand into the elements and then to use it in such a way that the resurrection body could become a physical sensory body, should this be necessary for those who are not yet spiritualised.

The whole city, in which no temple is needed, the New Jerusalem, will be built of *moral* substance, not of atoms and molecules or of various states of aggregation thereof, but it will be built of moral substance.

The moral quality that can become so strong that it assumes a physical character is the *conscience.*

Through our conscience we help to build the New Jerusalem, the bride of the Lamb, the body of Christ that will take the place of the earth when it is completely destroyed. The bride will be its physical body, but the substance of that physical body will then be our conscience.

In that time when the transition to an immortal body takes place, those people have the most perfect physical body, who have developed a very intensive and comprehensively working conscience. For us, conscience is something like an instinctive intuition that occurs and makes you feel that you have not done something in the right way, that you could have done it better.

You can imagine that this rather dull feeling-intuition can differentiate, refine itself and show its true nature in a multifaceted organism, which will then be the physical body. Every human physical body will be a part of that great earth-encompassing physical body of Christ.

Today I am emphasising that we should not think too lightly of the magnificent organisation of this new immortal body. It has all the splendour of the present physical body, but it is even grander because it has shed all aspects of death.

You can try to imagine in meditation that you have a body, which is not subject to the weight of the earth, which cannot become ill, which cannot die, which knows no physical pain, no defects or discomfort, but which shows an individual form. Then you can try to remember how in meditation you know that thinking, which is guided by the I, is situated entirely in the warmth-ether.

Because this activity is of pure will in thinking, the thoughts form in the warmth and we are not alone there, we experience the help of certain elemental beings in the meditation who help the thinking in the warmth.

With this experience we can go one step lower, to the element of air and experience there how spiritual breath as it were moves with the wind and how the pure element of the wind is comparable not only with the nervous system, but also with inspiration, with expiration, with that physical part which in the present body is the lung. There, too, there are helpers, the elemental beings who help take care of the body.

What we are now familiar with as the lung, consists in the future body of a penetration of the air with willed thinking, through which it becomes a pure blowing wind, but of which it can then no longer be said that the human being does not know whence he comes and where he is going, for he himself will be the conductor.

Then, with the willed warm blowing thought being, graciously active in us and also breathing outwards, we move on to the lower element of water. In the fully self-conscious mastery of this process, we are capable of giving that which we are in the elements an *outer form* as well which, although always in motion, can also impart a more or less stable form in the movement.

The real earthly element will then no longer be the material, but the essence of the material, containing the possibility of manifesting every substance that was once present on earth in the primal form. This is how we must then regard the jeweled splendour of the bride of the Lamb. The whole description of the precious stones and the pearls and the gold and the golden glass lake are imaginative images for something that we now know only in the weak thinking mind, but which someone like the Count of Saint-Germain already had some control over, that is, the granting of *the primal idea* to *the primal substance*.

In future, matter will no longer become that hard substance which you can bump against, but, for example, that liquid diamond with infinite colourful facets.

You can imagine the amethyst, the jasper, the beryl and so on in the same way; similarly, you can imagine the pearls and gradually gain a sense of what this biblical description of the New Jerusalem is in fact pointing to.

If then we do not lose sight, not lose heart, not for one moment, that what we are building is not only being built as a foundation for earthly existence without a mortal body, but that they are also the components for the building of the earthly body itself, which will be new and will come down from heaven with *human conscience as its substance*, then our imagination is one filled with reality.

Then let us envisage that we carry a body that is *not mortal*, that is *not born*, and that we try to *build up from the self-conscious thinking body*, through the formation of images, of imaginations, to such a degree that you could imagine that you could exist in such a body on earth. Dying would then no longer occur, but instead, for a time, you could decide not to expand into the elements, but to occupy yourself exclusively 'beyond the moon'. That would not be such a chasm, which death is for us now, for you would remain in the same world where you would retain the same consciousness, where you would still have the possibility to be associated with whomever you wish and are able to. Just as you can decide now on earth to go abroad for a few months and then return, you can decide to give your undivided attention to the soul-spirit world."

It was quiet for a while. It was clear that Philippe would not speak any further and Raymond took the floor and said:

"Thanks to my many years of occupation with the vision of the future of the singularity, it is not at all difficult for me to imagine that I could exist without a biological body. Only, when I compare the contents of what I used to think of as taking place of that biological body, with the knowledge of it of you people here, the contrast is almost unbearable.

I do really not want to dwell on the fact of my deception and only feel gratitude that I have been put on a path whereby this deception can be healed.

It is remarkable in fact how much the vision of transhumanism and posthumanism, based on artificial intelligence, resembles what is said here. Only it's trivial, banal, incredibly stupid, short-sighted and a complete slavery."

Johannes smiled and said:

"You are the one saying it..."

"I have to admit it, my words are inadequate for it, but on the other hand, of course, the very worst thing is that there is no knowledge of the truth of future human development."

"As you can see," said Johannes, "this knowledge does exist, but it is being kept from public sight with the strongest possible force. As soon as there is a moment when it seems that there is some interest in it, a countermovement is started, and that very young enthusiasm is nipped in the bud."

"Surely that seems very unfair!" said Raymond.

"On the other hand," said Johannes, "you are here now and going through a remarkable preparation for your profession as a university professor. We shall have to observe such events and simply disregard the many, many disappointments and failures..."

*

Johannes said:

"I also arrived at the *New Jerusalem* in my investigation, and because we have gone through such an extensive preparation, it now came to me very clearly in its full and glorious fulfilment as *a contrast to Babylon*, which is an imagination of the sinful body that lives wholly for lust.

When you imagine these two cities as described in the Apocalypse, you gain a profound insight into the difference between the jewel as it is used in Babylon and the jewel in the New Jerusalem. The riches and splendour of the kings and rulers of the earth decay simultaneously with that of Babylon, and the New Jerusalem descends in their place, the bride of the Lamb in full regalia for the wedding with her future consort...

You then see the physical body, depicted as an imagination, and are moved by the beauty and purity, but at the same time by the indescribable multifaceted nature and benevolence of this new body, in which no liar, no murderer, no criminal can live.

For example, the twelve senses, with which the human being perceives the environment, are now imagined as the twelve arches, which do not have to be closed because there is no longer any danger.

The wall of the city is built of jasper, but we must keep in mind that in this New Jerusalem there is no more *stone*, and that everything is as fluid and mobile and alive and changing as the liquid diamond.

If we want to understand what this imagination of the wall of jasper means, we have to delve into the primal idea, into the primal image of the jasper and then find as it were the skin of our new future body, with twelve new gates that have twelve foundation stones, whereby you would have to search again for each foundation stone in the primal image, in the primal idea and then bring it to life in the imagination.

An angel comes to measure the city and these measurements are given. They form an extraordinarily uniform structure, a square as long as it is wide, the wall according to human measurements, which are also angelic measurements.

Then we think of the second step in the building of the New Jerusalem: first there was the liquid diamond, which we find in the precious stone. Then there was the measuring of the inside of the temple and something similar is found here, in taking the measure of the New Jerusalem, in which you can sense that the new body will be formed according to an order and regularity that can be living.

What the *ark of the covenant* was in the Old Testament, we find here in the *taking of the measurements*, which is an indication of the formative forces, through which the new body is formed as precisely as it can be, if it wants to be both human and divine.

This brings us closer to the reality of this future non-material physical body, which will have a perception that will extend over the whole cosmos, but which can also turn inwards, to the microcosm.

The earth will have been transformed into the body of Christ and will stand in the universe "as a divine city, which is illuminated by the Lamb who shines as a lamp the light of the Father..."

Here we have an indication of the higher entities of being who can use this body as an instrument. As Philippe says, it is hardly possible to put it into words, and even the intellect is too small to grasp this greatness. Nevertheless, we must make this attempt and try to develop a premonition of what awaits us in the future, lest such aberrations as the singularity and trans- and post-humanism take us down the wrong path and keep us there!

So, the New Jerusalem will be our body, as the body of Christ. Of course, this cannot be expected in its full perfection in the sixth or seventh millennium.

But a preliminary phase of it will certainly occur, and that preliminary phase is also given in the Apocalypse in the letter to the church of Philadelphia. I think it is appropriate that we also absorb this and try to get a feeling for that collective physical body that we, although individualised, will receive in the future.

Revelation 3:

"And to the angel of the church in Philadelphiawrite; These things saith he that is holy, he that is true, he that hath the key of David, he that openeth, and no man shutteth; and shutteth, and no man openeth;

I know thy works: behold, I have set before thee an open door, and no man can shut it: for thou hast a little strength, and hast kept my word,

and hast not denied my name.
Behold, I will make them of the synagogue of Satan, which say they are Jews, and are not, but do lie; behold, I will make them to come and worship before thy feet, and to know that I have loved thee.
Because thou hast kept the word of my patience, I also will keep thee from the hour of temptation, which shall come upon all the world, to try them that dwell upon the earth.
Behold, I come quickly: hold that fast which thou hast, that no man take thy crown.
Him that overcometh will I make a pillar in the temple of my God, and he shall go no more out: and I will write upon him the name of my God, and the name of the city of my God, which is new Jerusalem, which cometh down out of heaven from my God: and I will write upon him my new name.
He that hath an ear, let him hear what the Spirit saith unto the churches."

"It is up to us," Johannes continued, "to try step by step to form imaginations of this future body.
Another aspect is the following. We have gratefully studied the teachings of Mani to gain an idea of how an elemental body may be formed in the future. I also wanted to highlight the ancient Hebrew Kabbalistic representation of Adam Kadmon as the primal man, who was also seen as being the whole earth as man and man as earth. The human being as paradise, but not the future man after the development of consciousness, but the paradise man before the Fall.
But it is good to include these categories, which were given there as higher human values, in the future expectations.
We must then imagine: The human being, not as standing *in* the realm of the earth, but *being* the realm of the earth, as the 10th category. Then nine other sacred qualities: the cross the foundation, the left leg the firmness, the right leg the appearance, the chest the personality, the left arm the perception, the right arm the imagination and then in the area of the head on the left side the intelligence, on the right side the wisdom and above, where the highest chakra is, the crown. I wanted to indicate that as a possible support for the development of us as individuals in the future, in connection with the non-mortal body. We need a certain primal struc-

ture to give the future a foundation and this being of the primal man, who was still the whole earth, is the representation of the *first Adam*.

We are now grasping the primal idea of future man, who will be the *second Adam*. All the wisdom of the human being rises up in me when I turn my inner gaze to these processes. The abundance and richness of it all make it so difficult, as Philip also said at the beginning this morning, to accept that you can only present one aspect at a time.

I could imagine that this beginning that we are making here now with forming a real image and idea of the future human being, that in the future we will imbue this more and more meditatively, one aspect at a time."

After a silence Eva said:

"Johannes, you have now 'opened' two vast themes. One theme is the imagination of *the New Jerusalem* as the body of Christ, in which we may participate. This imagination, which is given as a foundation stone, you might say, in the Apocalypse, could be expanded upon in meditation and then we would gain a completely different vision of what the human body was in its original purity and how this will be again in the future.

The other is then *Adam Kadmon*, who appears not only as a *new body*, but who appears as the second Adam, who is not only body, not only 'Realm', but also lives, thinks, feels, wants in that Realm, in a way that is unknown to us in our time. That actually requires a meditative development.

It seems to me that the Realm is the New Jerusalem and that the other nine have a correspondence with the constituent entities of Adam Kadmon. We should then be intensely occupied with that. What has come to us now is truly beyond comprehension."

She looked alternately at Philippe and at Johannes. Philippe said that it would be best if Johannes gave the answer. Johannes smiled and said:

"You have summed it up very well indeed! My closing words were also that this could be a task for the future, one that would be a spiritual 'hand full' on a daily basis... We are, as it were, just introducing the themes now."

Eva smiled very sweetly at Johannes and said:

"Good, Johannes. I will be patient..."

The following morning Philippe gave the next lecture.

"We have immersed ourselves in the non-mortal physical body and have come to know its jewelled nature. Johannes referred yesterday to the twelve gems and the twelve arches. Just as these refer to the senses, they also refer to the twelve zodiacal signs, to the configuration of the fixed stars, which in the microcosm will be the structure of a jeweled bride.

But it is not only a jewel, it is also a *living* jewel, and this is referred to in the second part of this image of the New Jerusalem, when reference is made to the river and the trees."

"Then the angel showed me the river with the water of life, clear as crystal, which flowed from the throne of God and of the Lamb. It ran through the middle of the street of the city, and on its banks, on both sides, were the trees of life, which bear fruit twelve times, once every month; and its leaves bring healing to the nations."

As we live as human beings on earth now, since the gender period, with which we began our reflections at the very beginning, we know two ether types from living everyday experience. These are the warmth ether and the light ether. We are familiar with warmth, and we also know light.

We are not only familiar with warmth as fire, but we also know it as body warmth and as the warmth of soul in sympathy. We are familiar with light that shines outwardly as sunlight which we are not aware of with normal consciousness as being light itself, but only in its illumination of objects and the colour of things, but we also know the inner light in every insight and understanding, also in every positive moment, when the heaviness of earthly existence seems to be lightened.

But the experience of the two higher ethers has been taken away from us. Before us stands the Cherub with the flaming sword. We are not allowed to experience the higher ethers. If we were to reach them without any development path, by underhand means, they would prove to be destructive. Remember the meditation on the elemental spirits:

You spirits of the (chemical) forces
paralyse my forces.
I will overcome you.
You spirits of life
are killing my life.
I await you in death.[9]

But that does not mean that a longing for these two lost experiences has not remained in us. We, as we sit here, have experienced this longing very intensely, because we have sought to rediscover these two ethers in the rightful way. We no longer have *power* in our thinking, we regain it in the thinking body; we have death in our thinking, we regain it in the *life* of our thinking body.

When the Word *sounds*, it has to do with the sound ether, but when the Word has *meaning*, it has to do with the life ether. The Word spoken of in John's Gospel is sound and is life.

We were allowed to retain warmth and light in a certain sense, but the coming of the Word in the flesh that has lived amongst us has brought

---

9 Complete text of the verse of Rudolf Steiner:
What I speak out of my physical body is illusory -
I must speak out of my etheric body,
to penetrate into the true reality:
1. you spirits under the earth press on the soles of my feet.
I step out over you.
2. you spirits of humidity caress my skin.
I press you to all sides.
3. you spirits of the air fill my inner being.
I unite myself with you.
4. You spirits of warmth ensoul my inner being.
I live in you.
5. you spirits of light fill my inner being.
I think with you.
6. You spirits of (chemical) forces paralyse my forces.
I will overcome you.
7. you spirits of life are killing my life.
I await you in death.
Thus I am, saying this, in the etheric body.
And you can come: Colors, sounds, words of the etheric world.
For Ita Wegman, October 1923.

about the possibility for us to *consciously* re-experience the fulfilment with sound-ether and life-ether.

That is the permeation of the ether body with Christ. And we know that in these higher etheric effects we *also find the astral light*, with which we can perceive and think in a way that belongs to initiation.

These are the river and the trees, the tree of life, in the New Jerusalem.

Warmth and *light* still belong to the *tree of knowledge*, but *sound* and *life* are the *tree of life.*

Not all human beings will simply have these higher etheric worlds at their disposal as a means of knowing, when the time comes that the body will no longer be of flesh and blood.

In the same way that not all the human beings *now* have sufficient inner strength to rise to the midnight hour after death where union with the world of the Divine Trinity is found, so not all human beings will *then* be able to come to living knowledge in the astral light of Christ. The old astral light (ancient clairvoyance) can be found, but firstly the soul's fulfilment with Christ must be sought and found, before this interpretation is found in the Christianised astral light.

But I am describing the state of the human soul that has made full use of the consciousness-soul state from the fifth culture period to reach the inner decision: I want to live for Christ and a thoroughly Christianised earth, an earth where everything has made way for Him, in which I then consciously participate. The thoroughly Christianised consciousness soul will have made this decision with itself.

These individualities, when using the non-mortal body, will have developed a distinctive way of knowing. What is sensory perception by means of the physical senses in our time will then have been completely "transformed" into the imaginative capacity underlying the senses. The thinking body will have developed to such an extent that it will have found the strength to form all possible sense impressions independently in an imaginative manner, thus creating a kind of fluid, a supra-natural "hyle"[10], in which reality – which will then be ethereal-astral-mental – can reveal itself.

If now, thanks to the development of thought, we can find that the idea underlies perception and that what the senses perceive is another

10 Greek for 'matter', in ancient philosophy it was a far reaching concept.

revelation of the same idea, then this idea will have found its way back into the thinking body to the true imagination, which we also have now, but which is immediately covered by perception with the senses. As soon as we are able to live with our power of thought in the senses and suppress the conceptualisation, we will find this imagination again and see it in the astral light in the full splendour and glory of the imaginative power.

Do not think that we will live in a shadowy existence when we no longer have the senses. What our senses have to offer us in terms of colour, smell, taste, tone, etc., is a pale reflection of what colour, smell, tone, taste are in the astral light. But all passivity *in perception* falls away and we live in an exceptional *inner image-forming activity.*

If I imagine the colour red, I thereby attract everything in the astral light that has an affinity with it, and if I unite this with the imagining of other qualities, this differentiates into an increasingly specific perception in the astral light, in which the reversal with the physical-sensory perception is a phenomenon, but this reversal loses its meaning when the physical sensory world has fallen away...

The crystal living river in the New Jerusalem is an imagination of the astral light. The image of trees growing on the banks of the river is the imagination of sound and life ether.

The different arts that we know on earth as representatives of the elements and the etheric types and also the old variant of these, the seven free arts, are laborious attempts to satisfy something of the longing for these – without the grace of sound and life ether.

In the future time of the New Jerusalem, all of life will be *art,* not as an attempt to experience something divine in the earthly existence that has been abandoned by God, but as a constant mercy of the divine presence.

We are, as it were, participating in the Christianisation of the etheric body of the earth, by connecting through the freely chosen consciousness-soul activity the wisdom that can be imagined in the etheric with the "I".

That activity – being able to *think* the etheric wisdom *with will* – is the *future love* and precisely that love is the *substance of the etheric body of Christ* that will be the future etheric body of the earth.

We join in the weaving of the garment, as Persephone once did, but who was lured away from her task to become active in the underworld – that is, the flesh and bone nature of the earth.

Then, in the time that we are now describing, we shall be freed from it again and together with her we shall jubilantly weave the etheric garment of the earth as being the etheric body of Christ, which shall be the etheric body of the earth.

Christ descended into hell after his death on Golgotha, that is, he passed through the nine layers of the earth right into its centre, recognising each layer as an evil transformation of his true Good Being and laying in each layer the seed for his reign. But no more than a seed, for he awaits those people who will take the aforementioned decision in their consciousness soul.

Then we still have to ponder the question: Which parts of the earth's inner being do we transform, when we work in forming the substance of the physical body of Christ through our *conscience* and the etheric body of Christ through our *love*?

Blindly we may trust that these transformations correspond to transformations of the earth itself.

But we must not remain blind."

*

"Johannes?" asked Philippe.

Johannes nodded and said:

"I can say something more about life in the immortal body, the ether body and the astral light. As you, Philippe, have described beholding in the astral light, this is indeed the beholding in the astral light of Christ.

In this way we are *alive* and have the consciousness not only of warmth and light but also of sound and life. It will be a great mercy for the people who are now working on their inner development, to be allowed to live in this very different way on earth during and after the sixth culture period.

What I find striking is the similarity again with the vision of the followers of the singularity and transhumanism, who imagine that the biological body, the brain, will be enriched with an artificial intelligence in such a way that they will have a much longer physical life – although not immortality – and will also receive support for their intelligence. We know that they imagine that what is now being played in a computer game outside you, could be played inside you in future and then in such a way that it projects itself outside you, so that you would hardly be able to distinguish what is virtual from what is real. A virtual world is then created in which you yourself are the creator. However, this creative quality has been created with the impulse of technology of artificial intelligence. Another conceivable possibility is that the algorithm of a certain personality can be determined, then uploaded into a supercomputer, stored there and, if the biological body remains necessary for its activity on earth, a new body can be grown from the frozen material of that personality, which is then fertilised with the algorithm and reinforced by all the possibilities of the technique of artificial intelligence, through which you could also imagine a kind of immortality.

When Philippe described the beholding into the astral light, this similarity occurred to me very vividly again, and I would therefore like to emphasise the difference once more, because in our case consciousness – when you are not meditating – is still less intense than the reality of the physical world. When you consider that difference, you have to say that in ordinary consciousness the thinking world lives a shadow existence. That is why it is so difficult to foresee what it will be like when the intensity of thought-consciousness, which we are familiar with in meditation, will be greater than what we know now in our physical sense existence. Here we still have the question of reality, and we think that if we would not have physical sense consciousness, we would end up in a shadow realm. Nothing could be further from the truth. The actual reality also lies in our thinking now, but when we look into the astral light, it will bring us a reality that will be infinitely more impressive than what the sunlit world can mean to us now.

That is one point. The other is the distinction between the astral light and life in the ether world. The two coincide in a certain sense, that is to say, the concrete perceptions in the etheric world come about with the help of the astral light, but that quality of *feeling of love* which is characteristic of the *etheric*, that is elevated above the *desire and wish character* which is peculiar to the astral world. Everything that is driven, that excites, that compels, that produces a wish-character, does *not* belong in the etheric experience.

This is not always so clear in literature. Perhaps we can only distinguish it so clearly since the resurrection of Christ into the etheric world, whereby the risen Christ actually appears – since about 1933 – in the etheric world.

Of course, there have always been initiates and gifted individuals who were able to perceive the etheric and who have always perceived Christ in it.

One of these gifted individuals was Novalis. In the case of Goethe, one has the impression that he was working from the source of pure astral light. But Novalis writes his poetry and his prose with the *tincture of the etheric body* in which Christ is present.

You can find it in the content, but you will find it above all in the effect of word, sound and rhythm. It is an exceptionally high-minded, idealistic, moral, artistic work.

Whoever is familiar with the experience of the ether body, whoever experiences the love impulse that is the substance, the purity, the tenderness, one might almost say the religious love impulse, recognises that Novalis writes from this source.

That is unique. I do not believe that it has occurred in history previously or later. Rudolf Steiner does not write like that either. I am convinced that he could have done so, but he set himself a different objective. He could also have become a miracle healer, but he set himself another task.

Anyone familiar with the experience of the etheric body will recognise this in the work of Novalis. The fairy-tale character that weaves through the prose work is, on the other hand, the contemplation of the Christian astral light. When you experience Novalis' work, you experience a non-terrestrial perception of being human and at the same time you feel a great love for being on earth, but for the new earth...

There are not enough words to describe this, but I will bring one of his spiritual songs tomorrow and read it to you.

The ether body is a macrocosmic being that also bestows time on earth, and that has to do with everything that lives, grows, blossoms, what is *in its becoming*.

We know that in the macrocosm there is a system of miraculously exact movements of the planets. Everything that is wise and mobile lives in the grace of this great macrocosmic being, the ether.

The highest part of that ether coincides with the astral world and thus has a penetration with soul. When we have developed our thinking body sufficiently, then our thinking is uplifted from a mirrored abstract shadow existence to a powerfully moving, concrete living being.

This, as Philippe described, will work back into the elements in the future, where it directs the creation of the non-mortal body. As far as the cosmos is concerned, it fully absorbs the cosmic intelligent wisdom. To the extent that it becomes imaginative, we live with our future capacity for knowing in the astral light and permeate the etheric. Insofar as we can read meaningful coherence in this astral light, we perceive the etheric, where the divine coherence of things and processes and beings is alive.

These three, physical body, etheric body, astral body, finally constitute the new earth, as the body, the etheric body and the soul of Christ. The macrocosmic being becomes earth. When a human being is allowed to take the first step into a life where death no longer occurs, that human being will have to learn everything anew like a new-born child. This will happen in the full self-consciousness that will have been acquired in the period of mortality.

The beholding in the astral light is filled with colour; the beholding in the etheric has a very different colourful character. In it everything that still recalls the memories of the senses is forgotten and it is the eminent coherences that are conquered by us as revelations in transcendental colourfulness"

Johannes remained silent and felt the exhaustion of his own etheric body, from which he and Philippe had to draw again and again in order to bring this living wisdom into consciousness. But like an after-effect, they were always flooded with new living health.

Johannes looked at Raymond and expected him to say something, but Raymond was too affected by the experiences that the words of the two men had triggered in him. He was reminded of an unknown, distant past in which it seemed that he himself had had transcendental experiences. He had to pull himself together with all his strength in order not to be taken into another consciousness with a tremendous force that he knew he could not yet withstand.

He looked helplessly at Johannes, who understood...

he next day Johannes stood up first. He said:

"I will read the ninth song of his 'Spiritual Songs', in which Novalis appears to know the future human being:

I say to all men far and near,
That He is risen again;
That He is with us now and here,
And ever shall remain.

And what I say, let each this morn
Go tell it to his friend,
That soon in every place shall dawn
His kingdom without end.

Now first to souls who thus awake
Seems earth a fatherland,
A new and endless life they take
With rapture from his hand.

The tears of death and of the grave
Are whelmed beneath the sea,
And every heart now lighe and brave
May face the things to be.

The way of darkness that he trod
To heaven at last shall come,
And he who hearkens to his word
Shall reach his Fathers home.

Now let the mourner grieve no more,
Though his beloved sleep,
A happier meeting shall restore
Their light to eyes that weep.

Now every heart each noble deed
With new resolve may dare,

A glorious harvest shall the seed
In happier regions bear.

He lives, his presence has not ceased
Though foes and fears be rife;
And thus we hail in Easters feast
A world renewed to life!

(Translated by C. Winkworth, 1858)[11]

When he had sat down again, Philippe stood up and said:

"We have now discussed some of the principles of future man, but of course the big question remains: How will we continue to live on earth as human beings, when earthly resistance and separation by death no longer occur? For example, the question arises: How will people still interact then? No more sexual reproduction, no more physical love, no more touching skin ... What remains of love and of the other emotions that exist between people, and how do they manifest themselves?

I said yesterday that the big problem is that from the present object-consciousness we imagine the imaginative consciousness as an everyday consciousness. Only when you have experienced and know the heightened reality of the ether world, the astral world and the spirit world through initiation is it absolutely clear that the interaction between people will certainly become more intense. If you have not been initiated, it is rather difficult to imagine that you could have real, meaningful encounters with people without the sense of touch, without eyes, without ears.

But it is not the case that we will not have those senses. We will just not have them in their present physical form. What precedes imagination in the awareness of perception with the senses will continue to exist. We will live just as fully in the earth sphere and on the earth and we will still be able to sense the environment, nature, the beings in that nature. Only the character of that perception will be quite different, but not less real. Nature, of course, will no longer be in the same state

11 In translations of this kind of holy poems the sounds and rhythms are lost, the notion more or less stays and some of the poetic force is still there.

as it is now, but what will be on earth will be perceptible to us, and even more so, because the limitations of space and time will be removed to some extent. We are no longer bound by place, we know the essence of time as it consists of a present and a past and a future, not only as abstract characteristics, but as living movements into which you can enter, as it were, and then go with the advancing flow of time, but also with the receding flow of time, and you can consciously choose to be at the point of confluence of those two streams, which we would now call the present.

When I consider the new situation that I have described so far, it might seem that every human being is entirely alone. This is certainly not the case. Social life will be very lively, we will still be engaged in conversation and exchange ideas. However, the way in which this happens will also be completely different.

It will still be the case that when you come close to another human being, you will feel when that other person enters your field of perception. You can also move into the other person's field of perception yourself. The difference will be that you have to be far more active. In the new situation you have to willingly accept the presence of the other person, because you form his presence, his form, his inner state. Not that you are creative in it, but that you are interactive with what is.

Destiny, as we know it, will no longer be effective in the same way. There will be more of a constant impulse to evolve within us, and the most important goal will be to develop love. But to be able to do that we need insight. We will have gained a great deal of that when we were still incarnated in a mortal body. When that time is over, we will still gain wisdom. The power of knowledge with which we will do that will be a form, which we only know now, when we *believe* something.

Science will give way to faith. Not the faith that the scholastics disputes were about, such as whether one should believe something that is nonsensical, or that one should only believe what reason can grasp, or that one should provisionally assume and believe something on the authority of wiser people. This kind of belief is not meant, but the belief that belongs to the *certainty of knowing*. When you know something to be true with certainty, then you believe in it.

That will be the power of knowledge and that faith will be the substance of the astral body of the earth, which is then also the astral body of Christ.

We are then still people striving for knowledge and we want to transform that knowledge into something *that is our own*, making us part of the whole with our own being through faith. This will be an important activity in the meeting of people.

But sympathy and antipathy will also continue to exist in all their glorious differentiation, not as a positive or negative aspect of feeling, but as a rich diversity of feelings that on the one hand portray the shape of the other person's soul and on the other hand will live in our own soul. Sympathy and antipathy will be important means of getting to know each other. Because the distance that now exists on earth – by means of the skin – no longer exists, it will be possible to infuse each other's souls in an extraordinarily intense way, temporarily merging completely with the beloved being and, in that merging, becoming aware of who the other really is.

The extremities in this are bliss and revulsion. When the soul is suffused with the impulse of Mani, it will have implanted the urge to transform all revulsion into bliss in itself. When it does so in the permeation of each other's souls, it plants, as it were, impulses of bliss in what it considers to be repulsive, while we should not underestimate how intensely the repulsiveness is *also* experienced and how strong the will to permeate has to be to plant bliss.

But we will not only have encounters with fellow human beings. We will also get to know the primordial images of nature as living beings, we will get to know the elemental beings as living beings, as companions, and we will also get to know the world of the higher Hierarchies with great shyness and reverence, because they are willing to behold us.

Yet we have a kinship with that world of the higher Hierarchies, and it is a kinship that has taken on a special form *on earth*, so that the encounters with other spiritual beings are of a different nature than what existed before in the spiritual world.

When we began these discussions here, I spoke of the descent of the Monad, of the specific individual Spirit of the human being, into the body. That was only possible when the soul, let us say, was healed of its very worst wildness. Then the Monad entered the soul as the great bringer of peace.

This Monad, which we then called the *"I"*, is the individual impulse in each individual human soul. It does not let itself be known, as it were, to a fellow human being in the same way as the soul lets itself be known. No one has access to the Monad but you yourself. But the Monad has no circumference, as it were, but has much more of an impulse-like characteristic, the fundamental tone in every incarnation.

Now that incarnation is a thing of the past, that fundamental tone frees itself from the obligation to enter into the flesh and determines the specific individual presentation of each person separately.

It is the impersonal individuality, an impersonal higher self, but that does not mean that it is a common higher self, because it is the individuality.

When you meet a fellow human being, you can be *one* in the physical body, because you live together in the New Jerusalem. You can be *one* in the etheric. And you can be *one* in the astral. But in the "I" you are one in yourself, undivided.

This "I" is the source of the love impulse, which all individualities have in common, when they have chosen what is good. But the *way in which* this love is developed, in which the impulse makes itself felt and *how* it makes itself felt, is completely individual and is the object of love between people.

Philippe's "I" is fundamentally different from Johannes's "I". Apart from all the external differences, apart from the personal differences, these two individualities are undivided. They do not melt together, but they fraternise. And this infinite variety of the signature of the individuality makes the human realm. Even when the individuality learns to say: 'Not I, but Christ in me', that does not mean that the individuality gives way to a general being, but it means that the personality, the personal "I" coloured by the soul, gives way to the *higher self*, which has its home in Christ. This is food for thought, for meditation. Every human being knows deep down how these parts of the being really are, but this deep knowing must come to consciousness in our time, so that we can actually learn to experience it. This will make it less and less difficult for us to have a concrete idea of the human being after the human being, of the human being who will live on earth when the realm of death has passed."

Beato said:

"Maybe I can go directly to what you are saying and ask my questions? I have not been so concerned with the future before and, as you know, I am very active in meditative life. But I have not done any independent research so far. My outward duties consist of saving people's lives through surgery, so it is a flesh-and-blood activity par excellence.

You may well imagine that the following question arises in my mind in particular: What is the point of being on earth, when everything is suspended in the air? When I think of this question, I immediately answer myself and say: The spiritual world cannot be compared to the virtual world, it is an extraordinarily real world, far more real than what we know as an earthly existence in sensory life. But apparently there is a spirit at work in man, and that person in this case is myself, who continuously wants to say: If there is no more flesh and blood, then existence has no more purpose. In other words, death and birth are necessary phenomena in order to be truly human, a flesh-and-blood person. If you are no longer that, then what are you? What is your duty? What do you still feel is your task? What is there still to be developed, if it is no longer through blood, sweat and tears?

I am aware, as I said, that that is a spirit speaking in me, which leads us into the illusion that only what is hard and dense is reality. I am aware of that, of course, but yesterday I attempted to form an idea of what you would do as a human being if you no longer had a body, if everything had become transparent. And I did not succeed.

What you told me this morning does give a little more insight into this, which is that every human being has a sanctuary as an individual self, to which only that person has access - maybe you can let someone in, I don't know. But in essence it is the sanctuary of the individuality and that creates a certain tension in being together with one's fellow human being in the etheric and astral world of the earth, there is a sense of something that needs to be bridged. These are only vague feelings that come to mind, but the fact that we have an individual I, does indicate something of a further possibility of working on earth because that individual I too makes the final and free choice for good or for evil. Of course, this is far from the end, when death no longer plays a role. But perhaps you, Philippe, can say something about this, so that we can gain more insight into working on earth."

"Yes, Beato, I believe that there is no better way to get to know Ahriman, the spirit of death and darkness, than to pay attention to this disbelief in a real spiritual world, which may not be able to literally touch the skin by the sense of touch, but where other mechanisms are at work, so that what happens there has a heightened realism. The mere fact of wishing to speak of it requires an effort, because that spirit does not want us to!

When we think of Greek mythology, we have images of processes that in fact take place in the spiritual world but, in order for the human being to be able to grasp them, are clothed in physical-sensory images. We have to follow the opposite path, which is to find our way back from the physical-sensory images to a pure representation of the spiritual world.

You see, what was depicted in those Greek mythological images are really the beings and the processes that take place there. We also all go through an extended life between two incarnations after death and before birth, and that is not free of events either, quite the contrary. But I agree with you, what is essential during this earthly development has to happen on earth. And your question is justified, it cannot be that life on earth takes place as it does now after death and before birth. It can only be possible that it is a genuine life on earth, that only the *vehicle* we use for it *will be different*, so that especially our knowledge processes and our behavioural processes will be different. The emotional life will largely remain the same.

When you no longer have a mortal physical body, you will no longer be bothered by the concerns of physical existence, such as food, drink and money. You will no longer have cravings for meals, thirst, hunger, digestive processes, excretory processes, bodily heat processes, procreation; you will be freed from all those things. These processes will be available in a metamorphosis for work on earth.

Rudolf Steiner expresses it in such a way that he says that the moon will have reunited with the earth. I do not believe that we should see this as a collision and merging of stone planets, but that it is the transcendental workings of the moon that are returning to the earthly activity, so that reproduction and so on are no longer physically necessary.

On the other hand, it is to be expected that the hardening processes we are already witnessing on earth and the loss of life of the earth will increase further, that the earth will thus continue to decay in this sense and that the mechanical technical development that is underway will continue in its flight. Possibly this will not be as fast as hoped for in the singularity, but it will continue, nevertheless. What is happening now in the electromagnetic field may have gained a certain visibility. I will have to go into that in more detail another day. But as it appears to me, I expect that there will be a group of people, in the more or less rightful human development, who from the end of the sixth culture period will no longer need to incarnate, but who will still be active on earth. I expect that they will have mercy on their fellow human beings who have not yet developed to that extent with their full loving Christian strength. But I also expect that they will have to deal mainly with the people who still *want* to be on earth in a mortal body with the help of all possible unnatural techniques, which will literally be inhuman. It will be so that the thoroughly Christianised souls will grasp the conscious impulse from within their selves to become active among these people who are left behind and who will, of course, not consider themselves to be left behind. They will partly, invisibly to them, be active as inspirational beings, but some will also feel obliged to condense themselves into the physical immortal form in such a way that they will actually be able to live among these people.

For then, in the seventh cultural period, the struggle of all against all will erupt and the people who no longer have to die will also want to participate with all their might, with all their strength in that struggle. The battle will not be fought with external weapons, but as it is known in the ultimate distress of souls, in the quarrelling, the warring atmosphere at soul level. When a war breaks out, it is not only the carnal violence that causes suffering, neither only the death of the loved one, but it is the distress experienced in the soul from which man suffers. We will work very hard on this for a long time to alleviate this suffering and to fight against evil.

There will be different wounds inflicted than at present, but these too will have to be healed. And while death is a release from suffering now, in the future such a release will no longer be a possible alternative.

But you must make an effort to empathise with all your imaginative power, with the help of all the inner knowing you have, to empathise with the suffering that will still be here on earth, even though the human being no longer has a physical body, that is, a mortal physical body.

Another image that you behold, when you immerse yourself in this, is that the new moulded immortal body is not *insensitive* to the environment and to the astral violence that takes place in it. As described in the Apocalypse, in the New Jerusalem itself the healing power is growing and flourishing, and self-healing always occurs. That is a description of the perfect Body, the City. Even in the seventh cultural period, development will be far from complete, and a *first onset* will descend from this Holy City. The suffering of chaos and the disruption of harmony that threatens, when a chaotic soul resides suffering in this new incipient body, is no less than it is today in the mortal body. Now it is so that the body finally gives way. Then it will continually take on the holy healthy form, but the process that lies between the attack and health will surely also call for help on earth. It is far from being the seventh heaven that we will find ourselves in.

After all, it is earthly life that is meant to develop the specifically human freedom and love. We are already living through the phase of freedom, but love is yet to come. What will then be asked of every human being, because their own I wants it in freedom, will not be comparable at all to the little love we are now developing on earth."

Philippe was silent.

Beato said:

"Thank you Philippe, it's dawning on me.... A related question then is: What will art be for man in future, when the mortal body is no more?"

Philippe said:

'The *essence of art* at present is that the earthly element in which tone or colour or real substance is expressed is transformed in such a way that it *makes* the *spirit visible* or audible or perceptible. That would be the essence of art, ideally, not the subjective stirrings of the soul, but the spirit itself that can be experienced thanks to the artist, a gift for people who do not have this experience on their own.

It is clear then that when you can live consciously in the spiritual world, you can be art itself, you can learn to shape the non-spiritual parts of your being in such a way that all these different parts of the being become a direct manifestation of the high spirit. That is to say, that the soul which remains becomes the manifestation of the spirit, that this is also the case with the ether body and the physical body, that is to say, that the soul will become a manifestation of *faith*, the ether body will become a manifestation of *love*, and the *physical body* will become a manifestation of *conscience* – of course, there are other categories that are used in this process.

Art then becomes much more of an art of making one's own being visible as a spiritual revelation. I can imagine that with this fourfold division you could make your spirit visible on earth, for people who are still dependent on the physical senses.

Just as it can be a graceful revelation when you are in nature and you observe the plant realm, the animal realm or a sunset, it will be a graceful activity for people who still have physical senses, when the spirit can condense itself in an artistic way and thus can reveal itself directly to these people..."

*

Philippe looked at Johannes and Johannes began to speak:

"I have three additions. When Beato asked the question about the purpose of earthly existence in the future, I suddenly saw in an image what had actually been done on earth in the past in a physical example. In our time, this is all taboo and the negative side is only seen, but of course it was also something very positive.

The image I had was that of the Catholic Mission and the Protestant Mission. These people sacrificed their personal lives completely, went to a developing country and gave all the help they could to the weak and sick there. Of course, the intention was to convert them as well, but that is not necessarily a bad thing. That there were wrong excesses there is also clear, but what I suddenly saw was that the good among the missionaries and sisters dedicated their lives to the purification of the soul and that with this purified soul they did everything in their power to do as much good as possible for their fellow men who were disadvantaged. When Beato asked this question and Philippe gave the answer, I saw the corresponding task for the future, which *we* are going to fulfil in any case, that the whole material earth with the people left on it becomes a kind of mission field for us and that we are going to work among these people, not to convert them to faith, but to convince them in their selves, so that they can really understand through and through how they should develop themselves in order to enter or remain in a positive stream.

And when Philippe was speaking just now, I had a great vision and insight into the future earth, the physical body, the sheaths of the human being, the I and being together in Christ.

I saw how we are on the way to working towards *everything becoming Christ.* Everything *was* Christ once, but we have been allowed to emancipate ourselves, to become ourselves. We can return to Him or not, but when we return to Him, it turns out that, just as everything was once made by Him, in the future everything must be given back to Him. Not now or in 5700, but in the course of the entire development of the earth, the earth with all beings that belong to it, but also with all beings that feel cosmically involved with it, will unite in Him. You have to try to grasp this literally, so that He is not only the encompassing Being, as it were, or the Brother who stands by you, but that the brotherhood among men is His brotherhood, that equality among men coincides with His equality with us, and that we have the freedom that is connected with our self, with our spirit, together with Him, that He will in no way force us into the spiritual life or prescribe anything, but that we will always have complete freedom in this.

I do not feel that I have now expressed in my words what I have just witnessed, it is simply not possible. I would like to say that the encompassing Christ will become even more encompassing, because everything will be transformed into Him. And it is *the human being* who has to take care of that transformation. Christ Himself will not do it.

So, when you speak of the task of us humans on earth, when we will no longer have a mortal physical body, it is a kind of activity like that of the bees who ceaselessly, without ever *not* wanting for a second, strive for a goal. Thus, we will do everything, absolutely everything, never *not* wanting for one second, to transform the whole earth with all beings into Him in a joint effort.

That will be something other than the former missionary or missionary work. We will have Him in His presence with us always, but not all people will have that from the beginning. It is up to us to see to it and to work for the formation of this true Christian community in a transcendental sense – and this is not a group of people who have united in a church and believe in an unseen Lord. Christ Himself is the church and we will be in Him and He in us, but we will also have Him beside us, every moment that we live from the pure impersonal I, the pure impersonal Self, we will have Him as the great Brother beside us: not only *in* us, not *around* us, but *beside* us or *facing* us – but not in a facing as antithesis, but a facing as encounter, so that you can really behold Him, by being beheld.

It is the higher human being in us, who is general, but also individually different, who can behold Christ face to face in the future and who does not then perish. What this will bring about in terms of emotional experience and insight is barely comprehensible. In art we have an indication here and there, in a poem by Novalis, a chorale by Bach, a few measures of music by Wagner... In the Bible in the Gospel of John... But it does not compare to what we will experience then..."

"How then should I imagine interaction with the higher Hierarchies?" asked Beato.

Johannes said:

"We are already fully part of Christ, in so far as we have not fallen away from Him. When the limitation to the beholding of the spiritual world has been dropped, we will be able to empathise with the essential characteristics of the beings of the higher Hierarchies better and better. We are already making an effort to do this and we know that what we are doing is also a reality, that by deepening our understanding of the *characteristics* of the different Hierarchies we will actually come into direct contact with those Hierarchies. But for many people this will still be a blind contact.

When this limitation disappears, then through an empathy with the qualities of imaginative and inspirational cognition, a truthful intuition can arise, in which the knowing human being merges completely with the being from the higher Hierarchies.

This is how we will deal with these beings, but it will not happen automatically. It is man's will that everything that is in the spiritual world should gradually reveal itself to the spiritual field of vision. It is not like watching a film in which you can sit back in your theatre seat and let the whole experience unfold before you.

Everything will be hard work, no being reveals itself that is not longed for, and that longing has to be expressed very concretely in the imagining of certain characteristics. Of course, this is already the case now, but we still have enough distractions in the world of the senses and we do not notice when these higher beings do not make themselves known. In a future time, when the world of the senses will have disappeared, it will depend entirely on own efforts.

Then there was something else I wanted to say. We have spoken extensively about the New Jerusalem, and I wanted to emphasise once more that in this city in which we are to live, the new future human body that lies far in the future, is a terrestrial body and will remain so when sexual reproduction ceases.

The characteristic of the earth is its mineral substance. We have also seen this. The New Jerusalem is composed of precious stones, pearls, gold and so on. It is an earth body and yet this mineral substance will no longer be hard stone.

It is not possible to express this in words of any kind. We have said: *liquid diamond.* But this liquid is not the liquid of water, although it is related to it. We have said: the primal idea of precious stones and minerals, that brings you closer to what it will be. But this primal idea has the mineral as its substance and then it becomes difficult not to see the stone.

Perhaps the essential characteristics of the senses themselves come close to it to a certain degree, but after all these too are known to us as *organs* which are very physical, but which you would not immediately recognise as minerals. So, you have to look for the similarities, using different methods. However, every time we look for such a similarity, we realise that it is *never an exact similarity*, but that by experiencing the different possibilities, we can come closer to an idea of how the mineral realm should be represented when it is no longer hard.

Leaves of plants also derive their solidity from certain mineral substances, but they are not as hard as stone. Yet the gates and walls of the New Jerusalem are not like plant leaves, but it may help us to obtain a clearer representation of them.

We can also study how the main minerals are related to the twelve zodiacal signs and thus get to know, for example, the four main directions in them - the Lion, the Eagle, the Taurus and the Man - Aquarius - as corresponding to four minerals: hydrogen, carbon, nitrogen and oxygen. Then you can become aware that you have found the components of organic chemistry and you know: the carbon is the diamond. In this way, too, you can deepen your understanding of the transcendental meaning of the earth as a mineral realm and the New Jerusalem as a city, in which we will live as in the body. The new future body is an earth body, the highest that the mineral realm could produce. In the Apocalypse, the bringing down of the New Jerusalem in the great perspective of time is at the point where the physical earth will pass into astral form. This will not be in 5700, nor at the end of the seventh culture period, but there will still be two full earth cycles to go through. So, what we are talking about here is only the very first onset of the spiritualisation of the earth and we have to keep in mind: The physical body is an earth-body and will still be so even when we will live in the elements to a greater degree!"

Philippe and Johannes met at the end of the afternoon to discuss progress. The two friends sat down at the table at which they had also done their morning presentations in the group. They looked at each other and Philippe said:

"Johannes, it is with great poignancy that I take in what you add each time. Of course, I know you very well, I know who you are and how gifted you are and – please forgive me - you know me too, but I do wonder: Why aren't you the one describing this whole vision of the future? Your way of describing it is really far more moving than mine, isn't it?"

Johannes's blue eyes were like the summer sky and laughter lines appeared at his eyes... He said:

"My dear Philippe, you must know that I would not be able to make these additions at all if I had not first absorbed your reflection. I do not find the insights you bring in the way you do, and what I add is inspired by listening to and experiencing your lectures."

Philippe said:

"I am sure that if you had taken on this task, similar insights would also come to your mind as a contemplation. And frankly, I wonder, why do I have to do it?"

Johannes shook his head and said:

"Because you are the only one who can do so. No Philippe, these insights don't come to me, not in that way - but in another way and that is what I offer as complementary addition to your content."

Philippe sighed deeply and said:

"Well, that's how it will be then... How are our friends Raymond and Els coping? You lunch with them every day. How are they coping with this?"

"You put it very aptly!" said Johannes. "Els is someone who absorbs these matters very easily. She is very good at unselfishly accepting things. She recognises everything we present. Actually, this is also the case with Raymond, except that in his life as a scientist, he has built up a solid wall between the actual individuality that lives in him and his person – and he is now breaking it down, brick by brick. Sometimes this awakens a certain amount of resistance in him, but on the whole I think he is a courageous man. He is someone who judges mainly on the basis of the degree of intelligence revealed by the person speaking. And because that is not lacking in us, in you and in me, he has a reasonable trust in us. That is actually quite ideal, that he does that, that he does not base his judgement primarily on the content of what we put forward. Then he would probably have no choice but to reject it. But he judges according to our spiritual stature and that makes him such a special person. So yes, they cope with it well. They work very hard at it too, every day after lunch they go for a walk and then they study and reflect and even meditate. Then in the evening they share their experiences with each other and the next day the programme starts all over again."

"Good," said Philippe. "I am glad we had this conversation because, as you can imagine, these morning lectures exhaust me, especially since the following day brings a further deepening and extension of the theme. I also have to process and experience this in the time between the end of our meeting and the beginning of the next one. This is of the utmost importance for health."

"Be assured of our gratitude and the respect we have for you and for the spirit that inspires you. I understand completely that it is not always easy and that you also have doubts about your human abilities. But let me reassure you: There is no one else who could do it the way you do. Not even Johannes."

Philippe began to speak.

"We experienced a culmination of the vision of the future human being in the words of Johannes yesterday. Today, I want to try to give a clear picture once more of how we will live then. When I speak of 'we', I mean people like us. Tomorrow, I shall try to present a picture of the constitution of the human being who has not been active in the development of the thinking body, and the day after tomorrow, I shall try to describe how the human being, who chooses to live on earth in a biological material body will be. I want to emphasise that this is not about discrimination, that we would say that we are superior to others. We are talking about people of free will, one wants to, the other one does not.

We now have our moments of meditation and when we have achieved a certain clairvoyance, we have achieved it because we have dedicated all our strength to learning to think in meditation in such a way that the will, *the thinker*, the I that thinks, not the person, but the individuality that thinks, produces the *thoughts* fully *consciously from himself*. When we do a concentration exercise followed by a meditation, we also concentrate the whole person into the meditative thoughts, so that there is a union of the whole person with his thoughts. This creates a completely different inner world of experience.

What is asleep in ordinary consciousness wakes up and what is dreaming also wakes up. What is awake in ordinary consciousness comes to a halt and allows itself to be completely determined by the new willed feeling-awakening.

When we direct our inner gaze to this – that is, not to what is thought, but to the new position we find ourselves in with regard to will, feeling and thought – then we have a preview of the future human being. The individuality will then have completely united itself as far as possible with the experiential world of the soul and will be able to unite everything that takes place in the experiential world of the soul with it just as consciously and knowingly as we do now with the thoughts. This requires rest, and in our time, we have to make great efforts to completely forget the form of the mind and to learn to think in that completely new and living way that is thinking with the thinking body.

Then, so many thousands of years later, we shall be fully accustomed to it, and there will no longer be any lifeless being-less thoughts, but everything will be life, revelation and being.

What is presently a world around us outwardly will then be a living world *within us*, and in the union with life, revelation and being within us, the activity of that other will shine through to us.

Our activity will consist in learning *to rest* and becoming completely *absorbed with our activity in the other*, through which the other beholds and inscribes itself in us, as it were.

In our experience the whole world will consist of world-thoughts which have no resemblance whatsoever to what we know now as thoughts, except for the fact that they are knowledge, that they convey wisdom, that we are intelligent beings through thoughts. The world thoughts are in this sense intelligent thoughts, which will then be our thoughts, but, as I have said, no longer resemble what we understand as thoughts now in any way.

Everything that is thought will be reality. Red is not an abstract thought, but an active living colour. Goethe made an attempt to describe colours in this way and still remains very abstract, of course. This description is still quite different from the direct experience of a colour, which has become a living being. This is an example of how world thoughts will have taken the place of our current thinking.

Our present feelings, which have a strong personal subjective character, will have given way to a resounding, tonal unity of forces. If thoughts, world thoughts, are a weave, then world feeling is a play of forces that makes this weave visible and in which lust and suffering, warmth and cold, sympathy and antipathy, are the active poles.

Our will has only just become kin with the essence of the spiritual world. Weaving and the play of forces are expressions of beings, and just as we form our thoughts as thinkers and have then finally formed them – being, interplay of forces and weave – we then live in an infinitely expansive world of these processes and beings. In meditation we live in a contraction of the state in which we will live when the clairvoyance we now pursue will be the 'normal' inner state. Now the world is, as it were, folded outwards and we are in the middle of it. Then it is inverted inwardly and we live as a unity in its periphery, yet merging into a multitude of beings. This rich, multi-faceted world turns out to be our I, which encloses this multi-faceted spiritual world as an individuality *and* can merge into it with the experience of all beings and processes, which then no longer have that abstract thought-character we know now – but still have a world-thought-character, through which we will *know* what we perceive very precisely.

With that inner world, which is simultaneously our environment, we will live in the elements on earth in a body that can be as broad as the cosmos, but that can also contract into an appearing entity.

The self and the body appear to be essentially kin.

Add to these experiences the presence of Christ himself, as described by Johannes yesterday, and you have an impression of the future man.

We are familiar with this inner state that inverts to a spiritual world in meditation in the following saying[12]:

'Penetrate soul depths quietly, and let fortitude be your guide.
Forget all former forms of thinking as you go into you,
To lead you to you.
Killing all self-light, spiritual light appears to you.

In your thinking live world thoughts
In your feeling live world forces
In your willing, world beings are at work.

Lose yourself in world thoughts
Perceive yourself through world forces
Create yourself out of world-beings.

Do not remain in the world-dreams by thinking-dreamingplay

Begin in the spirit widespaces and end in your own soul depths.
You will find divine purposes, knowing yourself, within you.'

We will want to make that effective on earth - and we will be able to do so."

"Please forgive me, Philippe," said Raymond, "I suppose it's my lack

12 GA 14, Rudolf Steiner, Mysterydramas.

of knowledge, but although I understand every word, the German, the relationship between the words, the sentences, I still don't understand what you are talking about. Perhaps you would like to summarise what you just said for me, given my lack of knowledge."

Philippe smiled and said:

"I'm sure it's not just your lack of knowledge. I have also noticed how difficult it is to express what is so apparent to me in the contemplation in meagre earthly words. So, I am very appreciative of your question!

When you consider how our present relationship of I and world is, you would say: I have the world surrounding me as I am at the centre, I have thoughts and feelings and my impulse to act within me, and that which is outside is for me saturated with reality, while my 'inner life' of thoughts looks like a shadow existence. I cannot possibly regard my inner life as the original reality and the world around me, which I perceive with my senses, as a consequence of that.

Then, when you start meditating and you proceed to bring *will into the thinking*, the will provides the power to make the thoughts more real, until they are so real that they have the *same quality of reality* as your sense impressions. And should you go further than that, the inner reality becomes even greater.

Thus, the importance of the world around you decreases in this respect, and the importance of the thoughts you think, of thinking in itself, increases.

When you succeed in transforming the thoughts into images and in preserving their reality, you begin to reach the realm of what we call Imagination. Then thinking takes on a symbolic form, that is, what was originally thought of in *thought forms*, abstractly rational, is *transformed into symbolic images* that have a reality character. That is the Imagination.

If you go even further in meditation, you no longer cast your inner eye on the symbols, but on the *activity* with which the symbols are formed. Then you come into contact with *the play of forces* that is also active in music and in the spoken word. This then becomes the new theme for meditation.

When you finally forget that too, only then do you come into contact with *the true being*, in this case, first of all, with yourself.

In meditation, this is initially not as significant a reality as the reality of the world around you, but that changes with practice. What I wanted to say a moment ago is that what you bring about in meditation in terms of actual perception of symbols, of the play of forces that form those symbols, and the being that produces everything from itself, becomes the future world for us.

Now it is only an additional gift to the outer world. Then the outer world will colour and sound internally as I have just described.

The inner world will be experienced in this way. Thus, a life on earth will come into being for us that consists entirely of inner perceptions, which then appear to us as worldly thoughts, as worldly forces and as worldly beings, living together with them.

The verse I have given is from the Master of the Occident and it expresses exactly what we do in meditation in the inner life.

It is now a question of trying to imagine that what can be practised here is a seed for what will become the content of our consciousness in thousands of years, when consciousness will have reached a heightened state, because what we have now forgotten and allowed to languish - that is the true emotional life and the true life of the beings in the will - will be experienced in the full awakening of consciousness. I hope that I have been able to express this more clearly now, but I am aware - and I say this every time - that the difficulty is that we are speaking about an inner life that becomes the essence of a worldly life and that it is so difficult for us to imagine this.

In ancient times - and this was still the case to some extent in Greek times - people were aware of how these high worlds had - and still have - an influence on the elements of the body. In the future, this will enter into the conscious control of mankind. I would also like to speak about that another time."

Raymond said:

"Can you say anything more about the individuality? I didn't quite understand that. Where is this in this whole process?"

"Yes," said Philippe. "When we speak of unselfishness or our personality, we speak of the incarnated person with his hereditary disposition, his family background, his nationality, his schooling and so on. All this has to be forgotten, so to speak, when you want to gain an impression of your own individuality, but also when you want to gain an impression of the individuality of a fellow human being.

So that individuality is not the person, but in the person, the individuality resounds in every detail.

In a very distant past as humanity, we have received the physical body in development, the ether body we have received in development and the astral body we have received in development.

Earthly existence is characterised by the gift of the Elohim or Exusiai, who give us the "I", i.e. the individuality.

It is only because of this that humanity, which was originally an undivided human being, is truly individualised.

This individuality is still being thought of by the high beings of the second hierarchy, this is a permanent thinking activity of these beings.

Since the coming of Christ, however, man has been given the opportunity no longer to be permanently dependent on the heavenly contribution, but increasingly to *create his own individuality* himself and to give it *the* form and content he chooses. It lies on the path of mankind to make the bestowed older parts of his being completely his own with his own free individual being.

This process will be further developed in the thousands of years that lie between now and the point where the human being is no longer mortal. If we consider that there are still 4000 years to go and we look back from now to 4000 years ago, we are in the period of 1000 years before King David! Then we can have an idea of how far the development will go in the next 4000 years, especially because the speed of change is increasing dramatically. What still progressed very slowly in ancient times, has accelerated in the last century of the consciousness soul. Therefore, it is barely conceivable what the possibilities for the individuality will be in the next 4000 years."

"But..." said Raymond, "it is not the case, then, that this individuality will ultimately merge into an undifferentiated divine whole?"

"No, we have to imagine that there is a process of increasing differentiation and individualisation, in which the individual will take complete control of himself and will not give up his individuality out of insight and free will but will place it at the service of the greater whole, while retaining the self-consciousness he has gained."

"You spoke of a sanctuary to which no one has the key, and no one can enter uninvited. So it is not the case that this individuality that lives in this sanctuary or that is this sanctuary is based on hereditary disposition?"

"No, certainly not! The body, which comes from the hereditary line and is mortal, is indeed to a certain extent an expression of the individuality, because he also tries to transform the physical body into his own image. But the spiritual individuality as such has nothing to do with heredity and must even consider it as a matter of fact to be overcome.

In 4,000 years, this conquest will be complete and individuality will shape the parts of the being without any interference from the hereditary."

Johannes said:

"In lieu of my contribution, I would ask you then to tell us about your insights regarding the effect of soul and I on the physical-etheric, as it is now and will be in the future."

"Yes," said Philippe, "I will do so. Although I shall miss your contribution very much.

As far as our time is concerned, of course, we must be constantly aware that a great helper can be called into our self-consciousness and that is Archangel Michael. He has the power and strength we need to spiritualise our intelligence. With his help, which we may freely request, we receive sufficient strength to transform our intelligent thinking to a reality, because by activating our will he enables us to become vigorous in our thinking. This creates an extraordinarily powerful, unselfish self-consciousness, and with that self-consciousness we finally achieve complete inner control over intelligent thinking. That includes the ability to behold that thinking. We receive the ability *to think and to be fully present* as a self-conscious being *simultaneously in the beholding.*

We, as striving people in this sphere, are familiar with this from our own experience and know that this self-conscious contemplation of thinking is a necessary accomplishment in order to then transform the other parts of being self-consciously.

When we are in conscious control of our thinking – which does not mean that we then think whatever we like, but that we consciously and actively observe and participate in the thinking we are doing – when we are in complete control of our thinking, then we can also penetrate into our *emotional life* with this self-consciously perceptive strength, where it is far more Christ Himself that we take in, because we begin to have a greater influence over the development of sympathy and antipathy.

It is not that we can arbitrarily have sympathy or antipathy at will, but we will succeed in the complete elimination of the personal element in it and in preserving the *objective part* and heightening it to a *perceptive function*, in which the feelings can be experienced in all degrees that are found between the utmost bliss and the very deepest suffering of deprivation.

So, as it were, we move with Michael as our force towards the subjective emotional life and overcome it completely. What remains is an ordered perception of the astral world.

Then we can penetrate still deeper into our being as it has been entrusted to us and this means that we can let all our accomplishments become a habit, but it also enables us to gain insight into what the ether body essentially is as a body of life.

We begin to see how the cosmic constellation of the sun and the planets continues to work in our life body as organic life processes.

Thus, we discover the scope of *Saturn*. Not only as an obscure planet in the firmament, but as an essential influence in our life processes, and specifically in the process of the dying life, where everything that is life and movement becomes *rigid*, so that we can say: this corresponds to the living nature of our *senses*. We see, as it were, the cosmic Saturn as life-activity in the whole area of our senses, where the most profound life in our bodies takes place.

As an antipole we encounter the Moon, the lunar sphere, which has to do with the most intense life of our etheric body and namely with the sphere of *reproduction*, while the senses are the quietest, the sphere of reproduction is the *most active*.

There are other planets in between.

In the middle, where our heart is located, we find the life of the solar sphere and that is the *circulation* of the *blood,* which is kept in motion by the sun. A cosmic vibrant life makes our blood flow.

Immediately adjacent to this, let us say upwards, in the direction of Saturn, is the planet *Mars* with its sphere, which is active around the heart, particularly as *respiratory* life, but also in the organ which we know as the *bile*.

The Sun represents the heart, the Moon the reproductive organs, Saturn the senses but also the spleen.

Downwards, under the sun, we find the organs associated with *Venus*. These are mainly the *kidneys*, but also the metabolic organs in general, it is the *metabolic life* that is associated with Venus.

Further down we find Mercury, who in our physical functioning, sustained by the ether body, ensures all movement, both the *movement in the body's fluids*, in the body's air, and also the movement of the *limbs*. The organ associated with this is the lung, but it is also the entire glandular system with the production and removal of fluids.

Upwards as its counter-pole we find the planet *Jupiter*, which is connected with the *thinking life* and in this sense is the life of the *nervous system* in the ether body. This already contains a little more life than the senses, but of course it still belongs to the tranquil receiving part of our physical body, which is sustained by the ether body.

The organ connected with this is of course the nervous system, but in the abdomen, it is also the liver.

This may seem like a summary, but this summary only comes to life when we, with the help of the power of Michael, try to make these images a reality, so that we learn to perceive them in our own etheric body as functions, which then in a condensed form become the actual organs and processes of our physical body.

Simultaneously there is a growing ability to work fully consciously in the activity on earth in such a way that our higher spirit being remains conscious in the will of any action whatsoever, be it through the sympathy and antipathy of the soul, or through the habitual life of the etheric.

In this way, we arrive at the essence of the different temperaments, an awareness which must precede the permeation with consciousness and supremacy of the earth elements.

In literature as is found in anthroposophy, we may read that in Greek times man knew that the relationship between the etheric body and the physical body is a phlegmatic one during winter, that is to say that there the mucous formation prevailed and still prevails, which we may observe for example in the occurrence of infections and inflammations during winter.

With the arrival of spring, this watery element began and is beginning to be replaced by the airy element, and the Greek was able to observe that during spring man has the sanguine temperament in the foreground.

Towards summer, of course, it is fire that begins to dominate and which is then accompanied by the emergence of the choleric temperament, while in autumn the tranquillity has returned and the earth element begins to predominate in the melancholic temperament associated with the processes of death and mineralisation.

We live in a time when it is possible to infuse these processes with consciousness from the mastering and spiritualisation of thought, and even to develop our own independent dominion over them.

In the coming period of about 4000 years, we will have the opportunity to develop this to a great height, so that ultimately it will be possible for us to form, from above, and maintain the physical body self-consciously without a material physical body.

Michael is the Archangel who now shows us the way and will stay with us. He is enveloped in the radiant garment of the higher hierarchies and especially of the beings associated with the sun. When we ask him to be our guide, he will show us the right way to receive full insight, feeling and ability to act from above so that we can permeate and transform our being with spirit and then will be empowered to be the first humans to fully self-consciously create an immortal body in all those thousands of years."

Eva asked:

"Philippe, will we have an immortal body in that future time that is still an earthly microcosm in a certain sense, with the sun in the centre, the moon and Saturn in the periphery, and the other planets in between with activities that are also important for our self-consciousness? Or will that no longer be necessary in that time?"

"We shall certainly have an extraordinarily fine and multifarious physical body, although it will no longer contain those particles of matter which make it mortal now. Just think of the New Jerusalem, the future physical body. It will be nothing less divinely complicated and differentiated, only our relationship to it will be one of love, as I have described.

The efficacy will be pure, as our spirit will have purified the astral body of all restlessness and unjust feelings and will have transformed the etheric body into a pure element of love, where, let us say, love has become a habit. But that will not be an ether body without any meaning, on the contrary!"

Els asked:

"Will doctors still be needed in the future?"

"Yes," Philippe said, "they will certainly still be needed, we will see that tomorrow, when we discuss the people who will continue to live on earth without a mortal physical body at that time, but who have not yet developed to the point where they can live their lives without the help of the higher hierarchies in the unconscious and of their fellow men in the conscious."

Philippe asked:

"Wouldn't you like to say something, Johannes?"

Johannes smiled and said:

"We are going far beyond our time... When I listened to you, I had the image of the rich spiritual world of the ether and the astral world. With regard to the ether, I had to think of the 'places' in the cosmos where the Hierarchies, with whom we will be able to interact freely in the future, reside, and with regard to the astral world, I saw us, as we will be clothed with *spiritual organs of perception*, as if these were ornaments.

In occult science we now call these organs *Lotus flowers*. In the future they will be characteristic of individuality. In oriental pictures we often see man drawn or painted with seven lotus flowers. When you seek initiation, you develop the flowers that have already been planted into magnificent organs. In the future we will learn to recognise ourselves by these, among other things.

Where you experience the sun, we have the *twelve-petalled lotus flower*. Six characteristics we have thanks to our own effort, and they point to a harmonisation of what we ourselves can develop in terms of thought, feeling and free will. The *heart* will be the organ of harmony.

High above that we find the *highest chakra*, which is also called the *crown* in initiation literature, the *lotus flower with countless petals*. There we have the living vision of Christ in us, beginning as the *beholding of thinking*.

In the polarity of this lies very deep below the area that we know as the *area of reproduction*, here is the *four-petalled lotus flower*. There also lies curled up the true power of love but then in the spiritual sense, in the very highest quality, which every human being on earth can develop.

Above the heart we have the lotus flower, the *sixteen-petalled one*, which is situated at *the larynx*, and which can be developed by ourselves to perfection, because we can accomplish the eightfold path of Buddha within ourselves.

Polar opposite is the *ten-petalled lotus flower*, which we develop by taking everything that comes from outside and is perceived with the *senses into our own hands*.

Between the larynx and the crown lies the *two-petalled lotus flower*, the *third eye*, the area of the power of thought. Concentration in thinking gives development to this two-petalled lotus flower. This flower has to be developed first, and that is what we are paying so much attention to here. The *development of thinking* is the development of the *two-petalled lotus flower*, and *beholding of thinking* becomes the development of the crown, the *multi-petalled flower*.

The lotus flower that lies between the ten-petalled and the four-petalled lotus flower is the *six-petalled flower*, which we now place in the area of the *prostate or the bladder*. We develop this through the complete self-awareness of the *harmony* between *thinking*, *feeling* and *willing*.

In the inner world, the human being carries the astral world, which is the emotional world of the moving planets in macrocosmic terms. But behind this, as it were, there appears to me an even greater human being who is universal, namely the macrocosmic ether. This is the cosmos of the moving planets, but then stripped of all wish and desire character, as a pure element of intelligent love. In that human being, who has the heart like the sun with his head in the fixed stars and his feet on the moon lives a still unborn child. It is the image in the Apocalypse of the woman clothed with the sun and her head in the stars who is pregnant, and who is an image for the pure astral body. Above that appears a figure that has overcome the dragon and that has more of an angelic form, we experience the Michaelic aspect, as Philippe discussed. That is the macrocosmic ether. The woman clothed with the sun is the rebirth of the old moon and the ether is the rebirth of the old sun.

When we delve into the astral form of the soul, we find the psychology of the planets; when we delve into the star form of the ether, we find the physiology, the occult physiology. The astral form belongs to the sixteen petalled lotus flower, the etheric to the two petalled one.

Now for us this is still an area of secret science, but we can try to imagine how we will be at home in these different worlds in the future time with self-awareness."

Hilippe looked tired and it was clear how much energy this task had taken of him and was still taking. But as he began to speak, he became much more energetic...

"We have painted the positive course of development exclusively so far, for those people who, in the sixth, seventh millennium, will have developed freedom to the fullest, accompanied by an unselfish self-awareness. This will enable them, while being *in* the midst of a situation, to be able to behold it from the *other side* and thus make freedom a possibility.

When you are completely immersed in something, without self-conscious reflection, freedom is no longer possible. But I have always said that this is the positive development and that not all humanity will be at that ideal level of development when the physical bodies lose their fertility.

We then have to distinguish between *two* possibilities: either the still imperfect human being nevertheless participates in the development and develops further *without* a mortal body; or the choice is made, with the aid of all possible technical-biological means, to continue living in an earthly body or possibly to move on to a more robotic existence while retaining intellectual faculties.

Today I shall discuss the first possibility.

If I say that part of humanity will not have reached the full development of human capabilities, this may be interpreted as discrimination. That is why it is necessary for me to explain this in greater depth first. This has nothing to do with skin colour, with nationality, with race, with religion, with origin. It has nothing to do with whether you belong in a tribe in Africa or are a member of a professorial college at a university. There are people who, in their previous incarnation, were farm labourers, and others who belonged to the highest realms known on earth. There are people who come from a team of cleaning staff, but they may just as well belong to the nobility who never had to do anything.

Of course, when the bodies have lost their ability to reproduce, there is no longer any question of people belonging to a cleaning team or to a college of professors, but I only want to point out by way of example that imperfect souls can be found throughout the earth's population, irrespective of race, birth, religion, schooling, entrepreneurial flair, intellectual talent and so on. This is about an entirely different matter.

If you look around you now, you can clearly observe that in the various population groups there is always a great diversity of inner development and that the person who is at the helm in terms of inner development often should not be at the helm at all.

Those people, who by the time the body can no longer be reproduced must continue to live without a physical body, but who by then have not yet developed the freedom and the loving capacity - let alone a self-confident spiritual perception and understanding - must then be assisted in their development in the same way as the human being must always allow after death at present. We have a certain freedom on earth, but when we die the whole choir of the higher heavenly Hierarchies comes and forms both the spirit body for us, which we need in the spirit, as well as the spirit soul and the 'spirit spirit'. Insofar as we have already been able to form these ourselves, we take them with us across the threshold of death, but the higher world intervenes with support and correction as far as the rest is concerned. Those who have gone before will also have a task to show us the right way and to guide us in our development towards the heights of the Spirit.

When we have reached the year in which the physical bodies have become infertile, this will be the situation in which these people, who are not yet independent, will develop further.

It is the selfishness that determines the development. The greater it is, the weaker the higher independent self is and we can imagine that in the astral world, where this selfishness thrives, a very important effect reigns through the presence of the imperfect souls. After death these are led to renounce selfishness in the Kamaloka. Now, however, they embody themselves on earth in a non-mortal body, but with the soul in the condition it would have been in had it incarnated in a biological mortal body. The astral community therefore becomes a very dynamic and troublesome area.

In the mortal body on earth, it is so that every person has his task, independent of the soul development, and that these tasks support each other, so that there can be spoken of a large organism which is humanity in its entirety, and in which one is dependent on the other to a certain degree.

We meditate on this when we meditate on the washing of the feet. It is a way of expressing gratitude towards all beings on earth – not only towards human beings – from the awareness that it is a divinely balanced whole, in which everyone has his or her own task.

Now we can very well imagine that the more developed soul has the task of assisting the less developed soul and that considerable energy and effort will be required from the more developed souls in order to become an uplifted harmonious whole. Just as the striving human being initially – and presently – makes the effort to create order in his own soul, so it will be in the distant future in a similar process, but then extending beyond the borders of his own soul and contributing to the greater whole.

Nevertheless, these presently selfish souls must be granted the opportunity to attain freedom. To enable this, it is necessary that a certain blindness remains, which gives them the possibility to work on themselves from within. This is what will take place. In the astral world there will be a large group of sleeping and dreaming souls who will not be able to wake up there, who will not be able to wake up at all in the etheric, who will only be able to have an awareness of themselves in the life in the elements. They will consciously go along with the flowing of water, the blowing of wind, the shining of light, being enveloped in gentle air and flaring up of fire from time to time. They will have a dreamlike imaginative awareness of meaning in those elements and they will be confronted sufficiently with the violence of the elements which will bring about a development self-consciousness.

Those who are more balanced will then be companions in the elements and in that sense be able to act as teachers and possibly also as caregivers. It is very easy to conjure up images of science fiction here, because if you imagine that among these people the battle of all mankind will break out against each other and you then also imagine the material kingdom on earth, where the fighting will also occur, and you try to find images for this, it can easily be the case that you see similarities with certain science fiction films.

We should not imagine it in this way. We cannot imagine it at all, neither with regard to the appearance, nor to the activity of mankind in that future time.

We are trying to do so now, but we have to recognise that there is a wide margin of possibility and probability.

Nevertheless, I would venture to form the following picture, that in the atmosphere of the earth, in which Christ is also found, a new earth life will unfold in which the physical existence of the human being will take place in the elements described, which may then through evil become those other degenerated elements of the mud or mist, the blazing storm, the darkness, the smoke and fumes of pollution and fire... In those sacred and profane formations of the elements, the human souls will express themselves and there will be wild battles between the various selfish soul-natures who do not want to acknowledge anyone but their own soul.

There will also be a group of people who have already come to terms with their own selfishness to some extent and want to curb it. This will be the situation in different variations.

You could say that this forms a middle class of souls. These souls may lapse into selfishness and then express themselves in anger, hatred, insanity... while they can also rise to the pure soul movements of quiet contemplation, faith, love and wisdom. When they reach out to the higher spheres, when they look upwards with their souls, they make it possible for the free, loving human souls to reach out to them and to act as teachers of healing through the divine spiritual word. The word will then resound through a spiritual organ of speech, which will give forth movements into the air and water, thereby resounding, but at the same time also shaping what should be done. The lower soul qualities will shape the elements into their evil form, and when you ask the question: Will doctors still be needed? Then here lies the answer, that the earth-atmosphere which is corrupted by the evil souls, can be healed by the activity of the holy soul-elements into the earth-elements. Christ in the earth's atmosphere obviously has full power to keep that atmosphere holy and healthy, but it is *man himself* who has this task. That is what He is waiting for.

The "I", the Self, which is not personal, shapes the elementary body from above into a perfect organism; the selfish soul whips up the elements and forms a wild, wild, lustful elemental body. The more the "I" is involved in shaping the body, the more peaceful and pure it becomes, and thus the inner state will become discernible right through to the external appearance."

Peter asked a question:

"What has not become clear to me is the following. You spoke about the washing of feet, that is an image for a creation in which all beings, processes and elements keep each other in equilibrium and there is also a consciousness and gratitude for it. Now I have to imagine that a part of humanity has an inner development that already possesses a certain dominion over itself and can accomplish a tremendous amount on its own. But what about those people who have not yet achieved this equilibrium and who are unconsciously guided by the higher beings and helped by their fellow human beings? What does the less developed soul then still contribute to the whole, except that it requires powers to be helped? What is their function for the greater whole? Surely it does not seem to me that it consists only in being an object for the higher beings to bring about development?"

"No,'"said Philippe, "you mustn't see it that way. If you think of the heavenly sovereignty without including earthly man, then you see a, let's say, highly differentiated harmonic collegiate, where the different beings fulfil very different tasks. The angels have a very special talent, but they also serve the higher beings.

This is how we should also imagine humanity on earth. Those people who have not yet attained full freedom and self-consciousness will be given a very specific individual task to fulfil on earth, in which they will serve that which is the earthly goal in its entirety in an active way, so that they can also attain self-consciousness and freedom through it."

"I may be going too far..." said Peter, "but can you also give an example of such a task?"

"Then you have to set the moral imagination in motion, Peter, to get an inkling of such future tasks.

You know that the angels take up our sense impressions and thoughts and transmit them, after spiritualising them, to the second Hierarchy, who then have another task in their processing, making them usable for the first Hierarchy.

So, I can imagine that there will be a need for mediation between the people still living on earth in dense mortal bodies and the already spiritualised human being. This spiritualised human being will then have self-consciousness and will be able to live with the higher Hierarchies and with Christ Himself as a brother. The human being living on earth in a hard physical body will have no possibility whatsoever to perceive the transcendental. The mediator's task will then be to get in touch with these sensitised people in such a way that they can form a channel for the transcendental workings of soul and spirit, through which these people, if they can be open to it, can still make contact with their lost soul and spirit, if that is the case.

That seems to me to be a good example for the task of these people who still have a craving for the sensual, but who no longer need to live in a mortal earthly body.

We can see that as a kind of Kamaloka for these people who then, by fulfilling certain tasks in a good sense and forgetting their selfishness for that purpose, gradually develop towards self-awareness and freedom."

Johannes said:

"It is in fact the case now that people with certain strong character traits or qualities, even if they are selfish, can do a lot of good in the world. When the dirty work on earth no longer needs to be cleansed because you are no longer living in a mortal body, that does not mean that there is no work to be done in a different way, which can only be done thanks to the fact that not all people have freed themselves from their selfishness and are in harmony. That it is an ideal for the distant future is, of course, obvious, but it must also be clear that the journey there is still a very long one and that we must be aware that disharmony can also bear *fruit* for a long time to come. An image of a holy society based solely on mercy is not the right one. We must remember the enormous power that will be expressed in the elements, because there will be souls stirring in them who are selfish and imperfect, but no less active. Then it is easy for us to imagine how the washing of feet will be in the world and how it will correspond to a Christian society. There must always be workers too, and I mean by that at the moment that we will continue to need selfishness as an active force for a long time to come, for example to reach, as Philippe painted it, the humanity left behind on earth."

Philippe began speaking again at precisely 11 o' clock.

"We have almost come to the end of our three weeks of working together here at our dear Institute in the mountains. Today it is my task to paint a picture of the future for mankind, who choose not to follow a central path to Christ of their own free will, but who want to remain extreme in the rigidity of the earth and in the development of technology. Raymond gave us a lecture on the singularity and transhumanism, which is the 21st century. In any case, we are witnessing an ever-accelerating development of technology, even if we do not agree with the idea that by the year 2040 artificial intelligence will have developed to the point where it will surpass human intelligence and will do so with increasing speed and significance. We will have to acknowledge though how fast and effective the technical development is.

Now, of course, anything can happen. Disasters can occur and interrupt the whole technological process. But let us imagine that in spite of disasters somewhere on earth the result of the technology will be preserved and can be taken up again and again for further development. When we then imagine a period of almost 4000 years of technical development, our powers of imagination soon come to a complete halt. Just as you can imagine a specific quantity of 100, 200, 1000... Beyond that it becomes difficult, it becomes so abstract, that we cannot possibly envisage the technological development over a span of 4000 years.

But what we do have is a remarkable passage in the work of the Master of the Occident[13] in which he makes a prediction for the future concerning the time we are talking about. He then says that at that time, when the lunar sphere will have reunited with the earth, a web will be found around the earth containing giant spiders, and that is a remarkable image. After all, we know that there is already a web spun around the earth and that people even call it that, that web is worldwide, and we walk, as it were, over that web of internet like spiders with our search engines and other related quests for knowledge.

When we imagine that everything that is technology now will take on a particular life in future, we have the extremely unpleasant vision of a

13 Rudolf Steiner GA 204 S. 244 ff.

technology come to life.

This, of course, is what science is striving for, not only to create technically perfect equipment, but also to give it life. That, too, could eventually outgrow human control. There could be an earth from which the true human being has withdrawn, but which has become imprisoned by the so-called Ahrimanic technical beings. This imprisonment is then, of course, relative; it is not to the extent that the earth would no longer be the body of Christ. But a specific area, that is the hardened electromagnetic atomic sub-natural area, might have become the sphere of life for the hardened technically-propagating humanity, which has replaced the original human intelligence with artificial intelligence. They will continue to make hopeless attempts to seize power in the cosmos.

It is hard to imagine what these people will be like; as I said, the makers of certain science fiction films have a particular ability to portray it. But I don't think our current power of imagination is sufficient.

They will be people who actually no longer deserve or want the name 'human being', because they will have eradicated everything that is freedom and love, and will have formed a society that is based entirely on selfishness and its control from the outside. This is where, in the seventh cultural epoch, the battle of all against all will finally break out. This cannot be helped, because no external system will prove strong enough to curb cultivated selfishness – only the inner being can do that.

So, we must imagine an earth that is totally hardened and that no longer has a living atmosphere. People live thanks to technology and breathe thanks to technology. Many of them will not have a soul nor an I in them, but will merely be technically reproduced bodies. The leaders, on the other hand, will be people with a soul and an I who have consciously chosen evil.

I don't think it's appropriate to elaborate further on this theme, because it's better not to use the imagination to stoop to such low levels. But I had to give a certain impression of it.

Perhaps you, Johannes, can give another picture of how the – let us say – middle class and the higher educated human being act on this mortal earth-man from the realm of the spirit?"

"In order to obtain a clear picture, we can meditate on the Revelation of St. John as a source of inspiration, and we will then understand that it is especially the blowing of the trumpets and the pouring out of the cups of wrath that will take place in this last period of the Post-Atlantean Age.

What is written there about what mankind will have to deal with on earth applies especially to those people who are hardened by their materialism. We know that in the spiritual world everything is being, and we must therefore remember that all those occurrences described in the Apocalypse as a result of the blowing of the trumpet and the pouring out of the cups of wrath are *beings*. In this sense, we can try to understand how the higher beings called angels in the Apocalypse fulfil their mission from God, but how lower beings are necessary to bring about the effects that are the consequence of the trumpets and the cups of wrath.

When there is mention of fire, of storms, of water disasters, of water becoming blood, among other things, it is human beings who fulfil these tasks, in alliance with the elemental beings. They themselves are the elements, people live in them and when those elements manifest themselves in their profane form, then it takes beings who fulfil those commands and who work in a higher command.

Because of the tremendously shocking effects that are unleashed upon people by these disasters, there will always be those who open themselves to something other than evil. We know this from the effects of fate. When you are shaken by fate, there is a moment of openness to the spirit.

After the Second World War we saw that an impulse towards freedom and love flourished everywhere, although it quickly stagnated in old habits. But this openness was present. However, it is not the case that you may say that the misery that is poured out over mankind and in which human souls have to participate, results in their consequently performing evil deeds. It is very difficult to put this into words in the right way, because of course it must never be thought that the crimes committed by people during times of war are the result of the benevolent divine impulse. It is not the virtuous divine impulses that want to destroy, but the virtuous divine impulses that urge us to purify and spiritualise. That is what God does. But the elements, for example, have to be led in a certain way in order to achieve that effect which the divine impulse intends, and it is distressing for those human souls to have to work in the evil elements. It brings them no pleasure! When the people who have been hardened on earth have been made receptive to this, then the higher human spirits can work in an inspiring way. They can use the good elements to convey an effective word from outside to these poor people who have remained behind, thus maintaining the openness in them and bringing about a gradual change in the state of their souls.

The freedom of these people lies in their willingness to open themselves up and to surrender to what is working in them and outside them, while others immediately close themselves off and harden even further in their resistance.

I have already said that in these three weeks we can only present an outline of what this vision of the future can offer us. We would have to approach and elaborate on it theme by theme. Philippe and I will be discussing whether we actually want to do that, and if so, how it should be done.

With regard to this theme, which I have just touched upon, the basis could be the meditative study of those two areas in the Apocalypse, which are the trumpets and the scales of wrath, but you really have to weigh each word in meditation in order not to lose the essence in the multitude of details. If you learn to weigh the words correctly, images of this future state of mankind will appear and we must be aware that we are talking about the Apocalypse in the Post-Atlantean era. When it is over, we will be just beyond the half way point through the earth's development. In the Post-Atlantean era the most important part of the earth's development is completed, but after that there is a long period of assimilation. That period also includes an Apocalypse, and the images we have in the Revelation of St John are relevant for that too, only you have to see them in a far more spiritual perspective. Thus, the Apocalypse has different time perspectives."

Philippe opened the day again and began to speak:

"There are still several themes that have not been mentioned and I will try to touch on them on this last day. Tomorrow we can then devote to questions and additions. The question is: When the body is no longer mortal, is there still procreation?

In occult literature we find descriptions that in the future the human being will no longer give birth to his offspring but will utter them. When we have become more familiar with this new body, we can imagine this more clearly. For we do not envision a human being of flesh and blood bringing forth a baby from the larynx, but we see how man is gifted with the creative word and is thus able, or at least will be able, to utter offspring.

When I explore this aspect in depth, I receive different answers to the question: will there still be procreation?

The first thing that becomes clear is that man's new body is not an absolutely permanent creation, but neither is it mortal in the same way as our present body of flesh and blood. The image arises of a soul spirit being that wants to be active on earth and, in order to be able to do so, forms an elemental body around it. Thanks to this body, further earthly activity is possible. Man can rest from this earthly activity by retreating from the elemental body and identifying with the spirit world. This is similar to what we do when we go to sleep; then we also withdraw from our physical body, leaving it in bed with the ether body and identifying with the spirit world, but we are no longer conscious. Then, however, we will be.

A withdrawal as prolonged as that which now occurs with death will then no longer be necessary. But you can imagine that this elemental body can be tainted by outside interferences and then it will be necessary for the person concerned to pronounce a new physical body by means of the creative word.

A very banal counter-image to this is the current method of three-dimensional printing. In this process, an idea is formed into a three-dimensional reality. This is an ingenious but banal technique. Inwardly, this can be seen in the pronouncement by the creative word of a new physical body, but on the highest spiritual level.

The second possibility is that the less developed souls are not able to arrange their elemental body around themselves and need the help of their fellow human beings, who can produce this body for them. This is far more comparable to the present-day procreation, except that it will no longer be sexual. In a similar way, hardened people who have opened up to soul and spirit and who are considered capable of living in a non-mortal earthly body may receive a body in this way. This will have to be brought forth.

The third possibility is a completely different reproduction. When man thinks and puts these thoughts into words, he or she also brings forth beings. Just as the elemental beings are offspring of the higher Hierarchies, so we humans also bring forth offspring through our thoughts and words, and in this sense, we pronounce our offspring, which have a disposition according to the nobleness or irreverence of our thoughts and words. This is already the case nowadays, but when humans will lead a purely transcendental existence, the way in which he speaks will be considerably more concrete and will also produce offspring that are directly perceptible.

Then there is the question of community building. Of course, we still have strong ties thanks to the blood relationship. This will disintegrate completely and be replaced by a soul relationship and a spirit relationship. Groups of people will live together in love on a basis of soul and spirit relationship. Just as the thirteen of us here are studying this subject in depth, we connect with each other in a kindred spirit and soul, and in this way the future community will be formed, and it will be able to develop intensely and make great circles around itself in the time when the human being will no longer live in as dense a body as he does now...

We are familiar with the heavenly council around Michael... As human beings we will form schools in which we will educate, will shape, will enthuse less developed souls for the pure spirit existence in Christ.

What we now know of love is a feeble flickering flame compared to the love that can then blossom between people. Love is now awakened by the body with the senses, but this is also a brake. When physical love is no longer active, this brake will be released, and we will be able to truly experience what love is.

Finally, there is the question of art.

When we have to imagine that everything that is abstract now will become a web of ghastly spiders in the future, the question is: Will art still be possible on earth?

We have studied the sacred elements as described by Mani and we may assume that the elemental body itself can be made into an object of art that will then be visible and audible to humans in their hardened earthly existence. You can imagine that this can even be brought about by a group of people...

The water element, which can also become a little more substantial, is the element in which a kind of plasticity can be achieved, so that the shape of the elemental body becomes an artistic design of soul and spirit, but also beyond that this plasticity can become visible. Finally, we also have the plant and animal realm, which has not been discussed at all.

The spoken word is expressed in the element of wind and has a resemblance there to what we know as eurythmy, which will then not only be visible externally in form, but will also be audible in tone and sound in a sensory-transcendental manner.

Just as we are familiar with the rainbow now, so will the colour be able to shine in the pure perfect element of light in forms thought up by the soul and spirit. Painting as we know it now will then be a real unfolding of a play of colours in the firmament. This is imitated on buildings, for example in France on Chartres Cathedral, in the evening. Then, a play of colours is projected onto the cathedral, a technical spectacle that I consider to be hideous. But when you imagine it as a play of colours formed by the Spirit and the soul on the threshold between invisible and visible light, then you have an idea of a future art form. Eurythmy also works with coloured light, but in this case, you should forget about the eurythmists and only look at the play of colours.

The pure gentle air is the element for tone. This area of art is also comparable to tone eurythmy to a certain degree. For the music of the future, we should carefully imagine something that lies between the audible and the visible, with sounding visible movement.

The fire of love will pervade all the arts and warm them with will, so that they are not distant revelations of beauty, but genuinely spiritual expressions in the elements. It will always be the love of the Spirit for the soul, for the ether, for the elements, for each other, which gives the body beautiful forms, gives the word effective divine expression, colours the heavens in accordance with the higher Hierarchies, makes the music sound like the divine harmony of the spheres and raises the togetherness of people to a divine human choir."

The four of them sat in the study for a closing exchange. Admittedly, it was not quite the time to say goodbye, as Els and Raymond would be staying in the house in the mountains for another week, but the three weeks of working together were over….

Els and Raymond sat opposite Philippe and Johannes.

As usual, Johannes naturally took the lead and began to speak:

"Philippe and I felt the need to have a final conversation with you. We see the others here regularly, but we are now saying goodbye to you for a longer period of time, and we have done something quite exceptional in these three weeks – we have invited two people to our discussions who have only recently come our way. Both of us have been absolutely sure about the soundness of our decision and nothing has happened in the past three weeks that could have raised any doubts, but we would like to have another conversation with you, in which we can express our feelings and experiences from both sides. Philippe has taken on this task for the past few weeks. You can also say: he has this task. And so, I would like to ask him first whether he would like to say anything."

Philippe nodded, sat back, looked thoughtfully ahead and began to speak.

"What I would like to say I would like to say to all of us and I will do so. But my wish to say this applies especially to you. In these three weeks I have given everything of what will be revealed to the beholding soul when it questions the future development of mankind, especially as far as the development of the body is concerned. If I had not focussed my inner gaze in that direction in a more enquiring way, I would not have had all these impressions, those impressions that I have given in the past week. It is not the case in modern initiation that this spiritual-scientific knowledge simply overwhelms you, as it were, or that you are filled with it in a spontaneous way. These impressions only occur when, with the power of pure living thought, you silently dare to move with the flow of time that comes to us from the future. This is a *stream of will*, and there is no way you can enter this stream with the outpouring of thought. But just as the will in our lives manifests itself in the course of all successive acts, so too, for the reality of the future, we must await that future. Then we can only perceive a sketch of it, with the help of a will power that has taken the place of thinking. When I look into the future in this way, then I am led or I lead myself to certain connections, processes, beings, developments, which are more or less visible in the beholding, but which, if you want to transfer them by means of the word, first have to be brought into a 'thought seclusion', whereby they then lose their living coherence.

And I must say that I have really suffered from this over the past few weeks. The inability that I have – which is a common human trait – to have to *convert* what can be experienced vividly within into *thought forms* that are fragmentary, incomplete, lifeless and, as it were, have fallen back into the present. With the inner eye, you can perceive future states that no longer or hardly contain anything of the here and now. If you transform these states into thoughts and words, you have to place them in the present, and in so doing they lose what is essential. But that is what there is. There is no other way to convey spiritual science than through thought forms expressed in words.

In the work of the Master of the Occident, I myself have exerted my will with all my might and have thus succeeded in guiding the lifeless thought forms written down in words back to the original living thoughts, feelings and will impulses of the beholding consciousness. Thus, I would like to ask for your co-operation, that what you have received – which of course does not come from me, although it happens through me – that you are able to set it ablaze with the help of the willpower that you apply with all your might.

In retrospect, I am also aware of the fact that obviously a lot more was not said than was; that these are really fragmentary impressions, because the present physical aptitude does not give us the possibility to render this spiritual totality. In meditation, I enter into an intuitive contemplation. If I put into words, in my lecture to you, what I have experienced in the spiritual beholding, then I lose so much that when I look back I constantly sense the voids that I would like to fill ..."

Philippe was silent. There was a hush, after which he began to speak again and said:

"I have spoken a great deal about the elemental body. Johannes has spoken to great lengths about the astral light. What was not mentioned at all in the discussion of the elemental body were the *beings* that are associated with the *elemental world*, that produce it, of which the elemental body is also composed in a certain sense. It was impossible for me to delve into that, because it would have become a proliferating and expanding whole, and I would not have been able to come to the main outlines. But it would certainly be necessary to talk about this at a possible later date. In the same way, the beings belonging to the astral light have scarcely been discussed, and the phenomenon of the astral light as a whole has not been expressed clearly enough - not because Johannes would not have been able to do so, of course, but because it is also a part of the greater whole that we have tried to describe and in which we inevitably remain incomplete.

However, I would very much like to hear a reflection of the past weeks from you, Raymond, and from you, Els, too – if you are willing to give one."

Raymond nodded and said:

"What I have experienced in the past few weeks is, of course, rather complicated. I don't know if I'm in a position to give a clear picture... I've been meditating daily for the last few months, like a novice, and I've been preoccupied – apart from the study of spiritual science – with essence, with the "I", the 'I am' as an essence, immersed in the question of the essence of the "I", which you acknowledge exists when you say: 'I am'.

And on the other hand, I meditated on the essence of numbers. For this purpose, I adhered to the theory of number of Pythagoras and Plato and asked myself the questions each time: Does the number one differ from the number two, for example, as far as the essence is concerned? Is it a different being or is the number as encompassing phenomenon the essence and the numbers individually not? In order to find out, I had to visit Aristotle's theory of categories. I knew it existed, thanks to my study of philosophy. I made these attempts on the basis of the guidance you gave, Philippe, when we met here in spring.

I came back here somewhat enriched by these meditations and this is how I listened to you. To sum up, I must say that I have become painfully aware of the abstractive effect of my mind. I have really been battling to restrain all the surfacing comments and to only focus on what you presented with all my willpower, as you call it. I succeeded, but it consumed too much energy, which otherwise could have been used for more profound reflection on what you were saying. That is one aspect.

The other aspect is more emotional, where I am deeply affected by this vision of the future. I have no doubt in my mind that it is true, and of course I have been amazed at your knowledge, your manner of speaking, your modesty, your prudence, behind which lies hidden a spirit, I would suspect, working with the whole choir of the heavenly Hierarchies and the all-encompassing divine being itself. So, I am not that abstract, that is a remarkable division within me.

Sitting here in front of you now, I feel, as I have expressed before, almost too small to be able to look into your eyes or to call you 'you'...

As far as the experience is concerned. We have absorbed everything without taking notes and we have practiced the exercises every day which we received as an assignment. I did take notes of these exercises and so did Els, so we have a wealth of information that we can take home and work with further. However, we are also aware that what you have revealed to us, cannot be looked up in any literature, for the simple reason that no such literature exists yet. I therefore hope that we will have a record of what you have said."

Philippe said:

"It's all recorded, I'll transcribe it and send it to you – but that will take some time..."

Raymond said:

"If I respond with regards to the content, I must say that it is as you have stated. We now have specific points of reference concerning the future development of humanity, as is possible in the best sense. But it provides an outline, and it creates a tremendous desire to delve deeper into the various elements, processes, beings, relationships and so on. To a large extent, it will be possible to realise this through the lectures of the Master of the Occident who has revealed many of these processes and relationships. However, to be able to see this in development towards the future is something completely different. As I said, I do feel a certain foothold. And, of course, most importantly, this is a majestic counter image to that impoverished vision of technical posthumanism. After all, that was the motive for gathering these weeks. It has worked out very well ... It may be that the vision of technical posthumanism is clear to me in detail, while spiritual posthumanism appears before me in fragments, but the splendour and the glory and the spiritual fulfilment and the depth of soul of the spiritual vision has become abundantly clear and, as it were, erases the relevance of technical post-humanism altogether.

I am not sure how to proceed with this and would like to ask your advice on the matter. What must not happen, of course, is that after these three intense weeks, we return home next week, get caught up in the treadmill of everyday life and gradually forget these weeks – until we perhaps come back here in a while. I intend to try to keep alive what you have initiated here."

Philippe said:

"I am very happy, of course, to hear that you intend to continue with this at home. I would like to say: Make it a meditative cycle, by starting at the beginning, doing the exercises as we did them together every day, day by day, and then when you have worked through the whole cycle, start again. Let these exercises inspire you in your studies. After all, in our time we really do make use of technical development, and that is fine, and we can easily discover which works of the Master of the Occident we should consult when we want to know something about the astral light or about the elemental beings. However, I recommend reading the whole book and not just a few pages. Of course, there are many other things in his books that you were not looking for. But above all, when you start studying, it is very important that you take in the details as part of the whole and not in isolation. So, if you find a reference to a book that talks about astral light, it may be only three pages... Then read the whole book anyway and only then move on to the next reference."

Raymond smiled and said:

"It is a pity that I did not get a chair in the spiritualisation of thought... But I console myself with the fact that when I work on this with all my might in my spare time, my other activities benefit from it, without anyone else having to notice.

That was what I wanted to say in the first instance, and it is the same as you described, but then of course on a higher level, that as I speak, I actually lose what I want to say and hope that some of it has been conveyed."

"I am very curious to hear what Els is going to say to us!"

Els looked at the gentlemen opposite her one by one and said:

"Do you think it is easy to sit opposite two professors and tell them what you think of them and then tell them what you think of their lectures?"

Johannes burst out with a warm peal of laughter and said:

"If it wasn't easy you wouldn't dare to say it, so it's not that bad and we're really very curious, very interested I should say, in your report!"

"Still, it's not easy," Els insisted. "In the past three weeks I have done my utmost to immerse myself as deeply as possible in listening to everything that was revealed there. I don't know where the idea of doing this came from, but somehow, it felt completely wrong when I simply started to just listen. It was as if something in me rebuked me sharply and said: You can't sit here like that! You have to use your imagination, which is so strongly developed in you. From that moment on I did so. While you were speaking, Philippe, I was constantly trying not only to listen to the words, but also to transform the words into visual representations. I have the feeling that I gained a lot by doing so although I have no recollection of what was given in terms of content. Perhaps if I go back into that imagination. Maybe it will come back into consciousness. But from my ordinary recollection, I have absolutely no memory of what has been discussed here in the past few weeks - except, of course, in a characterization of a few words."

She was silent for a moment and Philippe took the opportunity to ask her a question:

"Surely it is not the case that, as you sit here now, you are exactly the same Els who came here?"

"No!" said Els emphatically. "Absolutely not! I feel that I have led a whole life in these three weeks and become a totally different Els..."

'That," said Philippe, "is what has replaced what is usually your memory. When you direct your inner gaze to *the way in which you have changed*, then you have found what the memory does not allow you to find again..."

"I'll certainly try that later,' said Els cheerfully. "And it's not as if a blank wall becomes visible when I look back at the past weeks. As Raymond said, we practised intensively and wrote it all down. In that sense, of course, I still have the content at my disposal. But when you ask me: What were your experiences? I can't really answer that in concrete terms..."

Johannes shook his head and said:

"I can' t believe that! Will you try?"

Els sighed, remained silent for a while and then began to speak.

"I have had the impression that I was carried along in a *stream of time*, from a very distant past that did not seem unfamiliar to me, to a time that was drawing nearer and nearer. Somehow, I had the impression that the events you described, Philippe, whereby man has become an I-being, whilst simultaneously falling prey to Lucifer, comes to a standstill, in time as it were, at *the moment when the Christ being connects with the earth*. It is as if the whole development of mankind holds its breath there, time stands still, and *from that moment on time* essentially does not go from the past to the future but comes to that point *from the future*. It may be that this sensation was triggered by the way you described the events, it may also be that the power of my imagination brought me into the reality of the time stream. But I am sure that what I sense there is correct, and that after Christ the main stream of time comes from the future.

When we recognize from what you have said that this is the stream of the will, then since that time the whole condition of the human being in regard to his knowing, his experiencing and his acting has been completely reversed. And when you come into that flow of time, it is not at all strange that you can move, as it were, to further points in the future, then enter into that receding stream and then, in the moment, have an inkling of how it will be like then - or at least could be."

The three men were listening and looking at Els with wide eyes. Raymond had the familiar feeling that he was only a dull bourgeois, compared to the great spirit that Els concealed behind all her femininity. Philippe and Johannes were less surprised than Raymond, for they both, of course, had a profound capacity for insight. But they were nevertheless amazed by her way of expressing herself.

There was an expectant silence.

"And that is how I have tried," said Els, "also in the exercises at home – when you, Philippe, were delving deeper and deeper into the likely future - to really imagine that the *thinking body* is an existing entity and that it could become a foundation for earthly existence, just as our material physical body is now. Of course, I cannot grasp that at all, but I can imagine it, and so I have imagined that as a human being you have your footing in your thinking, that that is your standpoint, your body, and that from there you can surrender both in the direction of Earth Nature - which then consists of the elements – and also in the direction of Spirit Nature – which, as I understand it, consists primarily of the higher elemental world, that is, the ether world and what I do not quite understand is the astral world – that from your thinking body you can thus surrender in both directions. That seems like a spiritual correspondence with what is now life on earth and life after death. It remains vague and intangible, colourless actually, but not inconceivable.

I can imagine that you, Philippe, with your spiritual development are able to move from these premises, not by way of representation, but in an imaginative way, towards that area of the future, so that it no longer remains vague and inconceivable, but takes on a real character. Those are my experiences more or less. It probably sounds more impressive than it actually is in me, but in a way, it is quite remarkable that I understand something of it and that this understanding has only come about through the use of imagination."

Philippe nodded and said:

"It is admirable Els. You must have completely overcome the selfishness in the process of knowing in those moments, to come to this kind of insight."

Els said:

"They are more sensations than insights... But perhaps that perception is also insight. I would really like to continue with this, and we will do it at home as you suggested to Raymond. I hope, of course, that these lectures will be continued and that we will be welcome there again - or rather that you will plan them for a time when we can come too. I do wonder what it will be like when we are back in Amsterdam. What would this totally changed Els be doing in the unchanged circumstances? But that will take care of itself."

Philippe said:

"Now all three of us, Raymond, Els and I, have voiced our experiences. What is missing now is your report Johannes – if you don't mind my asking. Johannes, you have the last word!" said Philippe, smiling.

Johannes began to speak.

"During the past few weeks, we have responded to an impulse that we felt very deeply at Christmastime, and we have given a cautious preliminary expression to this impulse, which in a certain sense has given rise to a revelation of the future, an Apocalypse. We have not discussed the issues that will arise in the material existence of the earth, but have focused on Rudolf Steiner's remark in particular, who expresses in a number of lectures that in the sixth and seventh millennium, women will be infertile and man will live on in an earthly body which is no longer mortal – as in a mirror image of the body which became mortal at the beginning of Lemurian time. This statement by the Master of the Occident was our point of departure and we have been working intensively on it during the past few months, which finally led to Philippe being able to reveal a number of revelations in this field.

It's as you mentioned, Raymond, we don't have anything in the literature to go on, we can't look anything up. All that we know about it now is the result of an inner movement in the flow of time that comes to us from the future.

Of course, this flow of time does not reach its ultimate point at the moment when women become infertile. Time comes to us from a far more remote point in eternity. But as far as physical development is concerned, we have an ultimate point. And a point of departure as well, because the material mortal sensory aspect is coming to an end.

If you ask me what my experiences have been, then one all-encompassing experience emerges most strongly in my consciousness, and that is the experience of an infinite sorrow and sadness and concern for mankind. The human being has been chosen to be the stage for the struggle between *good and evil*, and the pain comes from seeing how relatively powerless he is to assume a position in this struggle.

The profound experience of the anguish resulting from powerlessness leads directly to the Being who has endured this in a form and degree that is not only inconceivable for us but also unbearable. Only that Being can transform the powerlessness, the impotence, in us into a specific form of power. But this does not make the suffering less – rather more, because from the powerless human sorrow you are enriched with the divine majesty of the Sorrow that lives in Christ.

I have lived in that sorrow during the past few weeks, in a human way of course, but also feeling guided by Christ Himself to be able to endure that sorrow. And through it all, the Triumphant Christ shines through. The Christ who endured the deepest imaginable pain and transformed it into the most supreme jubilation. That is the jubilation of the victory that goodness will eventually triumph over.

A deeply moving beginning in Goethe's Faust is when God says of Faust that Mephisto may go his way for a while, because the gardener knows that if the little tree turns green it will blossom and bear fruit in the near future. God already sees the little tree turning green, God also sees mankind "turning green", but the painful trials are far from over.

When the women become infertile and the reflection of the Luciferic temptation at the beginning of the Lemurian age sets in, we shall see the first signs of that victory. Death will no longer be able to overcome man, but that does not mean that there will be no more torment. For the battle between good and evil on the stage of the human soul continues. The pain in beholding it is great, but the 'greening' triumph of Christ through it is even greater ...

This is how I would like to describe my experience of the last three weeks.

We would like to invite you to our next working visit at Christmas time. The theme will either be the astral light and the astral world in which the future human being will be at home with an earthly consciousness; or the activity of the elemental beings in the elemental world, and the elemental light in which the future human being will live, if he wants to be active on earth.

This is not the moment to take leave of each other yet, as we have invited you to a farewell dinner with all the participants. And we do not say goodbye, but we do say: See you soon!"